Rawhide Robinson Rides the Tabby Trail

RAWHIDE ROBINSON RIDES THE TABBY TRAIL

THE TRUE TALE OF A WILD WEST *CAT*ASTROPHE

ROD MILLER

FIVE STAR
A part of Gale, Cengage Learning

GALE
CENGAGE Learning·

Farmington Hills, Mich • San Francisco • New York • Waterville, Maine
Meriden, Conn • Mason, Ohio • Chicago

GALE
CENGAGE Learning®

LIBRARY OF CONGRESS CATALOGING-IN-PUBLICATION DATA

Miller, Rod, 1952–
   Rawhide Robinson rides the tabby trail : the true tale of a wild West catastrophe / Rod Miller. — First edition.
      pages ; cm
   ISBN 978-1-4328-3075-5 (hardcover) — ISBN 1-4328-3075-9 (hardcover) — ISBN 978-1-4328-3083-0 (ebook) — ISBN 1-4328-3083-X (ebook)
      1. Cowboys—Fiction. I. Title.
   PS3613.I55264R392 2015
   813'.6—dc23   2015024240

First Edition. First Printing: December 2015
Find us on Facebook– https://www.facebook.com/FiveStarCengage
Visit our website– http://www.gale.cengage.com/fivestar/
Contact Five Star™ Publishing at FiveStar@cengage.com

RAWHIDE ROBINSON RIDES THE TABBY TRAIL

Prologue

The first night out the cats ran.

Rawhide Robinson watched helplessly as upright, hooked tails sliced through the prairie grass and flashed in the moonlight, accompanied by caterwauling the likes of which he had never heard.

A stampede, in the scheme of things, isn't all that unusual and, in fact, even expected on a trail drive. Any thrown-together herd is bound to be nervous and agitated and flighty at first, which invariably leads to a runaway or two until the critters calm down and learn the routine and grow accustomed to the ways of the trail.

Then, too, this particular herd, horde, bunch, band, group, gang, collection, crowd was comprised of felines, which was strange enough in and of itself. Add to that the fact that these cats were altogether unaccustomed to the wide-open spaces of the Kansas plains, acclimated as they were to a more confined urban environment, and, of late, the limited views available from within the narrow precincts of a railroad cattle car.

But perhaps we should back up in the telling of this tale and explain how it all happened, and why . . .

CHAPTER ONE

As the last of the cattle clambered up the loading chute and into the railroad car, Rawhide Robinson took off his thirteen-gallon hat and started swatting dust from his duds. The clothes were only a few weeks old; he'd bought them in town once the herd he'd trailed up from Texas was bedded down in the river bottoms where buyers could ogle the bovines like they were so many soiled doves lining the stair rail in a parlor house. The clothes he'd replaced with the new togs were left in a filthy heap on the bathhouse floor, the pants so stiff from three months' worth of trail grime they practically stood up without him. Only his broad-brimmed hat survived the purge, and it more for sentimental reasons than practical. It was so sweat-stained and soil-streaked and smoke-soaked only Rawhide Robinson himself could discern its original color. But Rawhide Robinson had put a lot of miles on that hat and it fit him. Besides, a cowboy doesn't quit on a hat so long as the crown holds its crease and the brim its curl.

New togs notwithstanding, few would notice Rawhide Robinson in a crowd of cowboys, for he was ordinary in every respect. He would not stand out, nor would he blend in. He was neither tall nor short, nor was he in any obvious way large or small. Not particularly slim, neither was he noticeably stout. His complexion and coloring and countenance were average, if anything. While you would not say he was easy on the eyes, you would not call him hard to look at, either.

In a word, ordinary.

But as anyone who knew him knew, extraordinary things happened to this ordinary cowboy. Tales of his exploits and adventures were told around campfires across the West, shared in saloons and bunkhouses, and retold aboard ships at sea. Which only goes to show that a man who falls somewhere between the mean, median, and average by most measures can also show up as an extreme outlier according to other analyses.

None of that was on Rawhide Robinson's mind just now. All that occupied his thoughts at present was the idea of riding the rails to the metropolis of Chicago, as he had on other occasions, to tend to the cattle aboard the cars and see them safely delivered to the packing plant, earning some extra jingle for his jeans in the process.

It was the late 1870s—or maybe 1880—or somewhere thereabouts, and Rawhide Robinson and a crew of cowboys had just delivered a herd of longhorn steers to Ogallala, Nebraska. The drive originated in the Nueces Strip of Texas and made its way north under the direction of one Carlton Q. Caldwell, as fine a trail boss as ever forked a horse.

Having accomplished his purpose and having nothing on his dance card, Rawhide Robinson elected to hire on with a cattle buyer and ride the cars to Chicago, seeing to the safe arrival of the stock and affording himself an opportunity to enjoy the myriad distractions of the big city, as he was wont to do from time to time as anyone familiar with his history would signify.

Whilst on a layover on a nondescript siding somewhere in the corn country, Rawhide Robinson rescued a discarded newspaper—the *Omaha Orator* it was—from a passenger coach and perused the publication to catch up on events, both international and domestic. A lengthy column in the paper, penned by a western correspondent, commented on events at a boomtown away out in the Arizona Territory called Tombstone. Seems there was a silver strike of major proportions there, and the place was growing faster than sawyers could saw lumber or carpenters could drive nails.

But the thing that caught Rawhide Robinson's eye was the passing mention in the story of a plague of rats and rodents infesting the place. The report claimed the bare-tailed, buck-toothed vermin were so thick that folks would mash them in their beds when they rolled over in their sleep.

As a result, cats were at a premium in Tombstone.

Nothing more was said of that situation in that particular piece of correspondence, but at the very moment he read it, an idea struck Rawhide Robinson like a sawed-off loblolly pine limb landing upside his noggin. All the rest of the way to the Windy City, his mind cranked on the notion like the gearbox on the locomotive pulling the train, and by the time he arrived in the city on the shores of Lake Michigan, he had it all worked out.

Or so he thought.

CHAPTER TWO

Once the beeves were off-loaded and secured in the slaughter-house—*abattoir* for the faint of heart—pens, Rawhide Robinson implemented his plan to deliver mousers to the mining town of Tombstone.

At first light, he set out into the city. But, unlike previous ventures there, on this particular occasion he was neither sightseeing nor on the hunt for celebratory undertakings.

No, sir, he was after street urchins. And, thanks be to heaven, they were as thick on Chicago's thoroughfares, boulevards, streets, and back alleys as the lice and nits in their hair. Owing to social conditions of no interest to this particular story, poverty-stricken youth on the lookout for the main chance were readily available for hire, which suited his plans to perfection. He soon rounded up a nice-size herd of ragamuffins and assembled them for a rascal convention in a vacant lot in the shadows of the impossibly huge Grand Pacific Hotel. (Not that Rawhide Robinson was residing in that luxury palace; the location was chosen strictly for convenience' sake.)

"Now, listen up, you young'uns," Rawhide Robinson announced to the assembled horde. "Here's a question for you. How many of you-all would like to earn some money?"

The response was a widespread raising of hands accompanied by shouts of affirmation.

"How many of you are willing to work for it?"

The response was the same.

"Well, you youngsters is in luck, as I am prepared to offer remuneration of a penny apiece for every alley cat, of any description, delivered to my possession at the rail yard."

Again, there arose a cheer.

"When I say 'every cat' I mean any and every feline animal that is in good health. I ain't interested in the dead and near-dead, and will be somewhat picky when it comes to cats that are maybe too old or too young to fend for themselves. Do you get the idea?"

Again, there arose a cheer, followed by a rumble of conversation among the waifs. Rawhide Robinson allowed the talk to wane, then asked, "Any questions?"

A hand shot up. "Youse don't care if they's toms or queens?"

"Nope. Males and females alike will fill the bill," said Rawhide Robinson.

Another hand, another question: "Color don't make no matter?"

"Don't care. Solid, striped, spotted, smudged, swirled, black, white, gray, orange, brown, dun, cream, long hair, short hair, shaggy or smooth—if they've got enough eyes and ears and paws and claws to fend for themselves I'll take 'em regardless of where their particular shade or hue falls on the spectrum, or be their appearance eye-catching or unpleasant."

"How's about teeth?"

"Teeth? I'll take 'em if they got 'em."

A giggle arose from the throng but the questioning imp persisted. "No, sir, what I means is, do they need a full set? Some of them furballs lose some o' their chompers in fights and such, or gnawing on grub. Do you care if they did?"

"No, young'un, that matters not to me. So long as they've got enough pearly whites to take their nourishment and latch onto rodents, it don't make no never mind."

"How's about fleas and lice?"

"I won't be payin' extra for parasites."

A barrage of similar questions overwhelmed Rawhide Robinson for half an hour until the industrious urchins were satisfied with the terms and conditions of the contract, and understood the details of the deliverables that would earn them the pay.

"Remember, a penny apiece. I'll take delivery starting tomorrow morning," Rawhide Robinson said to close the confab, then turned the urchins loose to commence the cat chase. Satisfied with the morning's activities, the entrepreneurial range rider retired to the rail yard where he negotiated the rental of a cattle car and had it shuttled to a siding. He scrounged lumber from scrap heaps and spent the afternoon knocking together ranks of shelf-like structures in the car so the cats could climb and recline in stacks and rows. He stowed hogsheads of water in the car.

Then, Rawhide Robinson sat down in the shade intending to contemplate feed for the felines. Instead, he reclined full length, propped his head on a pinewood pillow, tipped his thirteen-gallon hat over his eyes, and settled in for an afternoon nap.

"Sufficient to the day is the evil thereof," he whispered to himself as his breathing became slow and regular then morphed into raucous snoring.

CHAPTER THREE

While Rawhide Robinson slept, one Benedict Bickerstaff darted through the crowds and confusion of Chicago's streets and alleys calling a second confab of his peers. Eventually, a quorum of rascals and ragamuffins assembled in a vacant lot near Gunther's Candy Factory on State Street.

"Listen up, lads!" the boy shouted from atop the packing crate upon which he stood. "Pipe down!" Slowly but surely, the street urchins wound up their scattered conversations and all attention turned to the boy on the box. "Some of you knows me, some don't. But that ain't neither here nor there. What I wanna know is, how many of you is plannin' to catch cats for that cowboy bloke what we saw up by the big hotel on Jackson Street this mornin'?"

So far as Benedict Bickerstaff could tell, every voice in the crowd answered in the affirmative.

"Well, then, I've a proposition for you. That cowboy chap is offerin' to pay a penny apiece, is he not?"

Again, the answers came back in the affirmative.

"What with all the mousers hereabouts, we could all pocket a packet of cash off them cats. But we gots do it right; pool our efforts, y'know. So, you see, I've worked out a scheme to make it easy for us all to make a bundle. See, what I'll do is, I'll act as yer agent and simplify the whole shebang!"

This time, the crowd response washing over the boy on the box consisted of questions and inquiries phrased in an array of words, but all summed up by a demand from a big-voiced guttersnipe in the back row: "Details, Bicky! Tell us what ya got in mind!"

"Here it is, then. How it works is, you bring the cats you catch to me and I'll pay a penny a pair."

Benedict Bickerstaff's proposal was met with a chorus of catcalls from the crowd. "No! No!" he called out. "Listen up! Let me finish!"

Eventually, the riotous rumblings wound down to a decibel level conducive to communication and Benedict Bickerstaff bellered, "Shut yer pie holes, lads, and hear me out!"

When he again had the floor, the boy on the box outlined a plan whereby each evening he would station himself at a central point, shifting every night to a new neighborhood. As the others gathered cats, he would collect them at that central location and confine them to bags, boxes, satchels, sacks, and other suitable receptacles—all of which, he emphasized, he would provide through his own labor and expense.

"Think about it," he urged. "You won't have to worry about keepin' track of the cats you catch and havin' 'em scamperin' off whilst you pursue more pussies, will you. Nor will you have to worry about that wastrel standin' next to you there stealin' yer cats when you ain't lookin'. All in all, lads, you'll be able to spend twice the time catchin' kitties instead of all yer time tendin' tabbies—which means you'll pocket more dough in the end!

"Besides that," he added, "None of you will have to haul 'em down to the train yards. No! It'll be me, Benedict Bickerstaff, yer contracted agent, trampin' through the streets transportin' the tabby take, riskin' me neck at every intersection, bravin' the flyin' hooves of horses and crushin' wheels of carts and wagons, dodgin' coppers every step of the way whilst you lot curl up under yer covers and sleep the day away."

Back at the boxcar, Rawhide Robinson snored.

CHAPTER FOUR

Rawhide Robinson swatted at his nose in his sleep, attempting to shoo away the tickling tail feathers of the troublesome turkey buzzard perched upon his chest. The cowboy's dreams had transported him far from the Windy City to an unrecognizable world where he wandered aimlessly, and seemingly endlessly, through a desolate wasteland populated only by the decomposing carcasses of cattle. In the dream, the despondent cowboy collapsed in despair, troubled—and saddened—by the strangeness that surrounded him. Hence his uneasy repose and the visiting vulture.

As a cowboy, Rawhide Robinson earned his keep caring for cattle, so any harm that came to the critters was cause for anxiety—even in dreams. The only acceptable end for a bovine was a purposeful one, the result of which was fodder to feed hungry folks. And so the useless demise of the dreamland cattle kept the fretful vaquero swatting, awkward hands heavy with sleep, at the symbolic buzzard.

After whacking himself sharply on the proboscis a time or two, Rawhide Robinson awakened and realized the imaginary carrion bird was, in fact, only a flitting fly. But the odor of the putrefying herd still filled his nose, contributing to the cowboy's confused anxiety. He sat up, rubbed his face vigorously with the palms of his hands, and blinked rapidly to clear his vision.

The smell, he eventually understood, was real. The wind in the Windy City had shifted as he slept, so he was now downwind of the plentiful packing plants that turned cattle and hogs into beef and pork.

And therein, he also realized, lay the solution to his problem concerning comestibles for the expected cats! He would relieve the packers of the odiferous burden of disposing of the scraps and trimmings of their trade by turning it into a feline variety of jerky—a toothsome sustenance for traveling carnivores riding the rails!

He'd have to cogitate, of course, on cat capacity in order to determine an adequate quantity to nourish his herd for the duration of the train ride, but did not see the problem as insurmountable.

And so the plan was implemented.

Rawhide Robinson barreled and brined a bounty of beef (albeit the aforementioned scraps and trimmings) and set about hammering together drying racks and laying fires for smoking the meat when the time came, a chore easily accomplished given the heaps of scrap lumber between the rail yards and packing houses.

The labor having taken him deep into the night, and the restful effects of his afternoon nap long since dissipated, Rawhide Robinson collapsed onto his bedroll and surrendered once again to the arms of Morpheus, hoping, this time, that his dreams would be as fruitful as, but less troubling than, his naptime nightmare.

But he had barely closed his eyes when the aforementioned vulture returned and commenced tugging on the great toe of his right foot. The pinch wasn't powerful enough to be painful but proved a persistent annoyance. Then, much to Rawhide Robinson's surprise, the buzzard spoke. In a voice straight from London's East End—of which, of course, the cowboy had no knowledge—he heard his name.

"Mr. Robinson. Hey, Mr. Robinson, sir," the carrion eater

said with a tug on his toe. "Wake up. This ain't no time to be checkin' yer eyelids for leaks." Tug, tug. Tug, tug. "C'mon, pry open them peepers and talk to me. We got business, ain't we." Tug, tug.

Rawhide Robinson's eyes ripped open; he yanked his digits in the direction of safety and wrenched himself upright, tipping his thirteen-gallon hat off his head in the process. But it wasn't a buzzard that sat before him—it was a boy. A boy he had seen before. One of the boys he'd recruited to corral cats.

"Wha—wha—what!?" he said when finally finding his voice. "What do you want, boy? You darn near scared me plumb to death."

"Ah, it weren't me, were it. You was only dreamin' is all."

The flummoxed cowboy felt for his hat where it had fallen and screwed it down tight. He pinched the bridge of his nose between thumb and forefinger and shook his head from side to side like a coonhound with a tick in its ear.

"Thought there was a turkey buzzard gnawing on my piggies. Now, what is it you want that merits waking a man from his much-needed slumber?"

"Heck, mister, way you was a carryin' on and moanin' and groanin' under that there hat, you oughts to be thankin' me fer puttin' an end to yer nightmare."

Rawhide Robinson took a moment to pull his toes back through the holes in his socks and tug on his boots as he collected his thoughts. "I suppose you're right. Now, what can I do for you?"

"It's about them cats."

"Yes?"

"Well, see, it's like this. I've set meself up as agent for all the lads as lives on the streets, ain't I. Now I wants a contract with you, exclusive-like, for buyin' them cats you need."

"Contract, eh? Exclusive? Why would I?"

"Save you time. Since you only have to deal with me, you won't be racking yer brain about what's owed to dozens of urchins—only just me. Besides, I can make sure that all cats delivered is as ordered. I'll cut out all the bad ones savin' you time—that way, you can crawl under yer hat and sleep all you want on account of I'll be keepin' an eye on yer interests, won't I."

Rawhide Robinson laughed in spite of himself. "You will, will you? Just who are you, anyway?"

"My name's Benedict Bickerstaff. But that's a mouthful, so most calls me Bicky. Some Benny. Others B-B."

"Which do you prefer?"

"I don't care what I get called, long as I don't get called late for supper."

Another laugh from Rawhide Robinson. "Bicky, then. I like the sound of it. How'd you come to be living on the streets? Where's your folks?"

"Dead and gone. Mom, she died of scurvy on the ship from England and lies in a watery grave. Never made it to America like she wanted. Me little sister, she went over the side in a storm. Pap, he made it to Chicago and was workin' in the packin' houses but took sick and withered away. He's toes up in a potter's field. So it's only just been me these four years past, gettin' by on me own, ain't it."

"You're resourceful, I'll give you that."

"I don't care about that. Will you give me the contract?"

"I reckon so."

With a whoop and a holler, Benedict Bickerstaff jumped up and danced a jig.

"Calm down, Bicky, and sit yourself down," Rawhide Robinson said. "If we're to be in business together, we best get ourselves on the same page."

The boy looked downcast.

"Can't read, sir. Pages don't mean nothin' to me."

The cowboy laughed again. "Not to worry, boy. It's just a figure of speech. Just means we got to understand one another and what we're after so we ain't working at cross-purposes."

"Right."

The two entrepreneurs put their heads together and discussed the kind of cats desired, acceptable condition on delivery, schedules, and other niggling details. When finished, they shook hands as the sun rose over the city. Bicky started out in the morning light for the awakening streets of Chicago. But he stopped after a few steps and turned around to face his employer.

"One other thing, Mr. Robinson."

"What's that?"

"Price."

"Penny a pussy, just like I said before."

"Sounds fair enough, but think of all I'm savin' you by actin' as agent in this enterprise."

"So?"

"Well, Mr. Robinson, seems only fair we share in the savings, don't it. Suppose, instead of a penny apiece you pay me a nickel for every four cats?"

Rawhide Robinson thought it over. "I don't know, Bicky. That's a pretty hefty increase."

"Oh, pshaw! You goin' to lose sleep over a penny?"

"I reckon not. Four felines for a nickel, then. But make sure I ain't saddled with no useless stock. See that they're prime, every one."

"As you like it. See you in the morning, cats in hand. You'll see, won't you."

And with that, Benedict Bickerstaff ran off to spend the day in preparation for the evening when he would deploy his troops and undertake an effort to cleanse Chicago of stray cats.

Rawhide Robinson smiled at the boy's ingenuity and his own gullibility, stretched out on his bedroll, tipped his thirteen-gallon hat over his eyes, and soon snored in earnest.

CHAPTER FIVE

The ruins of a basement below where a burned-out office building once stood served as Bicky's headquarters for the cat-catching campaign. A jumble of bags and boxes, crates and containers littered one corner, heaped there by Bicky in preparation. Once the streets cleared of commuter traffic at the end of the business day he assembled his troops for last-minute instructions. Word of the cat hunt had spread throughout the society of street urchins and the army of operatives was bigger than he expected.

The pages of a discarded, water-stained ledger filled as each waif penciled his—or, occasionally, her—name on a line, or relied on another to witness the mark. A trusted friend, on the promise of payment for services rendered, supervised the books for Bicky, him lacking the ability to either write in the book or read what was written—recording and counting tick marks was the sum total of his ability to calculate, catalog, or chronicle.

With the paperwork out of the way, the young cat magnate climbed atop a crate. "You all know what we're about," he shouted to the assembled crowd. "It's cats we're after, ain't it. Alley cats. Stray cats. Don't be pinchin' no house cats. See, if folks start missin' pets and alert the coppers, the whole business could come crashin' down. So keep yer noses clean and stay in the shadows. Bring yer cats here and we'll credit you in the books. You have me personal word you'll be paid as soon as I deliver on the contract. A penny a pair, lads! Go get 'em!"

With a scream and a shout, a whoop and a holler, the assemblage of waifs hit the streets.

Benjamin Bickerstaff wrapped himself in one of the gunnysacks he'd collected and crawled into a packing crate, contemplating a catnap. But before the boy had time to settle into slumber, cats started arriving in batches big and small. Soon, the ruined basement was awash in critters of the kitty kind in more shapes, sizes, colors, breeds, and backgrounds than any one human ever imagined possible. Tabbies and calicos, long hairs and short hairs, corpulent and scrawny, bobtailed and big-eared, Siamese and Abyssinian, tortoiseshells and torbies, Persian and Burmese, toms and mollies—well, you get the drift. Calling them "cats of every description" would seriously understate the case.

Pencil dancing in the candlelight, the bookkeeper tried but failed to stay ahead of the game. Through the long night, the waifs came and went, ever and ever adding to the backlog of cats. When dawn lightened the eastern sky, Bicky the mouser mogul retired the troops, inviting them back for a repeat performance when the sun completed its circuit across the Chicago sky.

All morning long, Bicky inventoried the take and found that most every cat in the caboodle fit the specifications. All appeared to be ordinary alley cats, except for a few with fancy collars and perfumed fur. But, stripping collars and smearing the cats with mud and ashes solved that problem soon enough. The night's take was 672 felines—more than half the thousand Rawhide Robinson ordered. With luck, another night would complete the contract, Bicky figured as he loaded bags and boxes of cats onto the baggage cart he'd pilfered from the passenger depot at the train station. Once loaded, he set out on the first of many trips to the rail yard where wealth awaited.

The smell of food tickled his nose as he approached Rawhide

Robinson's camp near the switching yards. He looked around at
the makeshift drying racks the cowboy had erected, the low,
smoky fires underneath, and the meat strips hanging above. The
tickle in his nose turned into a twinge in his tummy, reminding
him it had not been fed for who knows how long. Bicky stopped
the cart and studied the strips of jerky, looking for a likely
prospect to invite to lunch. Just as he reached for it, Rawhide
Robinson's holler forced his arm and hand to retract as if at-
tached to a spring.

"Hey!" the cat customer yelled. "Don't eat that!"

"Sorry, Mr. Robinson, sir. Didn't think you'd miss just one
bit. And me belly button is bouncin' off me backbone, ain't it."

"All the same, don't be eating that. That meat's fresh off the
scrap heap. Not fit for humans, but I reckon the jerky'll be good
enough to keep the cats fed on the train."

Bicky screwed his face into a portrait of perplexity. "Train?
You're takin' the cats on the train? I don't guess I ever even
wondered what you wanted with all these pussies, did I. Are you
really puttin' 'em on a train?"

Rawhide Robinson laughed. "Sure thing. Sit yourself down
and I'll tell you all about it. First, though, line your flue with
some of this stuff," he said as he spooned up a bowlful of
cowboy-style beans. "Ain't no treat, but it's better than putrid
meat. Here's the deal, Mr. Benedict Bickerstaff," the cowboy
said as he watched the boy all but inhale the humble grub.

Two bowls later, the story had been told.

Bicky ran a grubby finger around the inside of the bowl,
licked it off, and asked, "Can I go with you?"

"Go? No! Why, you ain't but a kid. How old are you,
anyhow?"

"Seventeen on me last birthday, ain't I."

"Nonsense. Unless my eyes deceive me, you won't be seeing
seventeen for a good many years yet. The truth?"

"Fourteen."

"Fourteen? You sure? I'd guess twelve, judging by your size. Even so, going where I'm going and doing what I'm doing will test a full-grown man. No place for a button—let alone a runt."

"Runt! I ain't no runt! I'm plenty big for me size, I am."

Rawhide Robinson mulled that over for a moment. Then another. And yet another. "Even so," he finally said, "you're just a kid. Even if you are fourteen—which I doubt."

"Balderdash!" Bicky replied. "I'm every bit as old as you were when you were my age."

Again, the lad's logic rendered Rawhide Robinson temporarily speechless. The best he could tease out of his tangled thoughts was this: "Forget it, kid. Let's get them cats loaded."

Throughout the process of letting the cats out of the bags and boxes and shoving them through the cracked-open door of the cattle car, Benedict Bickerstaff harangued Rawhide Robinson with reasons why he should accompany him on the tabby trail. And the tirade continued with every load the waif hauled from his basement headquarters to the rail yard all afternoon long. The cowboy was relieved when the last cat of the day was loaded. The boy was disappointed as he towed his empty wagon back to town for another night's work.

And, with the sun already hiding behind Chicago's tall buildings, it wasn't long in coming.

CHAPTER SIX

Unlike the bountiful harvest of the night before, and probably for that very reason, pickings were slim for the street urchins when they lit out into the dark for the second cat hunt. Benedict Bickerstaff crawled into a packing crate as he had the night before, but this night he had ample time for forty winks four times over before the cats started straggling in.

All went well for a time, as Bicky examined the captured critters and his trusty scribe tended to the accounting. But, with a couple of hundred cats in the bags and boxes, deliveries took a decided turn for the worse. With cats being in short supply, the ever-industrious ragamuffins of the Windy City's streets and alleys started showing up with other creatures in costumes and disguises.

"Hold on there, you sneaky guttersnipe!" Bicky shouted at one point. "That ain't no cat—nor any relative of the feline race, is it! It's a itty-bitty puppy dog if ever there was one."

And: "You ain't foolin' me, are you, you devilish wastrel—thinkin' I'd fall for a Lincoln Park squirrel with a shaved tail. Take that vermin out of here and don't bring it back!"

And again: "Just because it's called a polecat don't make it no cat, does it. Off with you!"

There were skunks presented for payment. Raccoons. A fox. And, as if cleverness knew no bounds that eventful night, a baby pig in a fur coat.

All, of course, refused by the vigilant Benedict Bickerstaff.

Despite strict instructions to the whippersnappers to restrict the gather to alley cats, more than a few housecats arrived in the bunch. Being someone short in numbers, Bicky tossed them into the crates and carryalls, figuring that any cat left to wander the streets after dark must not be loved at home and so was fair game for cat snatchers.

He did set aside, in case of dire emergency, a few of the more civilized felines, including one oversized ball of fluffy white fur shampooed and scrubbed, primped and perfumed, with a velvet collar dangling a tinkly bell and a golden nametag inscribed "Percival."

(Had the *felis catus* equivalent of a herd book been at hand, all and sundry would be aware that the official name of this particular specimen was Percival Plantagenet. Imported from England by some highfalutin feline breeder to improve bloodlines, the cat wanted a more adventurous existence than standing at stud, so as it happened, "Percy" was actually pleased to be purloined and looked forward to any and all adventures that might come his way.)

"What's the count?" Bicky asked his bookkeeper after stuffing the last of the cats into containers and collapsing onto a crate. The scribe snuffed his candle and studied the rows and columns of figures in the silvery light of dawn. He added and subtracted, wrote and erased, crossed out and ciphered until satisfied.

"I make it three hundred and twenty-seven," he said.

"And how many yesternight?"

The scribbler turned back a few pages and read out the appropriate number: "Six hundred and seventy-two."

"How many altogether, then?" Bicky asked.

A few seconds of tongue thrusting and furious pencil scratching revealed the sum: "Nine hundred and ninety-nine."

"Well, if we have to add one more, we might as well make it a good one, hadn't we," Bicky said as he stuffed the immense fluffy white feline with the belled collar and brass nametag into a bag already writhing with captive cats.

"I'll be back," the mouser middleman said as he set out with a load of purloined pusses on his borrowed baggage wagon. "Them wastrels start showin' up askin' for money, tell 'em they'll get their reward soon as I settle up with Mr. Robinson. 'Round 'bout tea time, I should think."

He arrived at the rail yard to find Rawhide Robinson up and about and staring at his carload of cats through the gaps in the slats on the side of the cattle coach. Bicky climbed onto the corner of his cart to take a peek. The cats looked contented enough, perched on their shelves and climbing their ladders, hopping from one row to the next as well as up or down, not caring should a slip result in a fall, for, as everyone knows, a cat always lands on its feet.

Some lapped water from a long and low V-shaped wooden trough the cowboy had hammered together. Others scratched and shredded and chomped and chewed chunks of cowboy-created cat jerky.

"Ready for more?" the boy asked, eager to get on with the work and pocket the pay.

Rawhide Robinson nodded and slipped the door open. He set each container, one by one, inside the narrow opening, reached in, and removed the cats, one by one, giving each a quick once-over to assure suitability. As he worked, Bicky hectored the cowboy about joining him on the journey west, establishing a pattern that continued through the morning hours and Bicky's unloading of several cartloads of cats and the cowboy's loading them onto the train.

"Saved the best for last," Bicky said, grabbing Percy by the scruff of his neck and hefting him out of the burlap bag.

"Well I'll be a son of a gun," Rawhide Robinson said. "That's some cat. Fat as a county fair steer. He don't look like no alley cat, though."

"I can't make no guarantee, sir. I can only say he was snatched from the street in the wee hours of the mornin', wasn't he. Good thing, too, as he was about to be turned into a furry flapjack by the wheels of a runaway milk wagon," the boy improvised, removing his cap and placing it over his heart for effect.

Rawhide Robinson laughed, then tossed the oversized feline into the car. "Let's settle up, shall we?"

"Yes, sir!"

"According to my calculations, a thousand cats at four for a nickel comes to two hundred and fifty nickels, which adds up to twelve dollars and fifty cents."

"Aye, sir. That's what me accountant advised."

A gold eagle, two silver dollars, and a half-dollar coin made a satisfying clatter as they landed in the boy's palm. "Thank you, sir!"

"My pleasure. You did a fine job, you did. Here's a dime bonus," Rawhide Robinson said, flipping the shiny coin skyward.

Without missing a beat, Benedict Bickerstaff snatched it out of the air with his free hand. "Got to go," he said. "Time to settle up with me lads, ain't it."

"Goodbye now. Train leaves in the morning, so I won't likely be laying eyes on you again," the cowboy said to the boy's back, blinking away tears before they could form.

Bicky stopped and turned around. "You sure I can't come?" he pleaded.

Afraid his voice might fail him should he answer, Rawhide Robinson only shook his head.

The boy stuffed his hands in his pockets and his head drooped as he walked away.

This time, the cowboy's blinking failed to stop the tears.

CHAPTER SEVEN

Feeling himself the recipient of a king's ransom, Benedict Bickerstaff soon shed his ennui as the jingle of coins put a smile on his face. He dusted off the seat of his trousers, brushed the cat hair from his jacket, and strolled into the marble lobby of the Fourth National Bank of Chicago as if he belonged there. Footsteps echoing in the cavernous space, he walked up to a teller cage.

"Change this into smaller money, if you please," he said, slapping the gold eagle and a silver dollar on the counter.

The clerk leaned out to eyeball his customer, drew back a bit at the sight, adjusted his spectacles on his nose, cleared his throat, and said, "Where did you get the money, kid?"

"None of yer business, is it, you high-minded flunky."

Again, the teller drew back, this time wide-eyed. He said, "Don't be impertinent you little guttersnipe, or I'll have the police on you. Now, where did you get it?"

"I worked for it, not that it's any of yer affair. You this cheeky with all yer customers?"

"Are you this insolent in all your business affairs? If so, you useless waif, I can't imagine how you'd manage to accumulate this much money."

Not the least bit intimidated and lacking any inkling of backing down, Bicky said, "There's more where that come from, ain't there. Which don't make no never mind to you. Just change that for me and shut yer pie hole."

32

"How do you want it, then?" the banker said with a har-rumph and a tug on the lapels of his waistcoat.

"Gimme a half eagle and the rest in dimes and nickels and pennies. Plenty of each. And don't try to shortchange me. I'll be watchin'."

The teller picked up the boy's coins by their edges and walked into the vault, carrying them at arm's length. He returned in a few minutes and made a show of counting out each coin, arranging them in neat stacks on the counter. Bicky reached up and snatched the half eagle. "I'll take this," he said. "Put the rest in a bag."

As the clerk bagged the money, Bicky slid his remaining silver dollar and fifty-cent piece into one shoe and the gold half eagle into the other, then grabbed the sack and walked out of the bank as if he were accustomed to it.

He stopped at the door, raised his voice—partly for effect, but partly to enjoy the echo—and told the teller, "Just so's you know, you pompous twit, in future I'll be takin' me trade elsewhere, won't I!" Satisfied, he stepped into the streets with the poke stuffed safely inside his jacket.

A sizable crowd of catnappers was already assembled in the shell of the basement when Bicky arrived. He tossed the bag of money on the upturned crate that served as the bookkeeper's desk and its resounding thunk and clank drew a cheer from the eager urchins.

"Step right up, lads. Here's yer pay as promised. And don't never let it be said that Benedict Bickerstaff was ever less than honest!"

Bicky stepped back, arms folded and a satisfied smile on his face, as the boys, those already on hand and those still to come, pocketed their well-earned pelf and returned to the streets of the uncaring city more secure than usual, at least for a time.

"That's it," the ledger-handling lad said, giving the tattered and stained sheets a last once-over. He gathered the remaining coins—a dollar's worth—and offered them to Bicky. "Everybody's been paid. That's what's left over."

"Keep it. You earned it, didn't you."

"Bicky! You don't mean it! There's a whole dollar here!"

"Sure, I mean it. I couldn't a done it without you—too much to keep track of in me head, it was, and them scratches and scrawls on those pages don't mean nothin' to me."

"Holy cow!" the boy said. "Anytime, Bicky! Anytime you need help with ciphering or writing or reading, I'm your man."

"Thanks. But you won't be seein' me no more."

"Why not?"

"Headin' west, I am. I'm goin' for a cowboy, ain't I. That's the life for me."

Meanwhile, back at the rail yard, Rawhide Robinson was making ready for departure and seeing to the well-being of his investment. He filled water kegs and stowed them in the cat(tle) car, and rolled the two hogsheads heaped with his rough-and-ready jerky up a plank to provide provender for the trip.

By now, the oversized tom called Percy (for short) had established his place as top dog among the cats and ruled the roost from his catbird seat, perched atop the top shelf of the cat rack nearest the door (and the water trough and food supply). Abundant size and strength, reinforced by superior breeding and haughty attitude, made it easy for the no-longer-fluffy white feline to establish leadership over the assemblage of alley cats humbled by living and sleeping rough in Chicago's streets. And so, despite an occasional mewl or meow, all remained calm and quiet in the cat crowd under Percy's command.

The cowboy spent the waning hours of the afternoon finalizing arrangements for the railroad to send a switch engine come morning to latch onto his stock car and attach it to a train departing for points west. Then he treated himself to a restaurant meal to celebrate his last night in the city and the success—thus far—of his scheme to line his pockets at the expense of the rats of Tombstone, Arizona.

Returning to his makeshift camp, he packed up his belongings, stoked the campfire with more scrap lumber, and unfurled his bedroll in its glow. A final peek into the rail car to top off the water trough and toss handfuls of dried meat to his charges and it was off to dreamland for the entrepreneurial cowpuncher.

So deep and contented was his sleep that night that he failed to awake at the sound of the sliding door on the stock car, or notice the slight stir among the perched pussies protesting the violation of their privacy. But the cats, too, were more interested in snoozing than sounding the alarm at the interloper, so Rawhide Robinson and his recently recruited rat catchers aboard the rail car slumbered on in peace.

CHAPTER EIGHT

The train stopped to take on water out in the Illinois farm country near Mendota. Rawhide Robinson stepped down from the passenger coach to check his charges. The cats seemed content enough on their shelves, some sitting, others sleeping, some engaged in grooming, and others gnawing on sticks and slabs of dried meat. The cowboy (or, should we say catboy?) wondered at the quantity of jerky under consumption and the still-brimming water trough, shrugged it off, and returned to his seat.

But, when he found the same condition at the next water stop at Galesburg, suspicion got the best of him and he hopped into the car. He tipped the nearest water keg and thought it lighter than when he filled the trough before pulling out of Chicago. A peek under the lid of the jerky barrel also revealed less meat than he recalled.

Looking around the car revealed nothing out of the ordinary—only happy cats: well-fed, well-watered, and seemingly satisfied in every respect. Still, something didn't seem right. So, Rawhide Robinson grabbed the rim of the hogshead that held the meat and walked it away from the corner.

He saw a mangled cap and mop of decidedly un-catlike hair. Another shift of the barrel revealed a tattered jacket with upturned collar. Then, a pair of arms wrapped around drawn-up knees with a head stuffed between. Rawhide Robinson knew before he saw it that the face between the knees would be that of the erstwhile cat-acquisition agent, Benedict Bickerstaff.

After a moment, the head raised slightly, revealing one wide-open eye. Then, seeing the game was up, Bicky stood in the tight corner and brushed straw and dust off his jacket and pants.

"Mr. Robinson, how're you doin'?" he asked with a wide smile, as if his presence more than two hundred miles from home in a railroad car full of cats was as ordinary an occurrence as the rising and setting of the sun.

That prompted a situation seldom seen on any day the sun rose—Rawhide Robinson at a loss for words, his face drained of any indication that knowledge or awareness existed inside the head behind it.

"It's me, Mr. Robinson! It's Bicky!"

The cowboy shook his head like the clapper in a church bell, as if the motion would clear his mind, then lifted his thirteen-gallon hat and scratched his head as if to stimulate the brain beneath.

Finally, "Oh, I know it's you, Bicky. I'm just having a hard time getting my mind around why. Or how."

The boy shoved both hands in his front pockets and concentrated on the toe of one scuffed shoe as it scratched back and forth in the straw covering the floor.

It took a blast from the train whistle to alter the standoff and compel the confused cowboy to act.

"C'mon, then," he said, grabbing the boy by the arm and heading for the door. "Ain't no sense of you crowding in with these cats. There's plenty of seats in the car where people are supposed to ride."

Once the boy was settled into the seat facing Rawhide Robinson, the cowboy said, "Once we get to the next station, you'll find yourself on a train back to where you belong."

"What!? Where? Why?"

"Chicago, of course."

"What makes you think I belong in Chicago? Ain't a soul in that city cares about me, is there. Livin' hand-to-mouth on the streets, beggin' abusive citizens for bits and pieces, minin' dust bins for food scraps and cast-off clothes, sleepin' rough in back alleys and gettin' rousted by coppers all the time. No, sir. I ain't goin' back there."

Rawhide Robinson said, "Well, what am I supposed to do with you?"

"You ain't gots to do a blessed thing! I can take care of me-self. Been doin' it fer years, ain't I."

"But you're not in the city anymore. Out here, you won't be finding much in the way of tossed-out food or duds, nor alleys to sleep in. What do you intend to do to live?"

Bicky's face clouded over and his eyes rimmed with tears. "I'll get by on me own, won't I. Odd jobs and such."

The cowboy laughed, but not with any mirth. "You just don't see it, do you, Bicky? Odd jobs ain't that easy to come by out West. You'll starve."

The boy clammed up, sitting scowly and silent. Just when the monotonous clickety-clack of steel wheels on steel rails had Rawhide Robinson nodding off, Bicky said, "I could go with you, couldn't I. Help with the cats, like I been doin'."

"We'll be on the trail and away from folks for months. You've been living in that city with a million other folks. We won't see but maybe a hundred people from the time we leave Dodge City."

"That's fine by me," Bicky said. "All them people never did me no good, did they."

"We'll be sleeping on the ground under the stars every night, no matter the weather. It'll be hot sometimes and freezing other times. And we'll be out in it all the time, day and night."

"Ha! I did that in Chicago, didn't I. That don't scare me none."

"The grub we get ain't much good and mighty tedious. Bacon, beans, and biscuits most every meal."

"Long as it's regular, it beats what I been eatin', don't it."

Seeing his arguments weren't getting anywhere with the boy, Rawhide Robinson tried another approach. "I guess I got to admit you've done an admirable job keeping body and soul together," he said. "Still, it seems like you've been living by your wits. You know anything about working?"

That gave the boy pause. "No sir. There weren't no work for a lad like me," he finally said in a voice the cowboy strained to hear.

Then: "But I can learn, can't I! I ain't no dummy, Mr. Robinson."

"No. Bicky, I don't reckon you are. But I'm talking work. Hard work. All day, every day, and a share of every night. I don't know that a slip of a boy like you would be up to it."

"Let me try! You gotta let me!"

"You know anything about horses?"

"Sure! I seen 'em every day on the streets, pullin' wagons and carts, didn't I."

"But do you know how to hitch a team to one of them wagons? Could you rope a horse out of the remuda? Any experience saddling up? Can you ride?"

Again, the boy looked downcast.

They rode on in silence for a time.

"I'll tell you what," Rawhide Robinson finally said. "We pull a chuckwagon on the trail, chuck being the cowboy word for food. The cook runs that outfit and he'll be needing a helper—someone to help rassle pots and pans, wash dishes, haul water, gather wood and chips for the fires, keep those fires stoked, help pack and unpack the wagon, grease the axles, hitch the teams, lend a hand with the driving—and pretty much anything else he tells you to do. It's a job that'll test a fully growed boy. Might be too much for a button like you."

"I can do it!"

"Maybe so. If you don't, if you make a hash of it, you could make the whole drive miserable, and every man on it."

"Don't you worry about me, Mr. Robinson. I'm yer man. Just you wait and see. I'll do you a good job, won't I. Just see if I don't!"

The smiling boy pondered his new life for a few minutes, then asked, "What do you call it, this job of mine?"

Rawhide Robinson laughed. "I don't know as there's a name for the job. But there is for those who do it. Most of the hands will call you flunky. Some, depending on what part of the country they hail from, may refer to you as the swamper. Others might call you Little Mary."

"Mary! Anybody calls me Mary'll feel the bite of me fists, won't he!"

The cowboy laughed. "I reckon so. Them worn-out clothes of yours won't do. I'll have to stand you to an outfit once we get to Dodge and deduct it from your pay."

"Pay? You sayin' I'll get paid, like regular?"

"Sure. Not as much as the cook, of course, or even the cowboys. But there'll be money for you at the end of the trail, once I sell the herd. Less the cost of your outfit, of course."

"Oh you don't need to worry about that. I got money, don't I—I got six-and-a-half dollars, right here in me shoes!"

Again, the cowboy laughed, then reached out and rustled the boy's hair. "Well," he said, "we'll get you outfitted with proper drover's duds, one way or the other. Now, see if you can't get some sleep. You want to get rested up now, 'cause there won't be much sleep where you're a-goin'."

CHAPTER NINE

Benedict Bickerstaff hadn't stopped smiling since seeing himself in the mirror at the mercantile, topped off with a pint-sized thirteen-gallon hat almost an exact replica of the one Rawhide Robinson wore. Absent, of course, the sweat stains, the grime, the grease, the dirt, the manure, the soot, and other souvenirs of the trail.

In the shadow of the oversized hat, Bicky sported a hickory shirt still showing the wrinkles from where it had long lay folded on the store shelf. Atop that, a handsome vest and down below, woolen California trousers. Under it all, a pair of bright red long-handled cotton underwear. The shiny new ensemble stood atop a pair of high-heeled boots with green cacti inset into red leather vamps with mule-ear pull straps—a source of pride to the boy second only to the hat.

For the rest of the day in Dodge City, Rawhide Robinson walked the streets with Bicky stuck to him like a shadow. When the cowboy ducked into a saloon to recruit riders, the boy stretched out on the board sidewalk, peeking below the batwing doors.

Well into the afternoon, Bicky followed his employer back to the store where they started the morning. Waiting for them on the loading dock in the side alley was a grizzled geezer who appeared ancient to the boy. Pulled up beside the dock was a chuckwagon hitched to a team of stout horses.

"Bicky, this here is Sop 'n Taters Sanderson. He'll be kitchen

41

mechanic on our pending adventure. Which means he as good as owns you, body and soul."

"Rawhide, this button don't look big enough to heft a frying pan! Why, he ain't no good! It'll just make more work for me. I never signed on to wet-nurse no baby."

Bicky's neck and face flamed red and just as he opened his mouth to give the cook what-for, Rawhide Robinson said, "Now, come on, Sop 'n Taters, give the lad a chance. You got no cause to give up on him without he has the opportunity to prove himself." Then, to the boy, "Bicky, you help Mr. Sanderson here load the wagon. I'll go settle up with the storekeep and meet you down at the cattle pens."

The boy pitched into the work with a vengeance, determined to prove the old man wrong. He moved bags and sacks, boxes and barrels, cans and kegs, by any means necessary—he lifted, he slid, he rolled, he walked, he pushed, he pulled—and managed to keep the goods coming faster than the cook could stow them. Then again, the old man was fussy about what went where, shifting and moving things around repeatedly, some in the bed of the wagon, others in the chuck box, until satisfied.

When finally finished with the packing, a worn-out Benedict Bickerstaff helped the cook lash down the wagon cover over the bows, hefted himself onto the seat, and hung on as the team jerked the wagon into motion and made its way to the appointed meeting place.

"I got to admit, kid, you done right well with the loading. You're stronger than you look and you got spunk. You know anything about cooking?"

"No sir. Don't even know much about eatin', do I."

The cook laughed. "Don't worry yerself none about that. There'll be plenty to eat. Might not be much good, but there'll be enough to keep your gullet stuffed. As for the rest, you pay attention and I'll make a cook out of you."

Bicky said, "If you don't mind my sayin' so, sir, it's a cowboy I want to be, not a cook."

Again the cook laughed. "Not to worry, boy. You'll likely pick up plenty of know-how about cowboying. Besides cooking, you'll be helpin' out with the remuda—"

"Remuda? What's the remuda?"

"That's the horse herd, boy. Every cowboy needs a string of mounts on a drive, otherwise they get wore plumb out and ain't no good. Can you ride?"

"Course not. I'm a city kid, ain't I."

"Well, we'll fix that soon enough. We'll find you a gentle-broke horse and get you all practiced up. You'll be ridin' fine enough to jingle the horses in no time. Between watchin' the hands work and learnin' to handle the cavvy—that's another word for the remuda—you'll be on the way to makin' a hand. It's many a boy that came up the trail as flunky or a wrangler one year and made the trip next season as a drover—ridin' drag, mind you, but a cowboy all the same.

"But, for now, you're my flunky. If you hop to it whenever I gives you orders and pitch into the work like you did the loading of this wagon, we'll get along fine."

The sun hung low in the western sky when the wagon pulled up next to the carload of cats, which had been shuttled onto a siding at the far end of the stockyards. Cattle bellered in some of the pens and dust churned up by restless hooves hung in the air. Facing Rawhide Robinson where he stood was a handful of cowboys, and a couple of dozen horses stood hipshot and lazy in an adjacent pen.

Benedict Bickerstaff sat amazed at the situation. With nothing more than brief visits to a few grog shops along Dodge City's Front Street, where Rawhide Robinson appeared to do no more than laugh and talk and drink a few beers, he had somehow managed to outfit an entire trail drive.

"Well, boys, here's the deal," Rawhide Robinson said to the assembled company. "I aim to take this herd all the way to Tombstone, out in the Arizona Territory." He gave that a moment to sink in. "Some of you knows some of these other boys, some don't. So I'll take a minute for introductions.

"Most of you know, if only by reputation, Sop 'n Taters Sanderson. He'll be the dough roller on this trip, so you know you'll be well fed. Ain't no better trail cook nowhere than ol' Sop 'n Taters, so consider yourselves lucky. Next to him on the wagon is his flunky. Name's Benedict Bickerstaff. Call him Bicky. This is his first drive, so cut him some slack.

"This here tall drink of water is Arlo Axelrod of Uvalde, Texas. He's my segundo on this trip, so his word is same as mine. There's no finer hand." The next cowboy in line was as short as Arlo was tall. "Zeb Howard is out of the Snake River country. Met him on one of my forays into that part of the world, and I never expected see his face in Dodge City, but I'm glad I did. Johnny Londo there, and Tony Morales, they're a pair of aces from down Del Rio way. Top hands, both. Frenchy Leroux hails from the Louisiana bayous, but he's been up the trail enough times to know how to cowboy on dry land.

"Now, I know you're thinking this ain't a full crew for most drives. But we're only trailing a thousand head. And this herd will have to be handled different than most. Walk over to this cattle wagon with me, and you'll see what I mean."

And then—and then—Rawhide Robinson rolled open the rail car door.

CHAPTER TEN

When the rail car door slid open it seemed to those in attendance that it sucked all the air out of Dodge City, Kansas. While there is no official record of that airless event, there were those alive at the time who swore it happened, and they passed the story down to posterity. Word has it the birds stopped chirping, grasshoppers stopped whirring, flies stopped buzzing, dogs stopped barking, and cattle stopped bellering.

After what seemed an interminable silence, Arlo Axelrod finally spoke. "You gotta be kiddin', Rawhide! You expect us to drive CATS to Tombstone?"

"@^%$★" said Frenchy.

"?>+=#!" Tony said.

")&<=@!" said Zeb.

". . ." added Johnny, who was rendered speechless by this unforeseen and altogether surprising—and, we might add, disturbing—turn of events.

Rawhide Robinson said nothing, waiting patiently for the earth to right itself on its axis and return to its normal rotation.

Then, "That's right, boys. Cats."

He let that sink in for a time before continuing.

"Cats, boys, and I'll tell you why."

The trail boss told of the published news reports out of the southwestern boomtown chronicling the scourge of rats distressing the city and subjecting the citizens to unbearable misery. He related his contention that, pound for pound, this herd of cats

45

represented the most valuable livestock to ever take to the trail. And he promised to share the profits with the cowboys—an opportunity never presented them—or any other ordinary cowboys—in the entire history of trail driving in the West.

"But, Rawhide," Frenchy said, "we are *cowboys*. Our purpose is chousing cattle, not . . . not . . . not . . . pampering pussies!"

"I reckon that's right," Rawhide answered. "But you boys have a chance here to make history. You'll be doing something no one—cowboy or otherwise—has ever done before. We'll be setting the standard for this sort of enterprise for those who follow."

"Ha!" said Zeb. "What we'll be doin' is gettin' ridiculed. We'll be the laughing stock of the livestock business."

"It may be there'll be some of that," the trail boss conceded. "But what pioneer ain't been laughed at? Folks called Galileo crazy when he said the earth wasn't the center of the universe. They thought Columbus was nuts when he set out on his voyage across the ocean. Before Charles Blondin crossed the Niagara Falls on a tightrope they swore he'd never make it. Sakes alive, they even laughed at Lucy Walker when she set out to climb the Matterhorn! Sure, some will laugh. But you—you boys standing right here, right now—will have the last laugh when your names go down in history."

That claim got the cowboys thinking, but it was Rawhide Robinson's next contention that proved convincing.

"And think about the end of the trail. It don't make no never mind if it's Dodge City or Newton, Wichita, or Ellsworth, all the folks in these Kansas cow towns want is your money. And all the while they're pickin' your pockets they're looking down their noses at you. And sooner or later, they outlaw cowboys altogether and it's on to the next town, for more dislike and disrespect.

"You think that'll be the case in Tombstone? I say, 'No!' We'll be heroes, welcomed with open arms and accolades. Why, it won't surprise me if they throw a parade for us! March us right down Main Street amid clapping and cheering and all manner of ovations and honors! Yes, boys, unless I miss my bet, we'll be the toast of the town. The City Fathers are likely to present us with the key to the city. Drinks will be on the house, and your money won't be any good at any eating house within the Tombstone city limits.

"Newspaper men will line up for interviews. Photographers will beg you to sit for a portrait. When the history of that city is written, your names and your deeds will be prominent on its pages. Yessiree, boys, I do believe that what you're looking at here is more than a train carload of tabbies. What you ought to be seeing when looking at that clowder of cats is the opportunity of a lifetime. And it's an opportunity that you'll not see again. As the great Bard of Avon wrote in the classic play *Julius Caesar:*

> 'There is a tide in the affairs of men.
> Which, taken at the flood, leads on to fortune;
> Omitted, all the voyage of their life
> Is bound in shallows and in miseries.
> On such a full sea are we now afloat,
> And we must take the current when it serves,
> Or lose our ventures.' "

And, with those immortal words still ringing in the air, Rawhide Robinson turned on his heel and walked away.

CHAPTER ELEVEN

Rawhide Robinson's dramatic exit was short-lived. In fact, he only walked over to the stockyard fence, untied his saddle horse, and climbed aboard. He rode the few feet to where his cowboy crew stood, and said, "All right, boys, who's with me?"

The hands stood silent, studying the toes of their boots, occasionally peeking at the others from under hat brims in an attempt to discern their intentions. Finally, Arlo Axelrod hitched up the waist of his britches, tugged the brim of his hat down tight on his head, and said, "By golly, I'm goin', boys. Call me crazy, but I'm up for an adventure!"

It was as if a dam broke, spilling a wave of agreement.

"I may live to regret it, but count me in!" Tony said.

"I'm in, by %^!@?!" Zeb said.

"Me too," said Frenchy, somewhat subdued but clearly containing excitement.

". . ." Johnny added, still rendered speechless by the historic turn of events.

"Saddle up, boys," Arlo said. "Let's get them cats on the trail!"

And so they did.

As the men roped out and saddled mounts from the remuda in the stockyard pen, Sop 'n Taters educated Bicky in the ways and means of rail car chutes and ramps in preparation for unloading the cats. Once the cowboys were saddled up, mounted, and ready to control the herd, Bicky, familiar to the cats, walked into the car to chouse them down the ramp.

A small crowd assembled. A few pen riders from the stockyards sat their horses nearby, looking on. Railroad workers set aside their tools to watch. Birds perched on telegraph wires and fence rails. Even the cattle dogs who helped work the stock in the shipping pens trotted over to witness the excitement— some lying prone with heads on forepaws; others sitting on their haunches with heads up and ears erect; some on all fours, stiff-legged, leaning forward and trembling—but all fully alert with eyes intense and senses sharp.

"All right, Bicky, push 'em!" Rawhide Robinson hollered once he had the riders positioned to his satisfaction.

First, of course, was the king-size top cat, Percival Plantage-net—"Percy" for short. Thick, white fur licked and groomed into a bouffant to emphasize his superior size, the self-assured tomcat trotted out of the car. A brief dramatic pause allowed him to assess the situation—and the spectators to admire his form—then it was down the ramp with a fancy gait, tail held high.

A thousand cats followed, none as confident as Percy. But they followed his lead even though nearly frozen with fear. They glanced left and right at the mounted cowboys and the people afoot and on horseback—the spectators—farther afield. They looked ahead, past Percy's arched tail, down the long alley he was leading them into on the heels of Rawhide Robinson's horse, and then on to open prairie beyond. They looked long-ingly behind, into the maw of the rail car that had been their home these past days and wondered if leaving its cozy confines was wise.

And, of course, they kept one eye always on the stock dogs whose penetrating eyes caused them to tighten their ranks and step up the pace.

Once clear of the shipping pens and over the horizon—which

isn't that distant from the vantage point of a cat—the unfamiliarity of the environs severely agitated the alley cats. The relatively restricted boundaries of Chicago's streets had not prepared them for the emptiness of miles and miles of prairie. Accustomed as they were to limited sunshine, blocked by tall buildings, the cats knew not how to react to intense light from horizon to horizon. And, acculturated as they were to the noisy hustle and bustle of the busy city, the comparative silence of the plains proved deafening.

Anxious and uncertain, nerves as taut as a tuned fiddle string, the cats made their way to the bed ground away from town. Not knowing whence danger may come in this unfamiliar world, the felines strained their senses to probe both earth below and sky above. Intuiting there may be safety in numbers, they moved along in a tight group through the grass and brush.

The mounted cowboys took up familiar positions beside and behind the herd, but the compact size of the flock combined the point and swing positions, resulting in an arrangement with Rawhide Robinson in the lead as scout, Arlo Axelrod and Zeb Howard as swing riders, Johnny Londo and Tony Morales on the flanks, and Frenchy Leroux taking his turn riding drag. Unlike most drives, Rawhide Robinson intended to rotate the cowboys through the herding positions in recognition of the fact that all were experienced, trail-hardened drovers and deserved equal treatment.

Besides, he did not believe little cat feet, cushioned and padded as they were, would raise much dust, thus taking most of the unpleasantness out of riding drag. The only irksomeness the position might occasion, he supposed, would be the kitty litter left on the trail by a thousand animals. (However, Rawhide Robinson would soon learn—as would the rest of the crew—that cats tend to bury their waste, which made encountering that particular nastiness a rare possibility.)

50

Behind the herd—rather than ahead of it, as would be the case on the trail—came Sop 'n Taters and Bicky on the chuckwagon with the remuda trailing along.

Upon reaching the bottom of a shallow bowl well away from the city, the trail boss signaled the drovers to slowly mill the herd and let them settle in for the night. The cats remained bunched tighter than Rawhide Robinson might have liked, but he realized his charges did not need room to graze as cattle did.

Besides, he sensed their discomfort—worried about it, in fact—but assumed the cats would relax and spread out a bit once they became accustomed to the situation, and the calming blanket of darkness fell over them.

He could not have been more wrong.

CHAPTER TWELVE

The sun flirted with the western horizon as Sop 'n Taters struggled to set up camp. Being totally unfamiliar with the workings of wagons, horses, camp equipment, and the great outdoors, Bicky required constant supervision. Not that the boy didn't try—the cook admired the young lad's eagerness and quick mind. Still, there was a lot to learn.

And so twilight was fading as the cowboy crew circled the fire with steaming plates of spotted pup, fresh-baked biscuits, and fried bacon, accompanied by coffee so hot it would burn the hair off your tongue.

"Say, coosie," Frenchy said around a mouthful of rice and raisins, "I cannot recall when I so enjoyed spotted pup. Just the right amount of sweetness!"

The cook huffed and mumbled and said, "Think nothing of it. But don't get used to it. Weren't enough time to boil beans— but they're on the fire now, and that pot won't be empty till we strike Tombstone. Besides, I got to go easy on the raisins if you expect any hucky-dummy on this trip."

"I allow as how that would be a treat," Johnny Londo said. "But I got to admit that these here biscuits of yours is so toothsome as is that they would not be improved any by the presence of raisins."

Again, the crusty old dough roller harrumphed what passed equally for "thanks," "you're welcome," and "go to the devil" in his vocabulary.

Niceties out of the way, the men fell to eating with a vengeance, polishing their plates with biscuits until it left the tinware looking like it was coming out of the washtub instead of going in. Bicky, up to his elbows in soapy water, was grateful, but still scrubbed and scoured the plates briskly in an effort to please.

Bellies and coffee cups full, the cowboys spooled out bedrolls around the fire and sat or squatted or reclined on them, as blissful as contented cats. All, that is, save Johnny Londo and Tony Morales, who saddled night horses and rode out to relieve Rawhide Robinson, who had offered to delay his own supper and keep an eye on the herd until the first night guard arrived.

The men watched with interest as their leader wolfed down his portion and allowed him to settle in before barraging him with questions.

Arlo Axelrod opened with, "That went pretty well, don't you think, Boss? Gettin' the cats out here, I mean."

"I reckon so. Truth be told, I didn't know what to expect."

Zeb Howard wondered, "What's them cats gonna eat, Rawhide? They ain't like cattle who'll mosey around and eat the grass they're walkin' on."

"That's a question, all right. I don't rightly know the answer, but here's what I think. These plains is home to all manner of rodents—mice and voles and ground squirrels and prairie dogs and pocket gophers and kangaroo rats and such. Then there's all kinds of birds in the brush and fish and frogs in the streams. There'll be lizards and snakes along the way. What I'm sayin', I guess, is that these cats ought to be able to fend for themselves on the trail."

The cowboys thought that over for a few minutes, then Sop 'n Taters wondered how many miles he figured the herd would make in an average day.

"Well, that's another question," Rawhide Robinson said.

"Time will tell, that's for certain. But from all my noodling on the idea, I've come to think we ought to do as well as a cow herd; maybe better.

"These cats, of course, locomote on legs a whole lot shorter than a cow. But, you know, we move cattle slow so as they can graze all day as they go and not lose weight. We don't have to worry about that with these cats. And they do most of their eating at night anyways. We'll see how it goes. I figure we'll try moving along at a pretty good clip through the mornings and stop for a catnap while we have our dinner and catch a few winks ourselves, then push on until sundown."

"What about water?" someone wondered.

"A cat can't hold much, I don't figure. We'll overnight near water whenever we can, just like with cow critters. But I packed a couple extra barrels to haul water. When we make a dry camp, or have to push hard across a waterless stretch, I figure we can pack enough water to keep the cats going."

"I ain't never been out in that country we're headin' for," Arlo said. "And the fact is, I ain't got no clue how to get there."

Rawhide Robinson refilled his coffee cup, and, in the best "man at the pot" trail-drive and cow-camp tradition, refilled the cups of all who required it.

"First part's easy," he said after a sip. "We'll follow the Santa Fe Trail to Santa Fe—something like six-, seven-hundred miles. After that, we'll have to see. But back during the Mexican War a battalion of Mormon soldiers and a bunch of troops out of Missouri who were headed for Old Mexico took the trail to Santa Fe then followed the Rio Grande south from there. From what I read, them Mormon boys took a right turn somewheres down near the Mexican border to blaze a trail to California. If we can find that road, it ought to take us close enough to Tombstone that we can find our way from there."

The trail boss downed the last swallow of his coffee and

tossed the dregs into the fire. "You boys is all set for your turn on guard, I guess. Wake me and Arlo up for the last shift. Best turn in now and sleep while you can. I don't have any idea what might happen, but I'll tell you this: them cats is wound up like a two-dollar watch, and I'm a mite nervous myself."

Rawhide Robinson reclined atop his bedroll, head pillowed on the seat of his saddle, and tipped the brim of his thirteen-gallon hat over his eyes to block the glow of the full moon that hung in the eastern sky. Amid the somnolent chirp of crickets, coyotes on the surrounding hills commenced yipping and howling.

And that's when all hell broke loose.

CHAPTER THIRTEEN

Longshot Hawken sat in his camp atop a hill just east of Dodge City. A battered pan, no bigger around than a bear track, covered most of the smoldering fire before him, the remnants of the coffee it contained still steaming in the darkness of the approaching dawn. Normally, the old man still slept at this time of the day—or night—but he had been awakened by a ruction in the night and unable to return to his slumber.

Had the man been illuminated by more than moonlight, and had he been standing, his most prominent physical feature would be impossible to miss: Longshot Hawken was long. Every part of his body was stretched thin, from his elongated legs to his extended trunk and stringy arms. His neck, too, was tall and narrow, burned by the sun and crosshatched by age until it resembled nothing more than a basket-stamped leather cuff that might festoon the wrist of a shadow-riding buckaroo. In fact, the only part of Longshot Hawken that approached the horizontal was the broad brim of the Mexican sombrero atop the head that, like the hat's crown that sat upon it, was tall and thin and somewhat tapered, further accenting his height.

As the antique man sipped his strong coffee, he ruminated on the disturbance that disrupted his rest. He knew its approximate source from the soft glow of a campfire rimming a rise to the south of his camp, beyond the railroad and toward Fort Dodge and the Arkansas River.

Having spent the better part of six decades wandering the

West, there was little the old fur trapper, mountain man, buffalo hunter, plainsman, scout, and guide hadn't seen—or heard—before. But the night's commotion was a mystery Longshot Hawken's curiosity demanded he solve. So, as a silver ribbon low on the eastern horizon announced the dawn, he moved the picket pin for his pack mule to fresh grass, cinched his saddle atop the brown mule formally called Molly Fourteen, but just Molly for short, swung aboard with the dexterity of a much younger man, and sat easy as the mule ambled down the hill and toward the camp where he believed the answers he sought resided.

A few intervening swales and rises separated him from his destination and the sky lightened considerably as Molly covered the distance. Topping the final rise, Longshot reined up and eyeballed the camp below. At first glance, it appeared to be an ordinary looking drover's campground, much like dozens of such he had seen over the years between here and Texas.

At first glance.

But, as the mountain man blinked and winked and squinted and peeped and gaped and gawked and ogled, his astonishment amplified until he questioned the very veracity of his eyeballs. Nothing in his long experience, nothing from his explorations from the Rio Sonora to the Bow River, the Missouri to the Salinas, the Skagit to the Sabine, could explain the sight that lay before the eyes he no longer trusted.

Cats. Acres of cats.

Not the mighty cougar or puma or panther or catamount or mountain lion, with which he was intimately familiar owing to numerous encounters over the years and the presence of which would not have surprised him overmuch.

No. What spread before him was Rawhide Robinson's herd of kitty cats. As the old man watched, some of the cats sat and scratched and pawed and licked. But most slept, curled in furry little balls across the prairie as if deposited there by a cloudburst. "Raining cats and dogs" was a phrase Longshot Hawken had heard but always considered metaphorical. Besides, there were no dogs in sight, so that couldn't be it.

Failing to come up with any explanation, reasonable or otherwise, he gave heel to Molly, determined to raise the camp and further an education in the ways of the West he had long considered complete.

"Hello the camp!" he hollered after stopping a respectful distance from the smoking fire, according to western etiquette. None of the lumpy bedrolls moved. Nor did any of the picketed horses, heads hung low, stir at his presence. He rode closer and again raised the cry. Still nothing. Fearing the occupants of the camp had perished from some mysterious malady or dread disease, he dare not approach any closer. Instead, he rode toward the herd of reposing felines to await the arrival of one of the cowboys riding circle.

As it happened, Rawhide Robinson himself first completed his anti-clockwise course and whoaed up his leg-weary horse a few feet shy of the visitor. The cowboy dropped his reins to the mount's mane and fisted the blur from his itchy eyes. He hauled up the canteen hanging from the saddle horn, swished a swallow of tepid water around in his filmy mouth, and spat it in a splash to the dirt and grass below.

"Howdy," he finally croaked.

Longshot Hawken nodded once in response.

Ever the accommodating host, Rawhide Robinson said, "I'd offer you a cup of joe, but I suspect the pot has boiled dry."

Longshot nodded once, then said, "That's all right. I already had some. But you look like a gallon or three wouldn't do you any damage and might rinse some of that red out of your eyes."

"I reckon you're right." After looking around at the inactive cats Rawhide Robinson said, "These kittens don't look like they're going anywhere anytime soon. Let's ride to the wagon and see if we can't stir the embers and turn some river water and a handful of Arbuckle's beans into a hot beverage with stimulating properties."

"If it's a cup of coffee you're offering with all that folderol I suppose I could top off what's already floating in my belly."

Now it was Rawhide Robinson's turn to nod once, which he did, then picked up the reins and with a gentle nudge turned his horse toward camp. Longshot Hawken followed. As they neared, Longshot could see that no one had stirred in the interim. The horses still stood hipshot and jaded, the bedrolls unmoving lumps of canvas, the cook fire nothing more than graying embers emitting the occasional faint wisp of smoke.

"What's the matter with your crew?" Longshot wondered. "Of a normal morning there'd be cooking and cussing and other commotion." The mountain man reined up his mule at the edge of camp. "Them men ain't been struck with the plague or the cholera or some other infectious illness, have they?"

"Nah," Rawhide Robinson said with a yawn. "They're just weary. We was all up all night, or the most of it, ridin' hard. They was in the saddle most all yesterday afternoon, as well. It ain't never easy getting a herd ready for the trail, but these critters beat all I ever seen."

Longshot Hawken nodded knowingly, even though Rawhide Robinson's response did nothing to illuminate the situation. They rode on into the camp and ground-tied their horses (or, in Longshot Hawken's case, mule). Ever helpful, the old man added twigs to the fire and blew into the embers until the pile ignited, piled on larger limbs and a log, and fanned the flickering flames with his broad-brimmed sombrero until the fire burned bright. In the meantime, Rawhide Robinson filled the smoke-stained coffeepot from the water barrel and ground up and added a portion of beans and hung the urn by its bail from the hook on the cook's metal rack as the flames licked at the arrangement.

"I'd offer you vittles, but we ate all that was fixed. And it don't look like the cocinero is in any shape to be whipping up anything as yet. He rode as hard as the rest of us last night and I reckon he's earned his rest."

"What happened?" Longshot asked as he watched the pot.

CHAPTER FOURTEEN

"You never seen such a catastrophe," Rawhide Robinson told Longshot Hawken. "I came up the trail from Texas with a whole passel of cow herds for more years than I can remember, and all of that altogether never caused me as much trouble as these cats instigated in one night."

And so began his tale of woe to the old trapper.

He told how the herd of cats, though nervous, seemed manageable when they came off the cattle car, ambling down the ramp and trotting out of town in as pretty a stream as you could ask for. (Although Rawhide Robinson did not realize it at the time, the presence of stockyard herd dogs played a role, hanging about as they were with heads up and eyes alert, curious about the cats and ready to nip at their heels if asked, and passively intimidating the felines in the process.)

He told how the herd bedded down in the shallow bowl last evening but never seemed to relax. Rather than licking and stretching, scratching and grooming, as one would expect, the cats squatted and trembled, scanning earth and sky with anxious eyes.

He told how the cats ignored the arrival of the chuckwagon and the uproar around camp as Sop 'n Taters and Bicky—the cook and his flunky—assembled a hurried supper for the cowboy crew.

He told how the cats remained uneasy on the bed ground, owing, perhaps, to the unfamiliarity of the wide-open spaces,

61

accustomed as they were to the confines of the city and, of late, the even more crowded conditions of the railroad car.

He told how, under the spell of the full moon, an unknown number of coyotes, not-too-near yet not-so-distant, cleared collective throats and launched a social serenade.

And he told how, as if the yipping and howling were a cue, the world came apart.

"If I hadn't seen it, I wouldn't believe it," Rawhide Robinson said. "Them cats rose as one, just like a cow herd fixing to stampede. But when they bolted and ran, they didn't go in a bunch like cattle will.

"Not a chance. They ran this way and that, hither and yon, here and there, from Dan to Beersheba and hell to breakfast. And the racket! Land sakes, them cats was squalling and squealing, howling and yowling, setting up a ruction like I never heard!"

Longshot Hawken nodded once in agreement and offered, "I heard it. Woke me from my sleep and scared the socks off me—would have had I been wearing socks, that is. But you're right—it was a racket like I never heard before."

He searched for a metaphor, a simile, a comparison of any kind to describe what he had heard in the night.

"Sort of as if all the women in the Crow Nation was keening after their men went off to raid horses from the Blackfeet and ended up with their hair hanging from a Piegan lodgepole . . .

"Or, maybe like the screaming of them banshees them bog-trotting Irish folks always talk about . . .

"Or, the rumpus that would be raised was you to assemble a party of knife-wielding hog farmers and castrate a whole barn full of shoats all at once . . .

"Anyhow, it were a commotion. Didn't know what on earth it was—or even if it was earthly. Might have risen from the depths of hell itself, for all I could tell . . ."

Rawhide Robinson and Longshot Hawken mulled that over for a moment before the cowboy again contributed to the conversation.

"I once rounded up a herd of laying hens, and I'm here to tell you that fiasco was a walk in the park compared to this cat catastrophe. We had horses and cowboys running in every direction. Even the ol' cook saddled up. The flunky was up all night himself, keeping the fire going and the coffee hot—not that we had time for coffee.

"I'll tell you, them cats is just too quick to handle. Just when you'd think you had one lined out to head it off, it would duck and dive and twist and turn and then seem to plumb disappear. Why, they can hide right under your horse and you'd never know where they got off to.

"And all that caterwauling. Like to beat my eardrums to death. Gave the horses the heebie-jeebies. Turned the milk in the chuckwagon sour.

"Thing was, they didn't seem to want to go anywhere in particular. They'd just run one way for a while and then another, dodging each other as they ran. Didn't want to get together, but didn't want to go off by themselves, either.

"All things considered, it was the darndest thing I ever seen. Or heard. After several hours of chasing their tails and listening to that yowling it came to me that since they didn't seem to want to run far, there weren't no point in chasing them, trying to head them off.

"So, I had the boys ride circle around them, tightening the loop and slowing the pace as we went. Finally, them cats all just quit and plopped down on the prairie and fell asleep as if nothing had happened. The boys stumbled back to the chuckwagon and stuffed what food there was down their throats and hit the hay. Me and Arlo out there—that's Arlo Axelrod, my top hand—thought we'd best keep ridin' guard, just in case."

Longshot Hawken nodded once, then said, "That's some story. If'n I hadn't heard it myself, I wouldn't believe it."

"I *saw* it, and I don't believe it," Rawhide Robinson said.

The old man, still unsure of the situation and circumstances, inquired about the whys and wherefores of a herd of cats and Rawhide Robinson related his now well-rehearsed purpose.

"Tombstone, eh?" Longshot said. "As I recall, that's away down there somewhere near the Dragoon Mountains, or maybe the Huachuca Mountains, ain't it? Last time I was in that country there wasn't anything else there but my shadow. Since they found silver, they say there's a whole passel of people livin' out there on that mesa."

"People," Rawhide Robinson agreed. "And rats. Mice, too. But there ain't no cats to speak of—leastways not till I get there with this herd. Unless someone beats me to it."

Longshot Hawken laughed. "I reckon you're safe there, cowboy. Can't imagine anyone else has come up with such a harebrained idea."

"I sure hope . . ." the cowboy said, nodding off mid-sentence.

Tossing off the last of his coffee, the old mountain man mounted Molly and rode out to relieve Arlo Axelrod on guard. Part of his purpose in it was just being neighborly so the cowboy could get some sleep. But, for some reason he could not explain, Longshot Hawken did not think he was done with this outfit just yet.

CHAPTER FIFTEEN

Along about late afternoon, Rawhide Robinson and another cowboy rode out of camp at a gentle lope and intercepted Longshot Hawken and his plodding mule, still riding circle around the clowder of cats lazing on the prairie.

"Mr. Hawken, it's right neighborly of you to keep an eye on the herd," the trail boss said.

"Oh, that's all right. I wasn't up to much anyhow and Molly here was gettin' camp fever standin' around eatin' grass."

"I'm plumb embarrassed to have fallen asleep on you. It's altogether unlike me to pass up a chance to exercise my tongue. What say we let ol' Frenchy here take over and you and me go back to the wagon. The dough roller's got some biscuits on and has rustled up some other chuck. Made some fresh coffee, too."

"I'm obliged."

And so the unlikely duo rode back to the chuckwagon, now the scene of much more activity than during his previous visit. Cowboys were roping out horses from the remuda, bucking out the ornery ones, setting horseshoes, and otherwise readying the mounts for the trail. The flunky was chopping firewood. The cook saw the trail boss and the old trapper coming and poured a pair of tin cups brim full of blistering hot coffee. The promised biscuits, fresh out of the Dutch oven, were stacked and steaming on a couple of tin plates on the work table propped from the back of the chuckwagon.

Surprised at the generosity of the serving, Longshot grabbed a honey can and drizzled honey all over the biscuits on one of the plates. Witnessing the gluttony, the pot wrangler turned red and smoke shot out his ears. He opened his mouth to reprimand the mountain man, but Rawhide Robinson waved him off. The other plate of biscuits would have to suffice for the rest of the crew. Longshot was a guest. Besides, a heaping helping of sourdough bullets slathered in bee juice seemed little enough payment for most of a day's work riding herd.

Topping off the sweetness of his honey biscuits with a heap of salty beans and chuckwagon chicken—known as bacon in some circles—Longshot Hawken squatted near the campfire with a steaming cup of Arbuckle's coffee and turned his attention to his plate, seeking out the bottom of it with a vengeance. Once he found it, a rolling belch erupted from the depths of his digestive system, evidence of satisfaction with the chuck. He slid a worn Green River knife from a sheath on his belt and went to work whittling a toothpick.

"Think that sword you got there is up to that task?" a cowboy asked.

Hawken said, "I been packin' this particular pig sticker since the rendezvous of 1838. Fits my hand like a finger, it do. This ol' knife has skinned many a critter and carved up a wealth of carcasses, cleaved the joints and cut the quarters, it has slit fish bellies and sliced up rattlesnakes, scraped the bark off lodgepoles and stuck tie holes in lodge skins, chopped down a forest of saplings and shaved a mountain of tinder sticks. It has even stabbed attackers with ill intent and taken a scalp or two. So I don't suppose slivering out a toothpick will test it any."

He finished the whittling and set the toothpick to work at its assigned task and seemed to take an interest in the campfire, watching the smoldering coals with an intent look and wrinkled forehead.

"Say, Rawhide," he finally said. "How is it you propose to get these here cats to Tombstone?"

The trail boss, squatting on his haunches across the campfire, tipped his thirteen-gallon hat back on his head, sipped his coffee, and said, "Play it by ear, mostly, I suppose. Santa Fe Trail to start. Once we hit Santa Fe, I'm told there's a road south along the Rio Grande into Old Mexico. Somewheres along the way, we ought to be able to cut a trail west into that Arizona country, like them Mormon soldiers did away back in the Mexican War."

"I've rid all over that country," Longshot said. "And I say you've got the right idea. But the details, now, that'll take some thought."

"How do you mean?"

"Take the Santa Fe Trail, for instance—Cimarron route or the mountain route? That's a choice you'll have to be makin' soon."

"How soon?"

"Today. Maybe tomorrow. Day after, at the latest."

Rawhide Robinson pondered that for a minute or three, then said, "Don't know for sure. But I been leaning toward the Cimarron route as it's shorter, I'm told. What would you do?"

"Cimarron's shorter, all right. But it's dry and it's dusty. On the mountain route you're within spittin' distance of water most all the way. It's longer, sure, but it's rougher, too, out past Bent's Fort. You'll likely pay a toll at Raton Pass—don't know what they'd charge a head for cats. And goin' through them mountains from there to Santa Fe will test you for a fact. This late in the year, you might get snowed on. And, you might get run over by one of them stagecoaches they got goin' over that road.

"All told, to my way of thinkin', you're right to favor the old Cimarron route. These cats ought to handle it fine. Land sakes, you ought to could haul enough water for them cats—can't imagine the little critters drinks that much."

"Well, that's one decision made," Rawhide Robinson said. "Cimarron it is. And I already planned to haul water, just like you said."

"Good enough. Now, then, you'll have to decide where to cross the Arkansas. There's the Middle Crossings just beyond the Caches, just a long day, maybe two with your herd—say twenty miles—beyond Dodge. And the cats can probably walk across the Arkansas in some places along there for an easy crossing. Once across, it's sixty dry miles to the Cimarron River. But, like I said, you ought to be able to carry water for your cats.

"Or, you can stay with the Arkansas River another couple, three days out to Chouteau's Island and cross there—you might have to swim some, though. That crossing will put you maybe ten miles closer to striking the Cimarron River."

"Was it me, I'd cross early, there past the Caches," said Longshot.

Rawhide Robinson said, "Maybe. But maybe it'll be better to save them ten miles to get to water. Either way, once we're across, I don't suppose there'll be any trouble following the trail."

"Plain as the nose on your face, these days. Lots of paths and branches and such, but they all end up the same place. Wasn't so easy years ago—even ol' Jed Smith got lost out there one time, ended up killed by Comanches. But you'll have no trouble that way. Most of the Indians stay pretty close to the reserves these days."

Rawhide Robinson refilled his coffee cup and squatted at the fire again. He blew the hot off his drink and took a tentative sip. "You seem to have a good grasp of the facts, Mr. Hawken. What say I hire you on as scout and you ride along with us?"

Longshot Hawken thought that over for a moment. Then he

nodded once and said, "All right with me. Ain't nothin' else on my dance card just now. But I got to ask—you allow Molly in your outfit? I know how you Texas cowpunchers feel about mules."

Every cowboy on the crew looked to Rawhide Robinson to see how he would respond to that one. He mulled it over, then said, "You're talking about cowboys herding cats, here. And if you look around, you'll notice this crew ain't your ordinary bunch of ranahans. So I don't reckon a hardtail in the remuda will lower our social standing any."

"How about two mules?"

"Two!?"

"Two. This here's Molly Fourteen. Molly Twelve is back at camp. Don't ride him anymore, given he's a little long in the tooth. But he's a fine pack mule."

"Where's Molly Thirteen?"

"Ain't no such animal—thirteen bein' an unlucky number. Wouldn't wish that on any mule I ever met."

"And Molly Twelve is a 'he' you say?"

"Sure thing—much as a gelding can be a he, anyway. I know what you're thinkin'. *All* my mules is Mollies. Have been since the Molly I first rode from Missouri to the mountains way back when."

"I'd be honored if you and your mules would show us the way to Tombstone."

Longshot Hawken nodded once, checked the cinch on Molly's saddle, and mounted. "I'll break camp and be back here tomorrow."

With the sun kissing the horizon, Rawhide Robinson gave the crew marching orders for morning. "I'm thinkin' a pair, maybe four stock dogs might be worth havin' on this expedition," he said. "Them just bein' in the neighborhood sure kept them cats in line when they came off the train. And I reckon we could have used some pooches last night—might have cut that fandango short, had we had their help. So, I'll be ridin' into Dodge tonight to lay in the rest of the supplies and see about acquiring some drovers of the canine persuasion. You all just keep an eye on the cats. Two men on night guard at all times, two-hour shifts. I don't reckon they'll run—the tabbies don't seem troubled today—but, still.

"I'll be back tomorrow afternoon soon as I can get here with the delivery wagon and the dogs. You all be ready to move out and we'll see what happens when we try to herd these cats. Think of it as gettin' 'em trail broke. Don't suppose we'll make many miles, but we'll make a start of it. Any questions?"

There being none, the cowboy rode off toward town.

Tomorrow would be the day. Tomorrow, he would round up his clowder of cats and hit the trail on an adventure the likes of which only he, Rawhide Robinson, could imagine.

And an adventure the likes of which the world had never known.

CHAPTER SIXTEEN

The sun had barely started its climb when Longshot Hawken rode back into camp aboard Molly Fourteen with Molly Twelve trailing behind, without even a lead rope to keep him in line. Long days and weeks and years had taught the old mule that cooperation resulted in a much easier life, while recalcitrance only led to difficulty.

The mountain man unsaddled Molly, unloaded Molly the pack mule, and looked on as Sop 'n Taters and Bicky packed his possibles into the chuckwagon. Afterward, he squatted cross-legged at the fire with his rifle propped at his shoulder and a steaming cup of coffee in his hand. "You can call me Longshot Hawken," he said to the cowboys there assembled. "The trail boss has hired me on to scout this outfit, as I have been down this here trail many a time, and been through the rest of the country we'll be travelin' as well. I seen most of you yesterday, but never caught your names."

"Glad to have you with us, Longshot. Ol' Rawhide don't always observe the social niceties, so I'll handle the howdies. I'm Arlo Axelrod—you was kind enough to relieve me on guard—and I hired on as segundo. That Mexican-lookin' feller there is Tony Morales. Next to him is Johnny Londo. Zeb Howard is out with the herd now, you can howdy him later."

Longshot said, "That leaves this other one—I met him out on the herd ground. Frenchy, as I recall," he said to the cowboy.

"That's right, Mr. Hawken. Frenchy Leroux."

71

"Frenchy Leroux," Sop 'n Taters said with a laugh. "He's one of them Cajun cowboys from the Louisiana swamps. Me, I'm called Sop 'n Taters, and I'm the biscuit shooter on this outfit. I noticed yesterday you ain't got nothin' against biscuits."

"No, sir. I'm fond of 'em for a fact. I do believe I could eat a bushel of 'em."

"You darn near did, yesterday. I'll have to keep that appetite of yours in mind every time I mix up a batch of breadstuff. Though I have to say, Mr. Longshot, that your frame don't show no evidence of a fondness for food."

"No, it don't. I spent so many years half-starved out in the mountains that I guess this old body ain't caught up to all those missed meals yet. Who's the little feller?"

"That young man is Benedict Bickerstaff."

"Good heavens. His name is bigger than he is."

"I'm small, but all my parts work," the boy said.

"They do, do they?" Longshot asked around a laugh.

"That they do," the cook said. "These last couple of days he's worked his tail off. Ain't afraid to pitch right in. Learns fast, too. But you're right about the name bein' too big for him—so, he answers to Bicky."

"So, Bicky, how did you come to be part of this outfit?"

"I met Mr. Robinson in Chicago. I'm the one what gathered this here herd of alley cats, ain't I. I asked him to bring me along, so he did. Well, sort of, he did. I kind of had to stow away, didn't I."

The boy went on to recount the voyage from England on which he lost his mother and sister, and the sickness and death his father found in Chicago, and the years fending for himself among the other orphans, street urchins, strays, ragamuffins, and waifs in the streets and alleys of the Windy City.

With that, the cowboy crew seemed content to sip coffee and listen to the clatter of insects and cackle of birds. Johnny Londo rode out to relieve Zeb Howard on guard, but other than that there was little action around the fire until Bicky's curiosity got the better of him.

"That gun you got there—it's a big one, ain't it."

Longshot Hawken smiled and stood the rifle upright. "That there, son, is a genuine Hawken rifle, built long ago in St. Louis by my third cousin twice removed, Samuel Hawken his ownself. It's fifty-four caliber with a thirty-two-and-five-sixteenths-inch barrel. Overall, it's just shy of an inch over four feet long and weighs near ten pounds."

Noticing the blank look on Bicky's face, Longshot asked, "You know anything at all about guns, boy?"

"No, sir. Closest I ever come to one was them as was strapped to the side of the coppers in Chicago. I heard shooting in the night sometimes. But I don't know nothin' 'bout how they work or nothin'."

The old mountain man took a ball from his shot pouch and held it between finger and thumb. "This here ball is the thing, kid. This is what does the killing."

"That little thing!?" Bicky said. "I been hit on the head with bricks and boards lots bigger than that thing, ain't I, and they never killed me. How could that little thing hurt anybody?"

The cowboys laughed. Longshot Hawken reared back and flung the lead sphere, which landed with a thwack in the middle of the boy's forehead.

"Ouch!"

"That hurt any, boy?"

"Darn right!" he said, attempting to rub away the pain with the palm of his hand. "What'd you go and do that for?"

"This rifle—any gun, for that matter—will throw balls of lead at you a whole heap faster than that. So fast, in fact, you never see 'em coming. That little ball will punch a hole in your forehead goin' in and rip most of the back of your head off comin' out. This here particular gun has killed elk clean, dropped deer, stopped antelope, felled buffalo, and dispatched moose and bighorn sheep and grizzly bears and a heap of Indians. And it can do all that at a distance of four hundred yards. Don't never underestimate a gun, boy. Or the man what's holding one."

"No, sir," Bicky said. "Didn't mean no disrespect, did I. Just don't know about guns, is all."

"If you've a hankerin' to learn, I'll teach you. I reckon we'll have time on this here journey for a little schoolin'."

"Would you!? Could you show me about them little guns, too? The ones you hold in your hand?"

"That I can, lad. That I can. You just hold on to that there bullet, and one of these days I'll show you how it works."

Bicky looked at the lead ball with newfound interest, then, with anticipation all over his young face, tucked it carefully into a pocket.

CHAPTER SEVENTEEN

Rawhide Robinson sat horseback studying the Arkansas River as it wrapped around Chouteau's Island. The stream wasn't as wide here as it had been at the downstream crossings nearer Dodge City, but it was certainly deeper and the current stronger. He wondered if he had erred in opting to save ten miles of dry trail on the way to the Cimarron.

But the words Shakespeare put in Lady Macbeth's mouth—"What's done is done"—came to mind so he did not dwell on the decision. The river was there, and there was a crossing to make.

Sop 'n Taters and Bicky rode the chuckwagon across without incident. The river bottom seemed firm enough and not once did the wagon float. The boys pushed the remuda across and they made it easily without swimming.

But water that is shallow to a chuckwagon or a cow pony is something else altogether to a cat that stands, at best, two hands high. Add into the equation the fact—unknown to the drovers at the time—that cats dislike water and avoid getting wet at all costs, and a simple river crossing soon gets complicated.

The cowboys moved the herd to the stream's edge, much as they would any herd, but there the cats stopped dead in their tracks. Some dipped tentative paws into the water and soon withdrew them. Others extended claws and clenched a death grip on the riverbank. But all refused to use their paws to wade into the river. And no amount of hooting and hollering, no

75

amount of slapping coiled reatas against chap-covered thighs, no amount of whistling and whooping could convince them otherwise. Even the threat of heel-nipping cow dogs could not force the felines into the drink.

From his vantage point across the Arkansas, Benedict Bicker-staff watched the cowboys' and the dogs' frustrations grow at roughly the same rate as, but slightly less than, the cats' growing determination to hold their ground.

"Too bad we ain't got a boat," he said, as much to himself as to the cook standing nearby.

"Yep," Sop 'n Taters said. "It's a darn shame."

Bicky watched. And he thought. Among the thoughts sailing through his mind was the realization that, if you squinted your eyes just right, that dead, downed, and drowned cottonwood tree that had run aground upstream resembled the ship that had carried him across the ocean, what with its upraised limbs looking like masts.

As if bitten on the backside by a swarm of ants, Bicky commenced jumping up and down and yelling and waving his arms around.

"Mr. Robinson!" he shouted. "Mr. Robinson!"

It took awhile, but the trail boss eventually noticed the histrionics and forded the river to see what was up. He whoaed up as near to the babbling boy as the wary horse would allow, but could make no sense of what the flunky was saying. He turned to the kitchen mechanic: "What's got into him?"

"Darned if I know," Sop 'n Taters said. "He was just fine, then it was like a bomb went off in his britches."

"Calm down, boy," Rawhide said. "Take a deep breath or two."

Bicky composed himself enough to communicate, and quickly relayed his plan.

"I don't know," the cowboy said. "Sounds like a foolish idea to me."

"Foolish!" Bicky said. "Foolish! This, from a bloke what's herdin' cats?"

Rawhide Robinson laughed. "Let's try it. I ain't a man who's ever been afraid of being foolish."

Soon, he was crossing the river again, this time with Benedict Bickerstaff sitting behind the cantle of his saddle, hanging on as tight as he could while holding a bamboo fishing pole in one hand.

As you might expect, the cowboys were skeptical.

"It'll never work," Arlo Axelrod said.

"You must be nuts," Frenchy Leroux said.

"Crazy, that's what it is," said Tony Morales.

". . ." Johnny Londo added, once again rendered speechless.

"What's the fishing pole for?" Zeb Howard asked.

"Let's get at it, boys," Rawhide Robinson said. "It might not work, but it can't be any worse than what we're doing now."

And so the cowboys rode the river until locating the ideal fallen tree from among the hundreds in the water and along the bank. They selected a once-stately cottonwood, looped their reatas around various branches, and towed the tree to the appointed place.

A bit of maneuvering got the tree properly positioned, with the roots out in the river and the upper limbs reaching onto the riverbank.

"Well, there you go," one of the cowboys said. "What silly thing you want us to do next?"

"Be ready to ride when I gives the word," Bicky said.

"Hmmmph!" came the reply.

"Just shut yer pie hole and be ready!"

The boy reached into a pocket and pulled out a tiny bundle and unwrapped it to reveal a hunk of uncooked bacon, which he tied to the end of the fishing line. As the cowboys looked on, with expressions ranging from amazement to stupefaction to confusion to astonishment to consternation, Bicky dangled the pungent piece of pork above the perceptive proboscis of Percival Plantagenet.

The young angler effectively kept the bacon just out of reach of Percy's paws, tempting him with cunning feints and teasing maneuvers, increasing the cat's appetite with every move. Once he figured he had the cat well and truly hooked, Bicky flipped the tip of the rod riverward and the line reeled out and the bait dropped onto the tree trunk well out into the stream. Percy, of course, wasted nary a second leaping onto the tree and racing toward the lure of a bite of bacon.

And, to the amazement of all (except Bicky, who believed), the rest of the cats followed. It was a tight fit, but by clinging and clawing their way onto every inch of every branch, limb, twig, and trunk, all one thousand of the cats were treed.

The dumbfounded cowboys took their dallies, eased the slack out of their twines, spurred up their mounts, and towed the entire kit and caboodle across the Arkansas River.

CHAPTER EIGHTEEN

With the crossing accomplished, Sop 'n Taters and Bicky filled the kegs and barrels with Arkansas River water and the company headed south. They wouldn't make it far, having spent a good deal of the day getting the cats across the stream, but Rawhide Robinson determined to make a start of it.

It would be fifty dry miles to Wagon Bed Spring on the Cimarron River. The river was dry as often as not in most places, but, according to Longshot Hawken, the spring was reliable and within four days they'd have water enough to bathe in, if so inclined.

The crew—human, equine, and canine—pushed the cats late into the afternoon before the trail boss signaled a stop. Bicky hustled out of the chuckwagon and set to unloading the cooking paraphernalia. He dug pits for the cook fire and a campfire, gathered brush for tinder, pulled logs from the coonie slung under the wagon, and struck a match to the cook fire.

Sop 'n Taters got the coffee on and the biscuits in the Dutch ovens and set the beans to simmering while Bicky unhitched the team and clambered aboard the nearside horse (which Sop 'n Taters called *@#$%+, but Bicky called Brownie) and rode out to see to the saddle string, cutting out a half-dozen mounts favored as night horses and picketed them to graze nearer the camp so the night guards could make their selections.

With the cats bedded down, the cowboys rode into camp and quaffed down a welcome dinner, refilled coffee cups, and gathered around the campfire to unwind. Rawhide Robinson's responsibilities on this trail drive had overwhelmed his reputation as a raconteur, but, with the herd moving along as well as could be expected, the satisfactory performance of the makeshift cowboy crew he had recruited, the cooperation of the weather, and the absence of troubles from any outside source, he soon settled into old habits.

"Say boys, did I ever tell you about the time I . . ." he began, with a refrain familiar to all and sundry who had shared a campfire with the cowboy over the years. The men perked up, and Bicky, still toweling dishwater off his elbows, hustled over for a front-row seat.

". . . the time I rode a trail as dry as this one, up there in the Dakota Territory?"

"No, I don't believe I've heard that story," Zeb Howard said.

"It'd be news to me," Tony Morales said.

"I guess you better let me in on it," said Frenchy Leroux.

"Well, here's the deal," Rawhide Robinson said, scrunching down into a nest on his bedroll and tipping his thirteen-gallon hat back to reveal a lily-white forehead. "We was up north, not far from the badlands and a good distance from the Missouri or the Vermillion or the Cheyenne or any of them rivers up there. We had a mixed herd of some two thousand head, meant to stock a ranch up near the Canadian border. And, the fact is boys—and I'm not ashamed to say it—we was plumb lost. The sky had been clouded over for days, and without the North Star to go by we had no clue which way was up in that featureless land.

"Anyway, them cattle was as dry as the bones in Ezekiel's valley and if they didn't get quenched quick they would start keeling over. I was scoutin' around for water and came across a buffalo wallow. Now, we hadn't seen any buffalo for days, and them just small, scattered bunches. But, lo and behold, there was two mangy old bulls out in that wallow butting heads and bellering, on account of it was rutting season. Thing was, there weren't even any buffalos of the female persuasion around, so I guess they was doing it out of habit.

"As I sat there watchin' them old bulls, an idea occurred to me. See, that wallow was the lowest-lying place around there and I thought there might be water underground if I could only dig deep enough. And, by golly, I was right."

"Hold on there a minute, Rawhide," Arlo said. "How'd you dig down to water? And what's it got to do with buffalos?"

"What I done was, I cut me a couple of short poles off a scrawny old dead tree at the bottom of a coulee right near that buffalo wallow. Then I sneaked up on them old bulls and tied them to them poles—yoked them head to tail, I did, and slapped 'em a good one on the hindquarters to get 'em moving. Now, here's the thing. Each of them bisons thought he'd got the best of the other and had him on the run, which set him to chasing after him. Of course, the other bull thought the same and he set into chasing the other. 'Round and around they went, one chasing the other in a tight circle—never getting any closer, but always near enough to keep hoping.

"They ran and they ran and they ran and soon enough they wore a hole through the bottom of that buffalo wallow and it kept gettin' deeper and deeper. They was plumb out of sight by nightfall and by third watch you couldn't even hear 'em anymore. Come sunrise, I wandered down to the edge of that hole, and darned if there wasn't water rising up. Soon enough it was lapping over the edges of that hole looking as much like a regular pond as ever you did see.

"So, I mounted up and located the herd and by evening made it to that shiny new watering hole and every bull, cow, and calf in that herd drank their fill and never lowered the water even an inch. Then the clouds broke, with the North Star hanging up in the sky like a beacon. We pointed the wagon tongue so we'd know which way to aim the herd come morning, in case it clouded over again. And we ended up delivering that herd on time after all."

"Whoa up there, Rawhide!" Frenchy Leroux said. "What about them buffalo?"

Rawhide pondered that for a time, letting the curiosity of the cowboys rise to a fevered pitch.

"I don't rightly know, boys. I never seen 'em again."

He paused again, refilling his coffee cup.

"But I did see a newspaper later on up there in this town called Bismarck, and there was this report about some kind of excitement or other somewhere over in China on account of a pair of American buffalo had showed up out of nowhere."

"China?" said Sop 'n Taters.

"Nonsense!" said Arlo.

"Rubbish!" said Zeb.

"*Quoi!*" said Frenchy.

"Poppycock!" said Bicky.

". . ." said Johnny.

"Now, I ain't sayin' they was the same buffalo," Rawhide Robinson said. "I'm just tellin' you what happened. And every word of it's the honest truth."

With that, the cowboys crawled into their bedrolls. Sop 'n Taters gave the sky a once-over and, just in case, located the North Star, and aimed the wagon tongue in the opposite direction.

CHAPTER NINETEEN

Come morning, the cowboy crew started the day—even before morning coffee—by unloading planks stored in the bottom of the chuckwagon and nailing them together into crude V-shaped troughs, with a short section of plank nailed to each end as a plug and prop by which the troughs could stand. Water, bailed from barrels by the bucketful, filled the troughs.

By the time they finished, Bicky had the remuda pawing and snorting nearby and the cowboys roped out their mounts for the day.

The cats, not suffering yet for lack of water but glad for a drink, lined up at the troughs in groups as they were cut from the herd and driven in, with Percy, of course, leading the way. The dogs took a turn, then the saddle horses, and finally, the cowboys quenched their thirst with hot coffee, which beverage they also used to wash down a hearty breakfast of beans, bacon, and biscuits.

Longshot Hawken sat muleback aboard Molly Fourteen, ready and waiting to scout the trail. Not that it would be difficult to follow, with wagon tracks and ruts and paths pounded hard by years of traffic. Still, the trails sometimes seemed to tangle into a confusing maze, so the old mountain man's knowledge of the landscape likely saved valuable hours in crossing the Jornada.

Once the crew broke camp and Sop 'n Taters snapped the lines to get the chuckwagon rolling, the riders took up their positions and urged the herd into motion. It didn't take much, as the cowboys soon learned that with a few whistles and shouts, the dogs Rawhide Robinson wisely added to the company did most of the work. In fact, there was little for the hands to do other than ride along. Even though the cats raised little dust, the dry plain and steady breeze soon had the hands breathing through bandanas and wild rags tied bandit-style to filter grit.

The cats padded along without intermission that day, and the cowboys' noon meal consisted of leftover biscuit and bacon sandwiches eaten on the go, washed down with tepid canteen water. And so it was with relief the cowboys greeted the signal to bed down the herd at the end of a long, if uneventful, day.

But, as is often the case, a hot meal of bacon, beans, biscuits, and strong coffee perked up the saddle-weary—and bored—drovers just as the moon rose above the featureless horizon.

Benedict Bickerstaff, his day's work done, sat among the cowboys around the campfire. The feeling that he might, one day, be one of them cheered his soul. At the same time, the emptiness of the plain wrinkled his forehead and bent his eyebrows as he sipped at his watered-down coffee and cast suspicious glances into the distance.

Sensing the boy's worry, Rawhide Robinson said, "What's troubling you, button?"

"Oh, nothin' sir. Everything's hunky-dory."

"You keep looking out there like you expect to see something."

"That's just it, ain't it. There ain't nothin' out there to see. Not even a tree. Ain't seen even one tree since we got off the train, only except along the river. Don't trees grow out here?"

Frenchy Leroux said (with a sly smile), "It's the wind. Once a tree sprouts, see, the wind pulls it right out of the ground and blows it away."

"Naw," Zeb Howard said. "It ain't that. There's plenty of trees around, but they ain't got no trunks nor branches on account of they have to put all their energy into growin' roots so's they can reach down to water."

Bicky pondered those explanations, feeling the metaphorical tugs on his leg, until the trail boss spoke up.

"Don't listen to 'em, Benedict. They're having you on," Rawhide Robinson said. "The fact is, this whole country used to be lush with forest. Why, I recall when a squirrel could travel from the Canadian border to the Gulf of Mexico and never once touch the ground. Go the whole way, he could, crawling from limb to limb."

"What happened?" the boy asked. "Where'd they all go?"

"Well," Rawhide Robinson said, pausing to sip his coffee and squirm into a more comfortable seat on his bedroll. "I'm afraid that's my fault."

He said nothing more. Just sat and sipped his coffee and stared into the campfire.

"And?" Arlo said.

"What did you do?" Zeb wondered.

"Pourquoi?" the Cajun cowboy asked.

Bicky said nothing, but his eyes asked even more questions.

"Here's what happened, boys," Rawhide Robinson said softly as he roused himself from his private reverie. "It was one summer morning when I was just riding along through the woods minding my own business and singing a happy tune. 'Oh Susanna' was the name of the song, as I recall." A dramatic pause. "No, it might have been 'She'll Be Comin' 'Round the Mountain.' " Another pause.

"Get on with it! It don't matter what song it was!" someone said.

"All right then, but don't blame me if the mood's not properly set on account of a lack of proper musical context. Anyway, I was riding up on this lovely little meadow among the trees—not too big, maybe only three or four acres—when I spies this superb blood bay stallion all by his lonesome, just grazing as if he hadn't a care in the world. That horse wasn't no mustang nor Indian pony, I'll tell you. It was clear he came out of fine-blooded stock. Must have escaped from some rich man's wagon train or something. I knew he didn't belong to nobody nearby, on account of there wasn't anybody nearby.

"Anyway, I sat there with my eyes wide and jaw agape admiring that impeccable example of equine perfection. Like all horsemen, the thing most on my mind was how to get my saddle on him.

"I was, at the time, aboard a fleet little Spanish pony I'd traded this vaquero for when I was working on this spread down in Laredo. That Mexican boy had thrown in a clasp knife and his spurs for boot. Now, most of you has probably seen the kind of spurs those Mexican cowboys wear, but for the benefit of Bicky here, and anyone else not in the know, I'll tell you they had rowels about the size of that washtub you do dishes in. That big around, and with more points than I could count, despite the fact that my education included learning numbers."

Rawhide sipped his coffee some more and fidgeted with his position on the bedroll and adjusted the angle of his thirteen-gallon hat until the impatient cowboys urged him to get on with the tale.

"Finally, I determined to just go for it, and I built a loop in my reata—which, by the way, I had also traded that vaquero for. I untied from the saddle horn intending to take my dallies instead, which, as all you reata men know, is sometimes the best approach when putting your loop around a critter's neck in uncertain circumstances.

"So, I came bustin' out of the trees on a beeline for that stud horse. He didn't move a muscle. Just stood there with his ears up and nostrils flared and watched us come. I twirled my loop a time or two and fed a little more slack into it to make sure it was big and open enough to fit over that magnificent head and muscled neck.

"And darned if that hole in my rope didn't fly right and settle in perfect position. I jerked my slack and that's when the trouble started."

This time, the raconteur rose from his seat to refill his coffee cup, then stood staring out into the same distance Bicky had been studying.

The spellbound cowboys waited.

And waited.

Another outburst of impatience urged the storyteller back onto his bedroll and back into his story.

"Soon as my loop lit, that stallion leaped into action and hit his stride in no more than half a jump. I hadn't even time to dally before he hit the end of that rope. Every coil but one ripped loose from my grip and it was all I could do to strangle the end of that rope with every ounce of strength I owned in both hands. And even though my pony was running near top speed, that big horse was out of there like a shot fired from that there big ol' rifle Longshot Hawken carries.

"Then, like a sailing ship hit with a gust of wind, he turned on the speed and jerked me plumb out of my saddle. I'm tellin' you boys—and this is the honest truth—I never even hit the ground. Just flew through the air at the end of that rope with my cheeks flappin' in the breeze. Plumb scared I was, I don't mind telling you, but I darn sure wasn't going to let go of that rope, what with it having the finest horse I ever seen tied to the other end."

When Rawhide Robinson paused to sip some more coffee, Bicky filled the anxious silence with, "But what about the trees, sir? You ain't forgot about the trees have you?"

"Not a chance. In fact, at the time, I was worrying about that very thing. That meadow, you'll recall, wasn't all that spacious and I could see—which wasn't easy the way my eyelids was flutterin' in the wind—a wall of trees dead ahead.

"Then I could hear this screamy, scratchy whirring sound and had no idea what it was. Reminded me of a buzz saw, and it sounded like it was right behind me. I stole a glance, and darned if it wasn't my spur rowels, spinning so fast they weren't but a blur. That horse hit the timber with me a reata-length behind, and I'll be darned if them whirling spur rowels didn't start mowing them trees down like they wasn't even there. Talk about a buzz saw! Fact is, once I passed by there wasn't a tree left standing. Nothing but downed lumber in my wake."

"Ah, you're havin' me on, ain't you, sir."

"I believe he is, Bicky," said Frenchy.

"Sounds like it to me," Arlo said.

"I ain't telling you nothing but the truth," Rawhide responded. "Well, anyway, to wrap up this story and answer Bicky's question, that steed towed me from one end of the country to the other. He was determined to get away and I was just as determined not to allow it. Before he finally got winded, we'd laid waste to all the forests from the banks of the Missouri River to the foothills of the Rocky Mountains."

"Aw, Rawhide! That can't be true."

"Why, look around you, Zeb. See any trees around here?"

The cowboy ducked his head, as if to hide his shame behind his hat brim. "Nope."

"See. It's just like I said."

And, with that, Rawhide Robinson stretched out full-length on his bedroll and hid his smile beneath the brim of his hat. Tomorrow, he thought as he drifted into slumber, would be another day.

Soon he was snoring the night away while Bicky, in harmony with the cowboys, wondered at the veracity of his tale. It seemed improbable to all—save for the fact there were no trees.

CHAPTER TWENTY

Bicky dreamed about trees that night. Rich, verdant forests of deciduous trees with occasional patches of evergreens. Whether a reminder of his native England or the midwestern forests around Chicago he could not say. Like many dreams, it was masked by a touch of the surreal.

Still, when Sop 'n Taters toed him with a leather-boot alarm clock, his eyes snapped open and immediately looked around for trees. Alas, there were none. And he wondered if Rawhide Robinson's rowels had been their ruination, as the cowboy claimed.

Once he had the cook fire blazing he led the member of the chuckwagon team that doubled as jingle horse next to the wagon, climbed the spokes of the wheel, and hefted himself onto the animal's broad back. Riding out into the darkness before dawn, he found the remuda near where he expected and urged them toward camp.

He found the cowboys waiting and they were soon mounted and on the way to bring the cats to water, save Johnny Londo and Tony Morales, who hefted buckets of water into the troughs.

As cowboys and canines pushed the cats, Rawhide Robinson rode stirrup to stirrup with Arlo Axelrod. "Is it just me, Arlo, or do I hear some of those cats sneezing?"

"Couldn't say for sure. Ain't never heard a cat sneeze. But some of them's makin' some kind of strange noise. And I swear some of 'em's got the sniffles."

"Maybe we best rope out a few of them and look them over. Don't know as I know what to look for, but I guess it can't hurt."

Arlo thought it over, then said, "I reckon we ought to. That's what we'd do if they was beef critters."

They let the felines fill up with water and had the hounds hold them in a tight bunch while the cowboys discussed cat-roping techniques. No one, of course, offered any experience in the art, but they deferred to Tony Morales, the best roper among them.

"I don't know," he said. "Seems like a regular lariat thrown from horseback would knock 'em for a loop. We got any lighter rope?"

Sop 'n Taters rustled around in the wagon and located a roll of twine he carried to lash down the wagon cover and fly.

Tony looked it over, rolled its thickness between thumb and forefinger, and pronounced it suitable. He reeled off a twenty-foot length, figuring it a sufficient span for cat catching, and tied a honda in one end. At the edge of the herd, he watched and listened to catch a cat sneezing, then tossed a soft loop over the head of the offending tortoiseshell tomcat, snugged up the rope, and dragged the cat clear of the herd.

Once in the open, Tony hurried past the cat at an angle, deftly flipping the slack of his rope around the cat's hindquarters in order to trip him and roll him to the ground as the slack drew tight. All went as planned, except the cat flipped all the way over and lit on its feet, its back never touching the earth.

"Well, I'll be," Tony said as he tried the maneuver again, with the same result.

And again.

And yet again.

The cowboys laughed at the spectacle.

"@^%$*!" the frustrated twine tosser said. "Johnny, flank 'im down and hogtie him with a length of whang leather," the roper said.

Johnny Londo hooked an elbow around the rope and followed it to the cat, grasped the loop around the cat's neck (which required dropping to his knees, a cat being much shorter than a calf), reached across its back, and grabbed the flap of skin just ahead of the hind leg. He lifted and tipped with the aid of a knee and laid the cat on its side.

At least he meant to.

Instead, just before the cat touched the ground, it flipped itself upright and landed on its feet.

"C'mon, Johnny," Zeb said. "Don't let that cat get the best of you!"

Johnny flanked the cat again, with the same result.

And again.

And still again.

"&~^%@*!" Johnny said, stringing together more words than was his custom. "This ain't working!"

"Try legging him down," Frenchy said.

"You try it."

And so he did. But Frenchy had no better luck tipping the cat over using a front leg as a lever than Johnny had flanking him.

"Get another rope on him," Frenchy said with fire in his eyes.

Arlo reeled off another twenty feet of twine, tied a honda, built a loop, and threw as pretty a heel shot as ever was seen, snagging both of the puss's hind paws.

The men on the ropes stretched the cat as they would a cow critter and Frenchy waded in to tail the tabby down.

No such luck.

No contest.

Not a chance.

With every try, the cat twisted and turned and rotated and, without fail, its front paws hit the ground every time, grabbed a hold with its claws, and refused to fall.

Now, Arlo's dander was up.

"Here's what we do, Tony. Pull our ropes. Then, you forefoot him and I'll heel him."

And so they did. This time, with all four paws immobilized and airborne, the cat could not land on its feet. Still and all, he insisted on landing on his belly and would not be rolled, but that was good enough. Rawhide Robinson and Sop 'n Taters turned the cat this way and that, poked and prodded, palpated and percussed the furry feline from one end to the other.

"You know, I don't think there's anything wrong with him," Sop 'n Taters said. "I ain't no cat doctor, but he seems sound enough to me."

"I do believe you're right," Rawhide Robinson said. He released the cat and had the boys rope another one, then another, and still another. With their roping technique sorted out and perfected, the work went quickly.

The trail boss sat and thought, watching the cats as they licked and scratched, sneezed and sniffed. "They seem fine. I don't think there's anything ailing them. Maybe it's the dust."

Sop 'n Taters nodded in agreement.

The cowboy crew concurred.

"Well, we're burning daylight," said Rawhide Robinson. "Let's quit lollygagging and hit the trail."

CHAPTER TWENTY-ONE

Rawhide Robinson sat horseback overlooking his clowder of cats. The past two days, long ones, had finally got them across the dry Jornada and brought them to Wagon Bed Spring with the cats in reasonable shape. The tabbies had lost some flesh on the push, but having now gorged themselves on water, the rejuvenated cats stalked the brush and bushes hunting food.

Even Percy seemed himself again. The hefty tom, probably owing to his girth, had grown footsore and, rather than occupying his usual place at the head of the herd, spent the past day and a half perched atop a water barrel lashed to the side of the chuckwagon. Even from there, he kept an eye on the herd and from time to time—perhaps to lead by example, maybe to inspire his followers, or possibly for other reasons—he would hop off the barrel onto the iron tire of the wagon's rear wheel and trot along, facing backward as the wheel rolled forward beneath him.

The trail boss contemplated the actions of the top cat as he trotted along atop the wheel. It could be the tabby did it for purposes of slimming exercise. But he thought not, believing, correctly as it happens, that Percival Plantagenet admired his bulk, seeing it as a sign of prosperity, the result of a rich diet, and the upshot of superior bloodlines. In the cat's mind, thin and ropy alley cats were fine—in their place—but, clearly, he represented a grander, more evolved feline line and his leadership position was not only inevitable, but ordained.

Now, rested and refreshed from his chuckwagon interval, Percy snuggled into a comfy depression in the dirt, licking his paws and grooming his luxuriant coat, watching the herd much as the man on the horse, Rawhide Robinson, did.

The cowboy mulled over what he'd learned, so far, about herding cats. The use of dogs had been a lifesaver, he realized. With mere intimidation as their tool, they kept the cats lined out or bunched or spread, as circumstances required. While the tabbies had lost their fear of the dogs, they maintained a healthy respect—and a comfortable distance.

But that wasn't all. Curious coyotes skirted the herd continuously, but the presence of the pooches kept them at bay. Occasionally, one of the diminutive prairie wolves would venture near, only to beat a hasty retreat when the nearest dog gave chase. The cats, owing to sharp eyes and accumulated wisdom, understood the safety net the dogs wove around them and no longer feared the yipping and yapping and yowling of the coyotes, largely ignoring the menace that had once triggered a stampede.

Against his better judgment, but willing to follow the suggestion of his segundo, Arlo Axelrod, Rawhide Robinson no longer required his hands to ride night guard. That, too, was placed in the paws of the herd dogs with—so far, at least—satisfactory results. The cowboys, of course, were delighted with the development and, being better rested, were much more attentive during daylight hours in the saddle.

The cats and Rawhide Robinson had also come to realize as they made their way down the trail that, while danger at ground level was always a possibility to be guarded against, the real threat was overhead. Hawks, falcons, and eagles often circled in the daytime dome and owls sliced through night skies on silent wings, seeking out a meal that had strayed from the herd. Strength in numbers usually saved the day, and a coordinated

display of claws and teeth—accompanied by sibilant hissing—
usually encouraged the raptors to seek other skies.

A lariat, reeled out full-length by a mounted cowboy and
rapidly rotated in a buzzing arc above the herd, seemed to
confuse the predacious fowl and send them packing. And a
burst of anthill gravel blasted from the muzzle of an overcharged
fowling piece (carried in Sop 'n Taters's chuckwagon in the
event he happened upon a covey of quail, gaggle of geese,
congress of crows, rafter of turkeys, paddle of ducks, bevy of
sage hens, or other candidates for the stew pot to offer relief
from bacon and beans) proved prohibitive to persistent avian
predators.

Thus lost in thought, the sun slipped below the horizon
unbeknownst to the tabby trail boss. The bark of a dog awoke
him from his daydream—or dusk dream, as the case may be—
and Rawhide Robinson rode into camp for his ordinary—albeit
late—meal of biscuits, beans, and bacon. The drovers, fatigued
from the hard, dry, drive, were lethargic that evening, and one
and all tucked into their bedrolls early, hoping for a long and
peaceful night in dreamland.

Rawhide Robinson soon joined them. He did not know how
long he slept uninterrupted. It might have been a matter of
hours, or, possibly, measly minutes. He did not know, for a moment, what woke him. Storm? Stampede? Rustlers? Indian attack? His quick inventory of possibilities exhausted itself without
a conclusion and the cowboy sat upright and looked around.
Everyone in the camp was likewise engaged.

"What's going on?" Bicky said.

"Wha-wha-what's happening?" asked Sop 'n Taters.

"What is it!?" said Arlo Axelrod.

"*Ce qui se passe?*" Frenchy Leroux wondered.

"What the &*@#$?!" exclaimed Zeb Howard.

"*Qué está pasando?*" Tony Morales said.

"Wagh!" said Longshot Hawken.

". . . ?" Johnny Londo offered, confused beyond words.

The trail boss kept his own counsel.

The causes of their astonishment, their wonderment, their bewilderment, were many. Beneath them, the very earth rumbled; a gentle, but persistent shaking. The cook's canvas fly over the business end of the chuckwagon trembled. Hanging from an iron rod over the campfire, the coffeepot swayed slowly. The tin plates and cups in the chuck box rattled. The trace chains on the harnesses draped over the wagon tongue jingled. The glowing campfire coals rearranged themselves occasionally, licking up wisps of flame. Water sloshed in the washtub.

And under—or over—it all, an unrelenting hum or roar or reverberation or drone of some sort that seemed to come from everywhere, and nowhere.

"You know," Longshot Hawken said, "back when them big herds of buffs was still around, it was kind of like this when they was on the move."

Rawhide Robinson said, "But there ain't no big herds of buffalo anymore. Can't be that."

"Maybe it's one of them earthquakes," Arlo said.

Longshot denied it. "Nope. I was in an earthquake once in the Sierras. They ain't nothing like this. Nope, not at all."

"It's kind of like bein' under a railroad bridge when a train goes by, ain't it," Bicky said.

"But there sure ain't no trains around here," Tony said.

"I was in the Sandwich Islands once, where they have those big volcanoes," Rawhide Robinson said. "It's kind of like this before one of them erupts—but that can't be it, either."

"This is crazy," Frenchy said, "but it reminds me of being in the belly of one of them big steamships, like I was one time in New Orleans, loading a shipment of red beans and rice bound for Micronesia."

"Nah," Zeb said. "Ain't enough water in that Cimarron spring to float no boat."

". . ." Johnny said, his level of befuddlement more intense than that of his saddle pals.

"Hush up, now, and listen," Sop 'n Taters said.

And so they did. The cowboy crew sat upon their bedrolls, twisting their heads from side to side looking for a clue, tipping their heads at various angles listening for a hint.

Finally, awareness crept up Rawhide Robinson's face like a blush.

"Boys, I've got it!" he said. "It's the cats!"

"The cats?" came the choral response.

"The cats! They're purring! All one thousand of them is content and comfortable."

"You sure?" someone asked. "It's quite a racket for cats," someone else observed.

"It is," Rawhide said. "But like I said, it's a thousand head. Who knew how much commotion that many happy cats could make?"

"Hold on a minute there," Zeb said. "How's come they never done this before?"

"I don't know. Guess they've been fearful up till now. Fretful, perhaps. Maybe anxious or apprehensive or otherwise uneasy," the trail boss opined.

As if one, the cowboys rose from their bedrolls and walked toward the herd. Despite the noise, they were prone to tippy-toe, as if their presence might disturb the purring pussies. And they were careful in their stocking feet to avoid prickly pear and other thorny impediments.

Sure enough, the cats were serene and relaxed, each rolled in a furry little ball, purring away, making its individual contribution to the overall rumble.

Rawhide Robinson shook his head in wonder. "I don't know

about you-all, boys, but I'll sleep a lot better knowing them cats is content."

"Who can sleep with all this racket?" Tony said as they made their way back to the gentle glow of the campfire.

"You'll get used to it," Rawhide said as he stretched out on his bedroll. "Kind of relaxing, in a way."

And with that, Rawhide Robinson drifted off to sleep with, like the cats, a contented smile on his face.

CHAPTER TWENTY-TWO

All the talk around the breakfast fire was about the curious event of the night before, and how the persistent purring did, in fact, prove soothing, resulting in deep, dreamy sleep.

In due course, Rawhide Robinson prodded the boys along and they saddled up, packed up, loaded up, hitched up, mounted up, headed 'em up, and pushed the cats on down the trail. The day was an ordinary one—the cats traipsed along, flushing out and dining on rodents and reptiles on the way, held along the course of the trail by the herd dogs and mounted cowboys.

Along about late afternoon, Longshot Hawken rode over the horizon and informed Rawhide Robinson of a suitable bed ground with fresh water not far ahead.

With dinner out of the way, dishes done, fires fueled, and remuda at rest, Benedict Bickerstaff hunkered down next to the old mountain man. He reached into a pocket and pulled out the fifty-four caliber lead ball he kept there. The boy rolled the ball around in the palm of his hand, poked at it with his finger, and finally held it up for Hawken to see.

"Remember when you said you'd show me how to shoot?" he said.

Longshot nodded once.

"Well?"

"Well, what?"

"When?"

The old man tipped back his broad-brimmed sombrero, wrinkled his brow, scratched his grizzly beard, and said, "I reckon now's as good a time as any. Let me see if the boss objects."

Within minutes, the retired trapper rode off eastward along the back trail, the low-hanging sun at his back. Stretching ahead of him was Molly Fourteen's shadow and, in the distance, the silhouette of his sombrero. But, in between, his narrow frame barely blocked the sun, making for a most curious pattern of light and shadow. Behind, Bicky plodded along aboard the broad, bare back of Brownie, the wheel horse from the chuck-wagon hitch.

Once distant enough to not disturb the herd, Longshot Hawken espied the countryside to make sure they were alone. He dismounted to assemble a low cairn of rocks, then led the boy some fifty yards distant and the both of them dismounted.

"This here Hawken rifle is more dangerous than a rattlesnake, child, so always approach it as if it's ready to strike. Be ever careful and always assume it's loaded and ready to fire." He showed the boy the nipple and explained the absence of a percussion cap and how the rifle couldn't fire without one, rendering it—mostly—safe.

"Newer rifles load through the breech, or through a magazine of some sort," Longshot explained—then explained "load," "breech," and "magazine." After that, he opted to forego comparisons and stick to the Hawken itself. He reeled off the involved parts: muzzle, hammer, nipple, triggers, patch box. He showed and explained the functions of powder horn, shot pouch, starter stick, ramrod, and caps.

"Now, you're goin' to load the rifle. Just do as I say."

And Bicky did. He poured the requisite amount of powder down the muzzle and pounded the buttstock on the ground a time or two. He set a patch atop the barrel, added a ball, and used the short end of Longshot's starter to punch it into the hole, turned to the long end, and pounded the ball down the barrel. He pulled the ramrod from the thimbles and, with effort, shoved the ball down and down until it stopped, then gave it an extra shove to be sure it seated properly against the powder.

"She's almost ready," Longshot said.

He showed Bicky how to pull the hammer to full cock and cap the nipple. He reiterated the purpose of the double triggers and cautioned the boy to beware of the minute amount of pressure the front trigger required to fire the rifle once the rear trigger was set.

He explained how to aim the rifle by lining up the rear and front sights.

"It's a snap with this particular rifle, as I had the iron blade sight on the front up there replaced with brass—easier for these old eyes to see, you see."

"Right," Bicky said.

"Ready?" Longshot said.

"Ready," Bicky said.

"Line up on the top rock on that pile I made and fire away."

History does not record the final resting place of the bullet Bicky blasted out of Longshot Hawken's Hawken rifle, but the rock at which he aimed did not feel even the faintest hint of a breeze from its passing.

Longshot Hawken extended a hand with a smile and helped Bicky up from the ground upon which he lay as a result of the rifle's recoil.

"Kicks like Molly Fourteen, don't she?" he said as he picked up the Hawken.

Bicky dusted off the seat of his pants, picked up his hat, and screwed it down tight. "Gimme that thing," he growled.

With furrows in his brow you could plant corn in, the boy repeated the ritual of loading the Hawken as Longshot looked on. He hefted the heavy gun to his shoulder and looked for the target, waited until it came into view, pulled the set trigger, and when the target rock landed atop the brass sight he braced for the impact and touched the trigger.

This time, the stone perched on the pile exploded in a puff of dust.

Longshot said, "Land sakes!"

"Hit it that time, didn't I," Bicky said.

"That's some fine shootin', child. Load 'er up and let's try it again."

The result was the same, so Longshot retreated another fifty yards and the boy's aim remained true. Likewise at two hundred yards, which the trapper declared sufficient for the marksman's first time at shooting.

"He's a natural," Longshot told the cowboys when they rode out of the falling darkness and into the campfire's light. "Regular deadeye, he is."

"What'd he shoot?" Zeb asked.

"A whole pile of rocks," Longshot said. "Picked 'em off top to bottom slick as you please."

Bicky rotated his shoulder and rubbed the tender spot, still feeling the effects of the Hawken's kick.

"Ah, that ain't nothin'," Zeb said. "Rocks sit still. Ain't like a critter. And rocks don't shoot back, like a man will."

"Still, it's this child's first time even holdin' a rifle and I say he done fine."

"I did, didn't I!" Bicky said.

The long, lean mountain man patted the boy's back with a bony hand. "That you did, boy. That you did."

Sop 'n Taters said, "All right, eagle eye, you best turn in. Mornin' won't stand still for any more of your boasting."

The boy plopped onto his bedroll and pulled off his high-topped boots. "Can I shoot some more tomorrow, Mr. Long-shot?"

"We'll see, son. We'll see."

When the boy's breathing settled into a steady rhythm and the smile on his face stopped twitching, Longshot Hawken sidled over to Rawhide Robinson. "I ain't blowin' smoke about that lad's shootin'," he said. "He's got the knack for sure."

"I ain't surprised," the trail boss said. "The boy's sharp as a tack and eager as a beaver. Picks up things right quick, too."

"Say, Sop 'n Taters," Longshot said. "Could you use some camp meat?"

"Always," came the reply.

"You bet," came a cowboy's voice out of the darkness. "Something, anything, besides bacon would be downright pleasant."

"Now just you hush," the bean boiler said, "or the only thing you'll be workin' your jaws on is a cool water sandwich. You'll eat what's put in front of you and savor the flavor of every spoonful.

"Still and all," the cook said, "a little fresh meat would add variety to the menu."

Longshot Hawken thought a moment, then said to Rawhide Robinson, "I think what that boy needs along about now is a little huntin' trip."

CHAPTER TWENTY-THREE

Another ordinary day on the trail led to another ordinary evening around the fire.

"I don't believe we've lost a single head, have we, Arlo?" Rawhide Robinson said.

"No, according to my reckoning. Near as I can tell, every cat's accounted for."

Benedict Bickerstaff, toweling dishwater off his arms, said, "How'd you know?"

"What do you mean, boy?" Rawhide Robinson said.

"What I mean is, how do you know how many cats we got? With 'em all spread out and movin' 'round, you can't count 'em, can you?"

Rawhide Robinson said, "Well, you're right. Of course you can't count every cat."

"So?" the boy said.

"Well, it's like this, see," Rawhide Robinson said. "What you do is, you count their ears."

"What?"

"Yup. You count their ears, and then you divide by two."

"Balderdash!" Bicky said. "Ain't no way you could do that."

"Sure you can. It ain't easy, but it can be done. Not as easy as countin' cattle, but it's possible."

"How do you count cattle?"

"Well, you see, they're higher off the ground than cats, so you can see right under them as they trail along. So what you do, see, is count their hoofs. And, of course, divide by four."

"Poppycock!"

"It's always worked," the cowboy said. "Close enough, least-ways. So I was somewhat surprised when counting cats turned out different—counting ears, instead of hoofs."

All the cowboys nodded in agreement. Bicky remained bewildered.

"I suppose you could chalk it up to my limited experience with critters of the feline type," Rawhide Robinson said.

"You've had experience?" Arlo said. "This is the first time I ever been around cats, to speak of."

"Me too," said Sop 'n Taters.

"Même ici," Frenchy said.

"Likewise," Longshot said.

"Nor I," said Tony.

"Same here," said Zeb.

Johnny Londo, in an unusual effusion, said, "Where you been around cats before, Rawhide?"

"Not housecats or alley cats, mind you. But I was around other cats this one time. Fact is, I invented a whole new kind of cat."

"Do tell," the cowboy crew said as one.

Rawhide Robinson ambled over to the campfire and refilled his coffee cup.

"It was springtime in the Rockies," he said as he made his way back to his bedroll by the campfire. "I was on my way to rep on a roundup and got caught in the mountains in a late snowstorm. Snow piled up to my horse's belly in no time and showed no sign of stopping. Seein' as how I was headed uphill where it could only get worse, I rode into this little canyon and found shelter under a rock overhang and spied a cave there in the back wall.

"I pulled the kack off my horse and unloaded the packhorse

and poured them each a bait of oats. Gathered what I'd need to make coffee and fry up some bacon and ducked into the cave. It was a mite gamey in there, and I could hear something rustling around farther in, but figured it was bats or pack rats or some such and didn't pay it no mind. Anyway, that cave was dry and I figured once I got a fire lit it would be warm, and that was good enough for me. So I dragged in a heap of deadfall and built a fire there by the opening where it would draw good and I set into boiling coffee.

"That's when the trouble started," he said, then paused as he eased himself onto his bedroll and rooted around till finding a comfortable spot. He set his coffee cup aside and pulled off his boots one at a time, each requiring a good deal of effort accompanied by grunts and groans. He stretched out his legs and wiggled his toes, noticing the great toe on his left foot working its way through a thin spot in the fabric. By tomorrow at this time, he thought, it will have broken through.

"Rawhide!" Sop 'n Taters said.

"Huh?"

"Good heavens, man, get on with it!" Zeb said.

"Yeah, tell it," said Longshot Hawken.

"Right," Bicky said.

"Talk on," said Frenchy.

"Hold your horses, boys," the raconteur said. "Hold your horses." He tipped back his thirteen-gallon hat, picked up his coffee cup, and blew and sipped and blew and sipped.

"Here's what happened," he finally said. "And as sure as I'm sitting here what I am about to tell you is the honest truth. There I sat in that cave, slicing bacon into a skillet, when I hears a scream that set my hair on end. Then came all this hissing and spitting and growling from the back of the cave—out of sight, you see, so I hadn't the vaguest idea what was making all the racket.

"Then, these four cats came springing out of there. They wanted to quit the place altogether, I believe, but my fire blocked the cave opening. I'll tell you, them cats went right berserk. Running in circles, climbing the walls, scratching and biting at me, swatting me head to tail, smiting me hip and thigh."

"What kind of cats was they, Rawhide?" Arlo Axelrod asked.

"I didn't have time to consider it at the time, you see," the storyteller said. "But what they was, was baby mountain lions. Their mother must have been out hunting, I suppose, looking at it in hindsight. Couldn't say how old those kittens were, not being educated in the ways of pumas. But they were about twice the size of these alley cats we're herding. Bigger, even, than ol' Percy. Anyway, you can't imagine the confusion of cougars in that cave.

"Boys, I had to defend myself or I would have been shredded like cabbage for sauerkraut. And there I was, with nothing in hand but a butcher knife and a frying pan. I didn't want to kill them, them being but babies and me being the one to cause the conflagration. But, like I said, I had to do something so I set in to swinging away with both hands.

"What happened was, I sliced the tails right off all four of them puny panthers, and whacked each one sharply on the snout, which mashed their noses near flat. Thus discouraged, they crawled back into their corner. Needless to say, I hightailed it out of there to seek shelter elsewhere, not wanting to be in the neighborhood when that mother mountain lion came home."

"That's quite the story, Rawhide," Zeb said. "I imagine them cat scratches left a few scars."

"That they did, boys. But that ain't the half of it." Rawhide Robinson rose from his bedroll nest and again ambled to the coffeepot for a refill. When he was once again seated, his audience demanded, in sharp language, the completion of his tale.

"Well, I never knew about it for years, on account of not

visiting that mountainous region again. But, somewhere, I came across some naturalist's scientific report on the flora and fauna of the Rocky Mountains and he referred to a new feline species discovered in the high country. *Lynx rufus* of the cat family Felidae is the fancy name, but bobcat is what it is referred to commonly.

"The distinguishing features of the species is a bobbed tail and a flattened face. From the engraved illustration, I recognized right off that my defensive attack against them cougar kittens spawned a whole new breed of cat."

"Poppycock!" young Bicky said.

"Can't be," said Zeb.

"Nonsense," Sop 'n Taters said.

"Absurde!" said Frenchy.

Rawhide Robinson interrupted the denials: "Now, hold on there, boys. Any of you ever been to the Rocky Mountains?"

"No."

"No."

"No."

"Non!"

"Longshot Hawken here, he's spent years in them mountains. So, tell us, Longshot—you ever see any bobcats out there?"

"Why, yes. Yes, I have, Rawhide. Peeled the hides off a good many of them and seen a good many more."

"And their looks—do they look like what I said—short tail, flat face, and so on? Like their faces got whacked with a skillet and their tails slashed with a knife?"

"Sure enough."

"So you see, boys, it's just like I said."

With that, Rawhide Robinson rolled himself in his sougans, wiggled his toes to see if his sock yet maintained its integrity, tipped his thirteen-gallon hat down over his eyes, and let the

resonant purring of a thousand cats lull him to sleep.
None of them, by the way, being bobcats.

CHAPTER TWENTY-FOUR

Longshot Hawken rode over the horizon, looking, from a distance, like a big sombrero floating above a mule. As the illusion neared, the mountain man's body took form, looking first like a thread, then a post, and, finally, like a fabric-covered rack of bones thin enough to slide through a cinch ring.

"I declare," Rawhide Robinson said when the scout reined up before him. "If it weren't for that sombrero of yours, a man could believe ol' Molly Fourteen was riderless."

"The size of shadow he casts is no measure of a man," Longshot Hawken said. "Besides, what I lack in width I make up for in height."

"I reckon that's so. Still, you'd have to run around in a rainstorm just to get wet."

"At times, that very thing has proved an advantage. Speaking of water . . ." Longshot Hawken went on to describe the trail immediately ahead—where water would be found and the location of a suitable bed ground. Then, "Do you suppose that dough roller of yours could get through the day without the services of young Bicky?"

Rawhide Robinson removed his thirteen-gallon hat and scratched his head. "I don't see why not. What you got in mind for the boy?"

"I spied a bunch of antelope yonder way. I figger it's time the lad tossed some blue whistlers at something besides rocks and peach tins. Put some fresh meat in the pot, besides."

The trail boss agreed and Longshot rode off at an angle to intercept the chuckwagon. Benedict Bickerstaff held the lines. Sop 'n Taters, hat pulled low, slept through the bumps and bounces. Percival Plantagenet trotted along atop the iron tire of the right rear wheel, eyeballing the progress of the herd. When satisfied, the vast cat hopped onto the lid of the water barrel lashed to the sideboard, wrapped himself in a furry ball, and closed his yellow eyes.

The mountain man rode alongside the wagon for a spell, then said, "Say, boy, you still got that bullet I gave you back in Dodge?"

Bicky felt around in a pocket and answered in the affirmative.

"Well, wake up that slumbering cocinero. Me and you got places to go and things to do."

"I'm awake, you old rascal," Sop 'n Taters said. He tipped the brim of his hat back and eyeballed Longshot. "What is it you're up to?"

"I got a hankerin' for fresh meat. Me and this child is bound for antelope. I spied some away off yonder," Longshot said with a nod in the general direction of his intended travel.

"Hmmph. I suppose you'll be wantin' vittles to take along."

"It would be a pleasure."

"Well, then, I better pack a double portion to see you out and back—for unless I miss my bet, you'll come home empty-handed."

Longshot Hawken nodded once. "Could be. Depends on how young Bicky there shoots."

"That settles it, then. I'll make sure I pack plenty."

Bicky snorted. "Blarney! I'm a right deadeye, ain't I. Don't you worry none about me!"

"I'm told you're a right hand at shootin' rocks," the cook said. "But rocks don't go too good in a stew. Even salt and onions don't help 'em none. Besides, it ain't no chore to kill a rock—they stand still."

"Just you wait. You'll see."

Longshot rode off to the remuda to fetch Molly Twelve while the cook and his flunky raided the chuck box for a bag of leftover biscuits and slices of fried bacon. When Longshot returned aboard Molly Fourteen with Molly Twelve in tow, the boy elbowed his way aboard the mule, the old man tied the feed bag to his saddle horn, and the unlikely pair rode away.

"Antelopes is curious critters," Longshot told the boy some hours later when he stopped atop a slight rise to point out a small band of pronghorn way off in the distance. "Sometimes, a man can hide hisself in a shallow wash, tie a rag or set his hat atop a stick and hold it up, and sometimes them goats will walk right near just to see what it is.

"But they're skittish, too. And once they run, that's the last you'll see of 'em. They can outrun a horse for certain, and run a good long ways as well."

He explained how they would ride a wide arc to get downwind of the antelope and stay out of sight as much as possible in the approach, sticking to the low places on the gently rolling plain. This they did and when they were as close as Longshot felt comfortable being, they ground-tied the mules. Longshot handed Bicky his prized rifle.

"Get that ball of yours and charge yer weapon but don't cap it yet," he said.

They dragged themselves by their elbows to the crest of the rise separating them from the pronghorn band and peeked over the top. Longshot studied the herd and pointed out the target.

"I believe that fat doe will make the best eatin'," he said.

He explained where to aim for the best kill as Bicky pulled the hammer to full cock and slipped a percussion cap onto the nipple. Trembling, the boy found his target and struggled to control his rapid breathing, pulled the set trigger, exhaled slowly, touched off the powder with a gentle squeeze of the trigger, and watched the antelope—and everything else—disappear behind a cloud of white smoke.

When the haze lifted, Longshot Hawken said, "That's some fine shootin', child. You drilled her square."

Bicky waved the last of the smoke away and saw the other antelope still nearby.

"Gimme a ball!" he said.

"Ain't got one," Longshot said.

Bicky looked, and, sure enough, the mountain man's shot bag wasn't hanging from its usual place off Longshot's shoulder.

"Ain't got one! Why not?"

Longshot smiled. "We only needed one antelope, so we ought not need more than one bullet. And you already had one."

". . . !" the boy said, stricken with the same loss of words that often affected Johnny Londo.

"You wasn't fixin' to miss, was you?"

"No . . ."

"Well."

"But I could've, couldn't I."

The mountain man nodded once.

After cleaning the doe, Longshot Hawken hefted it across Molly Twelve's withers and Bicky's lap for the ride back to the chuckwagon.

Bicky's disbelief rode along with them.

"One bullet!

"I can't believe it! I coulda got three more of them beasts, couldn't I. But you got no bullets.

"One bullet!"

Longshot Hawken dropped back to ride behind the boy so he could stop trying not to smile.

"Only one bullet!"

The mountain man turned in the saddle and lifted the flap

on his saddlebag, just to assure himself the bulging shot pouch still rode safely.

"One lousy bullet!"

CHAPTER TWENTY-FIVE

"I can't tell you how much I appreciate the taste of fresh meat," Zeb Howard announced to the cowboy crowd assembled around the campfire as he licked antelope fat from his fingers.

For the past few days, Sop 'n Taters had graced their tin plates with antelope steaks, roast antelope, antelope stew, beans and antelope, antelope and biscuit sandwiches, antelope soup with rice and desiccated vegetables, antelope chili, antelope sausage, a meatloaf made from chopped antelope and wild onions, and a rich broth brewed from antelope bones, which proved an ideal dip for softening leftover corn dodgers and biscuits.

"Right fine, this antelope," Frenchy Leroux said with a satisfied rub of a full stomach.

"It is a pleasant change from bacon," said Tony Morales.

"Yep," Arlo Axelrod offered around a rolling belch. "A man could get used to eatin' antelope."

Longshot Hawken sat beside the fire with a whale-oil-soaked cotton cloth affixed to his wiping stick, cleaning the barrel of his trusty Hawken rifle. "I could not agree more," he said. "Maybe one of these days I'll have to give young Bicky here another bullet."

The witticism triggered a laugh from all assembled, save Benedict Bickerstaff, who said, "You can all go to the devil! I shot that antelope, didn't I. You ought to be thankin' me, not makin' light of me. Maybe next time I get a bullet—if ever I do—I'll miss, just to show you lot."

"Aw, Bicky, we don't mean nothing by it," Johnny Londo said in a rare display of vocal prowess. "Any time you get an itch in yer trigger finger, fire away. The menu around here has improved considerable since you shot that goat."

Sop 'n Taters said, "Indeed it has. Gives a man a chance to trot out his culinary skills and apply his gastronomical talents to something besides Mexican strawberries, sow belly, and shooters.

"Not that those ordinary comestibles from my mobile kitchen is anything short of sublime," he added.

The contented cowboys refilled their coffee cups—for it is an undisputed fact that the stimulating liquid drips and dribbles its way down through the cracks and crevices in even the fullest stomach, meaning there is always room for joe. Or jake. Or java. Or jitter juice, murk, or mud. Whatever you call it, cowboys always enjoy brewed bean juice of an evening, finding the hot beverage conducive to conversation, companionship, and comfort.

With everyone settled, Rawhide Robinson tipped back his thirteen-gallon hat and voiced a familiar refrain, "Say, boys, did I ever tell you about the time . . ."

The "boys"—including those with considerable years on them who respond to the label only in a general sense (meaning Longshot Hawken and Sop 'n Taters) and those who rightly deserve the description (meaning Benedict Bickerstaff)—wriggled and squirmed their respective frames into restful and relaxing aspects, knowing they were in for another enjoyable—but likely lengthy—true tale of bravery and daring in the Wild West.

". . . I participated in a sharpshooting exhibition against the renowned markswoman Annie Oakley?"

"No, Rawhide, I don't believe I've heard that one," one cowboy said.

"Me neither," said another.

"Nor I," another added.

"Pas moi," someone said.

"Do tell," said another.

"Well, I'm a fair hand with a rifle, although my nature forbids my boasting about it. But, one time in my travels I paid the price of admission to see the aforementioned little lady do some for-sure fancy shooting.

"Then, not wanting to embarrass her with a public challenge, I waited around afterwards cooling my heels till all the autograph seekers was gone. When finally I got the opportunity and challenged her to a shooting match, her handlers wanted to negotiate stakes and odds and all such, but I told them I was only interested in the competition, and did not wish to take unfair advantage of a youngster like Miss Moses—that being the name Miss Oakley was born with.

"They wasn't going for it, only being in it for the money, you see, but Annie, she had a competitive streak a mile wider than she is, so she told them to put a sock in it and roll out the guns and ammunition."

Rawhide Robinson paused to wet his whistle and collect his thoughts. His audience fidgeted.

"Now, Annie, she had herself quite an arsenal, even back then. All manner of firearms for various kinds of shooting, with special-made rounds for all occasions. Me, all I had was an abused and misused 56-56 Spencer repeating rifle I was packing at the time; one I was given in trade by an Army veteran of my acquaintance. But, rough-looking though it was, its aim was true so I reckoned I'd get by.

"We started the soirée with paper targets tacked to trees. Which immediately caused a row. See, Annie, she put every one of her shots in the bull's-eye in a pattern you could cover with the tips of two fingers. But them judges claimed I'd hit but one shot, with all the rest so far off I hadn't even scorched the paper. We bandied and bickered and quarreled and quibbled to no end until I ordered up a lumberjack with an ax and a rip saw. Fella name of Bunyan, as I recall. Well known in certain circles, he was.

"Anyhow, he sliced through that tree trunk slick as a skinning knife through axle grease, and there was the lead from all six of my shots lined up in one hole as neat as beads on a string."

"That sounds like some shootin'," Tony Morales said.

"Indeed it does," said Frenchy Leroux.

"I'll second that," Arlo Axelrod said.

Johnny Londo, often at a loss for words, said, ". . . !"

"Boys, that ain't the half of it," Rawhide Robinson said. He hefted himself up from his bedroll and ambled over to the coffeepot, filled his cup, and, in the best "man at the pot" Western tradition, offered to top off any cowboy who requested it. By the time the niceties were dealt with, anticipation among the cowhands was boiling over.

"C'mon, Rawhide, get on with it," said one.

Said another, "What happened next?"

"*Alors quoi?*" someone said.

"*Y entonces,* Rawhide?" another asked.

"Well, next thing, one of them assistants of Miss Annie's took a sheet from a newspaper and held it up sideways, with only the thin edge showing from our vantage. That young gal took aim and fired and that page parted right across the middle as if sheared by scissors, leaving that feller with half a sheet in each hand.

"Of course I was obligated to match her prowess. When the smoke from my shot cleared, that assistant down the way was still holding up the page like before. Annie's entourage started chortling and guffawing as if the contest was over—until that

newspaper page was turned in our direction," Rawhide Robinson said.

At that point, the trail boss paused as if to take a sip of coffee, but, in actuality, in a deliberate hiatus to build tension.

It worked.

"Dagnab it, Rawhide, quit yer ditherin' and tell us what happened!" Sop 'n Taters hollered as every head in the crowd nodded in agreement.

"All right, all right—loosen up your hatbands and relax. I'll
get to it," he said—then paused for another sip.

"What happened was, my shot—as intended—had trimmed a
tidy window out of the center of the page. And when that feller
bent down to pick up the piece I had cut out with my leaden
shear, he held it up for one and all to see that it was the
advertisement announcing Annie Oakley's Exposition of
Extraordinary Marksmanship there in that town, including, of
course, the date, time, place, and price of admission."

That assertion was greeted with a mixed chorus of declara-
tions of admiration and suspicion, with those esteeming the
cowboy's shooting skill holding, perhaps, a slight majority.

Rawhide Robinson continued.

"You'd a thought that would convince those folks of my
superior abilities as a sharpshooter, but such was not the case.
I'll tell you, boys, the barrel of that old Spencer rifle of mine
belched smoke and fire until it was too hot to touch. But, still,
they trotted out contest after contest.

"Annie shot the cigarette right out of an assistant's mouth,
after which I took my shot, with which I just grazed the end of
a quirley and set it alight. She shot down a dime tossed in the
air, after which I turned an airborne ten-cent piece into a nickel
and five pennies. Someone produced a deck of cards, and Annie
had the six of hearts tacked to a tree a far piece away and
proceeded, with six shots, to shoot a hole in every single red

spot. My card was the five of spades. I instructed the assistant to nail it up facedown, and still I obliterated every one of them obscured spade symbols pretty as you please."

"Now hold on a minute there," Longshot Hawken said. "I've seen a heap of shootin' in my time, and done a fair bit of it myself, and I ain't a-buyin' it."

"You're pullin' me leg, ain't you," Bicky said.

Zeb Howard said, "C'mon, Rawhide, admit it. You're feedin' us a line of @&^$%★."

"Absolutely, positively not," Rawhide responded. "It's the honest truth, every word of it. But I understand your skepticism. Them folks at the time didn't believe it either. So, I drew four more cards at random—their suit or number unbeknownst to me—and had them tacked up just the same. Then I fired away and blew the suits off every one of them cards. They turned them faceup to reveal the four, three, two, and ace of spades. Boys, I had shot myself a straight flush!"

"Oh pshaw!"

"No way!"

"I no lo creo!"

"Codswallop!"

"★+%#@!"

"Still and all, boys, that's an accurate account of what occurred. But, even at that, they still wouldn't give up. They allowed as how I had done well, so far, but doubted my luck would hold. So they started tossing these little glass target balls skyward, in singles and in bunches, and we'd take turns bursting them with rifle fire. It went on and on and on and on and on and on and on and on with neither me nor Miss Moses ever missing a shot.

"Finally, I said, 'Boys—and Miss Annie—this ain't never going to end, and I am down to my last cartridge. So, let me propose a final shot.' I explained what I had in mind, and they agreed that if I pulled it off I would be declared the winner, as it was so outlandish a suggestion that even the great Annie Oakley would not attempt to match it.

"So, I levered that final round into the chamber, licked my finger and held it up to test the wind, then took aim and fired—at nothing, it seemed. Then, we sat down to supper and, since it was coming on dark, retired for the evening. Come morning, Annie's entourage gathered and treated me to a sumptuous breakfast—sliced ham, as I recall, with fried spuds and onions, scrambled eggs, grits, fresh tomatoes, buttered English muffins, steeped tea, coffee, of course, and—"

"—Enough, Rawhide!" someone interrupted. "We don't care what you had for breakfast! Get on with the story!"

Rawhide Robinson tipped his thirteen-gallon hat back, scratched his chin whiskers, and sipped his coffee. "Sorry, boys," he finally said, "but it was a breakfast worth remembering. Especially in light of what happened next."

Again, he paused.

Again, his contrived reticence nearly fomented a mutiny.

And so he continued.

"Well, not long after the dishes was cleared, I called for the feller whose job had been tossing those glass balls in the air. I told him to be ready to toss a target on my command. Then I requested silence and those assembled complied.

"I listened.

"And I listened.

"And I listened.

"I'll tell you, boys, I like to have burst my eardrums so intense was my concentration on the auditory environment.

"Then I heard what I was listening for, faintly, oh so faintly. It was the sound of my bullet flying through the sky, coming toward us from the opposite direction in which I had fired it. The sound grew and grew and got louder and louder—but still beyond the hearing of all but me, as only I knew what to listen for and only I possessed the acoustic sensitivity to discern it—until I judged the time to be right and issued the command for the ball to be tossed, which it was, and just as it reached the apex of its flight, it burst into a bajillion pieces."

"What?"

"Huh?"

"Que?"

"Well it's simple, boys. I had shot plumb around the world and still hit the target. And if you don't believe me—an eventuality I cannot imagine—just you ask Annie Oakley."

". . . !" came the response, as all assembled were stricken with Johnny Londo's loss for words.

CHAPTER TWENTY-SIX

Rawhide Robinson let loose a whistle, raised his right hand high, and waved it in a tight circle. At once, the cowboys commenced letting the herd drift and looped the leaders into a loose mill on the ground where they would bed down for the night. The stop was earlier than usual this day, for some loose spokes on the right rear wheel of the chuckwagon required attention. (Loosened, perhaps, by the pounding paws of Percival Plantagenet as he plodded along atop it on occasion.)

Besides, Rawhide Robinson figured, the cats—and the cowboys—were due an extra hour or two of rest and he liked the look of the land. Although dry, the area was pockmarked with gopher mounds and prairie dog holes and brush was abundant, suggesting the presence of birds and rodents and reptiles for feed.

The country was open and level for miles in every direction, save for a conical hill Longshot called Round Mound. Atop the hill was a curiosity—a Sibley tent perched upon the eminence that continued the slope of the knoll. No other sign of life was evident, so Rawhide Robinson dismissed the canvas shelter without further thought.

But, later, as the sun slipped under the edge of the horizon, after he swallowed a last bit of biscuit softened with the sop from his bacon and beans and dropped his tin plate into the wreck pan, the entrepreneurial trail boss sipped from his refilled coffee cup and eyeballed the landscape. With a start, he noticed a faint glow washing the walls of the hilltop tent and a wispy haze lingering over the smoke hole. "Longshot!" he said.

The wizened guide rose from his squat in a singular motion and stood beside the cowboy before, it seemed, even taking a step. "What's up, boss?"

"Lookee there," Rawhide Robinson answered with a nod of his head toward the hill.

"Would you look at that," Longshot said. "I'd a sworn on a pack of prime beaver pelts that camp was abandoned."

"Me too." After a moment or four of contemplation, Rawhide Robinson said, "I reckon we had best ride on up there and see what there is to see."

The horseback duo (with Longshot, of course, being "horseback" aboard a mule) espied a pair of picketed horses as they angled around the hill to reach the top. They reined up a respectful distance from the tent but before either man had a chance to hail the camp, a booming voice from within seemed to shake the canvas. "Longshot Hawken, you ornery excuse of a two-legged fur-bearing fire-breathing free-trapping buffler-running tender-footed pilgrim, you may as well fall off that spindly imitation of a mount and come in. And bring that saddle tramp with you. Coffee's almost hot."

Once he managed to pick up the bottom of his jaw and reconnect his brain with his voice box, Longshot whispered, "Well, if that don't dampen yer powder. If that ain't Buckskin Zimmer I hear, I'll skin a grizzly bear with the splintered end of a lodgepole."

"Buckskin Zimmer?"

"Better light and come on inside, Rawhide. You'll have to see for yourself as there ain't no explainin' Buckskin Zimmer."

The drovers ducked through the door flap and stood for a moment examining the accommodations. In the middle of the roomy tent a shallow firehole lined with stones housed an efficient blaze. A blackened kettle hung from a hook on a leg of the tripod that held up the center pole. From another leg, a bent-up coffeepot steamed, with most of the mist shooting out a split seam halfway up the side. A tussled-up buffalo-robe bed pallet, a stack of spindly firewood, a pair of scuffed-up rawhide panniers, a jumble of parflêches and other containers, a well-worn McClellan saddle with a bridle laying atop it, a double-rigged sawbuck packsaddle with breeching and breast collar, a water bag fashioned from a buffalo paunch, a long-barreled Sharps buffalo gun, a short-barreled Henry repeating rifle, a brace of Model 1858 Remington cap-and-ball revolvers, along with belts and bags and boxes and pouches and horns and tins of ammunition associated with each firearm, lined the walls of the circular tent—but all Buckskin's goods and chattels barely made a dent in the available space.

The tent's sole occupant lounged against a backrest of peeled willow sticks. A grizzled beard framed a wrinkled face below a head of thinning gray hair pulled back and bound with a leather thong. Since any other eventuality would destroy the harmony of the universe, Buckskin Zimmer was clad entirely in buck-skin—a beaded and fringed shirt, still handsome despite a chronology of grease and grime and blood stains, similarly smutched britches festooned with a row of tarnished conchos up each leg, and, of course, moccasins.

Finally, Longshot Hawken said, "Mighty roomy for one ol' man, Buckskin."

"That it is. The United States Army gave me this tent—although they didn't mean to. I found it in the quartermaster's storeroom at Fort Fetterman one night after a spell of guiding them blue-coated idiots on an Indian campaign. Didn't look like anyone was using it at the time, and there was a whole stack of them there, so I requisitioned me this one," he laughed. "It is a bit much, I'll grant you, but it keeps my belongings out of the weather. And it don't get to smelling so rank in here should my personal hygiene lapse from time to time."

Rawhide Robinson and Longshot Hawken lowered themselves to matted grass that served as the floor of the tent. Zimmer reached into a parflêche and rattled around and emerged with a pair of dinged-up tin cups and handed one to each of his guests. "You gents are welcome to coffee, such as it is. I'm afraid my pot is injured and its capacity reduced to four-and-a-half cups. Suits me fine, but tends to run short should company come. Which it seldom does. Anyway, help yourselves. We'll add water and beans as the need arises."

When it appeared that Longshot Hawken and Buckskin Zimmer did not intend to engage in conversation, Rawhide Robinson—abhorring silence in such situations—opted to open the ball. "How is it you came to choose this particular location to pitch your tent, Mr. Zimmer? You are kind of exposed up here, ain't you?"

"Yes, but it don't matter much, these days. Ain't enough wind this time of year to be any bother. All the fight's gone out of the Indians and they're mostly penned up on reservations anyway so I don't anticipate attack from those quarters. Not too many travelers along this old trail these days and them few that do come along is so green around the gills that they present no danger. And should brigands with ill intent happen by, I can see them coming from a long ways off and assess the threat. But that has yet to happen."

Rawhide Robinson mulled that over for a time, then said, "You are off the beaten path out here. Why so far from civilization?"

"Because it is so far from civilization. I cannot tolerate the stink of human beings in bunches. Nor can I countenance the contrary ways of the current crop of cabbage heads overrunning the West. Sooner or later I'll sniff the stench of settlers on the wind and pull up stakes for a less-populated place, but that time is not now, not yet."

"Been out here long, Mr. Zimmer? Out west, I mean?"

"Stop calling him 'mister,' Rawhide, or he'll take on airs," Longshot said.

Buckskin laughed. "He's right. Not about the airs, but about the 'mister' part. Just call me Buckskin. But, to answer your question, I've been out here a while."

Longshot Hawken laughed. "A while my eye. This child is about the onliest man still livin' who has been in the West longer than yours truly. When Buckskin Zimmer first came west you could still see Zebulon Pike's footprints. He trapped for beaver and other peltries, collecting enough skins to upholster the whole world. This randy ol' man wintered over with more Indian bands than I can name and married up with women from more than a few of those tribes. He led bullwhackers down this here Santa Fe Trail when it was too fresh to raise dust, hunted buffalo with the Métis on the Red River Plains, supplied meat for steamboats on the Missouri, showed mapmakers and so-called explorers the way to go, scouted for the Army, guided wagon trains over every trail there is and some he invented, hunted buffs for the railroads, and harvested tons of hides from both the northern and southern herds. He knows the Californios and Texians and their ways, the Spanish Grandees and Mexican peons of the Southwest, the English and the French and the Russians of the Northwest, the missionaries, the Mormons, the miners, the loggers, the fishermen, and the drovers. All that and then some, not necessarily in that order. Suffice it to say that if there's anywhere in the West Buckskin Zimmer ain't been, then no one else has been there either."

Now it was Buckskin Zimmer's turn to laugh. "There's truth in what he says, but, I fear, too much of it. I'm an old, old man and most all of that is simply a function of the years. But, now, my time has passed and it is a chore just to keep coffee in the pot and meat in the pan. A man like me can't hardly scratch out a living anymore."

The old man paused for a moment, then: "What I want to know from you two is, what's the deal with all them cats? In all my years, I ain't never seen hardly any of them critters here in the West, save a few with them Celestials what worked the mines and built the railroads."

That question, as you might imagine, resulted in a lengthy explanation of the trail drive and its purpose, along with a recounting of various adventures along the way.

"Well, boys, that proves my point," Buckskin offered.

Rawhide Robinson asked, "What's that?"

"If there weren't so many people out here, including out there in Tombstone, there wouldn't be no rats."

Neither of the guests could argue with that.

"Then again, if there were no rats, they wouldn't need cats. Which circumstance would have deprived me of seeing my old friend Longshot Hawken again, and the opportunity to meet you, Rawhide Robinson."

And, he thought, a chance to maybe make some money.

"It surely has been a pleasure, Buckskin," the cowboy said around a stifled yawn. "Well I'll be a son-of-a-gun, Longshot!" he said, noticing the tent wall brightening with the dawn. "Darned if we ain't chin-wagged the night away. Rattle yer hocks, you old reprobate—we got a herd of cats waitin' and we're burnin' daylight."

The timeworn trapper followed his guests through the tent flap and watched them angle down the hill toward the herd. Through a battered brass telescope, he studied the cats as they roused from their slumber, stretching and scratching. Buckskin Zimmer mimicked their actions as he pondered the potential market for pussy cat fur.

CHAPTER TWENTY-SEVEN

Rawhide Robinson and Longshot Hawken ambled down the hill in the gray light of dawn.

"Quite the feller, that Buckskin Zimmer," the cowboy said.

"That he be," the old mountain man agreed. "He's everything I told you. But, I didn't tell you everything."

"Oh?"

"Not by a darn sight. Now, understand, I can't swear to this from any of my own knowin', but the fact is, it's been rumored for years that the old man's fingers is a mite sticky. Oh, nobody ever caught him at nothin', but many's the time another man's traps in his company came up empty, even after being sprung. At the same time, ol' Buckskin seemed to catch more beavers than he had traps.

"Them traders kept a close eye on him at rendezvous and at forts and never saw nothin', but their stores always seemed to tally up short when he was around. Even the Indians was suspicious—which is why he took up with so many different tribes. After a time, they'd always send him packin' without ever any explanation as to why.

"And so on. There were complaints from some of the wagon trains he guided and he was never welcome back in some of the settlements and no army outfit ever hired him twice nor let him inside the walls of their stockades a second time. Still, like I said, no one ever proved anything. Might have been nothin' but talk, for all I know. But I always keep one eye peeled whenever

Buckskin Zimmer's around."

Breakfast was over and the hands were mounted when the pair rode into camp. Up to his elbows in the wreck pan, Bicky said, "You missed chuck, didn't you, boss. Don't you and Mr. Hawken be comin' 'round beggin' for leftover sinkers when yer belly starts complainin'."

"Oh pshaw!" said Sop 'n Taters. "Don't pay no attention to that boy. I've set aside plates for the both of you. Bacon, beans, and biscuits aplenty," he said as he poured coffee for them. "I swear boss, sometimes that Benedict Bickerstaff gets too big for his britches."

Rawhide Robinson laughed. "Why, I swear, coosie, if I didn't recognize that boy's voice, I'd have sworn that was you talking. He ain't saying anything he didn't learn from you."

The two hungry men kept at their breakfasts, then sat back and sipped coffee as the cook and his flunky struck camp. "Looks like them boys got the herd goin' all right without our help this mornin', Rawhide."

"Sure thing. They're good hands. I reckon if they were going off in the wrong direction you'd have said something by now."

"Oh, a blind man could follow the trail through this country. It wanders some and spreads out here and there, but the general direction's always the same. We'll strike Rock Creek—Carrizo Creek, as some calls it—less than ten miles ahead. But it's unlikely we'll find water there, this time of year. But I figger we can push on another four, five miles past that and make another dry camp, then we'll be in easy strikin' distance of water at Point of Rocks tomorrow."

Rawhide Robinson took a last sip of his coffee and tossed the dregs into the dying fire. "We ain't getting any closer sitting here jawing. Let's ride."

From his perch atop Round Mound, Buckskin Zimmer watched the strangest trail herd he'd ever seen, or hear tell of, fade into the distance until nothing but a faint haze of dust remained. Then he set to folding his own tent, loading his packhorse, and lighting out on his own.

His trail took him south toward an encampment of off-reservation Comanche he happened to know about. An old Indian healing woman had a particular herb in her apothecary he thought might come in handy.

Then, if all went well, he would head west and overtake the herd somewhere near the crossing on the Canadian River. The storm clouds gathering on the horizon should not affect his plan.

CHAPTER TWENTY-EIGHT

Throughout the day, clouds streamed overhead, growing thicker and heavier with each passing hour. Rawhide Robinson and Longshot Hawken sat horseback—and muleback—watching the sky.

"Reckon we're in for some rain?" the cowboy asked.

"Couldn't say. There's water in them clouds, but lots of times it don't want to fall on this country. Storms just keep on goin' and dump their load somewheres else. Could be we're in store for some thunder and lightning, though. We'll see."

"I don't know how them cats will react to a storm. Sure hope they don't run."

Longshot Hawken laughed. "I don't suppose many folks know what to expect from a herd of cats in any circumstance."

With that, the guide rode ahead, searching for a likely looking spot to overnight. He doubted he'd find any sheltered place, given the featureless landscape, but there just may be a shallow somewhere. Rawhide Robinson rode around the herd, alerting the cowboys to keep their eyes peeled and use the dogs to keep the herd close.

By late afternoon the wind came up. The clouds lowered, painting the landscape a dark and ominous gray. But the day, while fraught with tension, passed without incident and the drovers finally turned the anxious cats onto the bed ground Longshot located.

Thick clouds prevented knowing exactly when it happened,

but the sun dipped below the western horizon, introducing a thick, heavy darkness. The dogs sat trembling and anxious at their various stations around the herd and the cowboys rode circles around the fidgety cats.

Then the glow of lightning appeared in the distance. At first there were no visible bolts, only bright flashes illuminating clouds from within. Slow, rolling thunder accompanied the light show. But the electric storm moved ever closer, and soon lightning arced across the sky and thunder cracked almost in unison. Other lightning bolts smashed into the prairie, with strikes in every direction. The very air felt charged, standing cat fur on end and making it sparkle.

The cowboys dismounted and stepped away from their horses before huddling as low as possible. They stowed spurs in saddlebags and any chaps festooned with metal conchos were rolled and stowed. Even metal fillings in teeth caused concern.

But the cowboys were in for a lesson that night.

Unlike cattle, the cats did not rise and run, despite the severity of the lightning storm. Instead, they huddled ever closer until the herd looked—at least when lightning flashed—like a variegated carpet with deep pile. As the storm weakened and blew on toward the far horizon, the cowboy crew, one and all, breathed again. And the first time each exhaled it was with a giant sigh of relief.

The clouds thinned, then broke apart, and here and there stars winked and twinkled. Then, as if by magic, the veil disappeared altogether to reveal stars so thick and bright you could read a newspaper by their light.

One by one, the cowboys rode into camp and stripped their saddles, then redecorated themselves with whatever metal trimmings they had earlier hidden from the lightning, and they strapped spurs back onto their boot heels. The saddle mounts rejoined the remuda and the hands likewise herded up around

133

the campfire, grateful for the blistering hot coffee Sop 'n Taters
had boiled and brewed and had ready and waiting.

Little was said as the late supper made its way down the
drovers' throats. Each man seemed content with his own
thoughts, and more than one silent prayer of thanks made its
way up through the once-threatening sky.

With the meal safely stowed inside hungry stomachs, the
mood lightened and the cowboys set to swapping stories and
lies about the storms they had survived on the trail and in
roundup camps. Each attempted to outdo the other, and
Rawhide Robinson looked on and listened appreciatively, waiting to take his turn. He had long since learned that his storytell-
ing prowess more often than not left the audience in stunned
silence and prompted other tellers of tales to stow their stories
for another day, so he waited until all others had made their of-
ferings.

But when his turn came around, Rawhide Robinson was
ready.

As was often the case, he started out with, "Boys, did I ever
tell you about the time . . ."

After a chorus of responses in the negative, the raconteur
launched yet another true tale of bravery and daring in the Wild
West.

"We were pushing a herd north a few years back and the
weather thickened up much like it did today. Only it wasn't no
dry thunderstorm. No siree, rain was coming down by the
bucketful—until, that is, it starting dropping by the barrelful.

"Night came on with no let up. Eventually, the cattle ran, as
cattle will in such conditions, and when they stopped they were
scattered hither and yon across the prairie. Thing was, we
couldn't see past the curl on our hat brims, let alone see any
cow critters.

"Oh, when lightning would flash we might catch a glimpse of

one skating past and maybe some others standing around here and there, but then the lights would go out and there weren't a thing we could do but sit and stew. I'll tell you boys, it was altogether frustrating to be rendered helpless by something you can't even get a hold of. But darkness—and, by the same token, light—exists in that curious realm of things that are there, but, then again, they ain't there. I mean, can you touch darkness? Or light? Can you hold them in your hand? Can you feel them? Hear them? Smell them? How, even, can you talk about something as ephemeral as darkness? What can you—"

"Oh, for heaven's sake, Rawhide, knock off the philosophizing and get on with your story!" some cowboy said, and all the other cowboys concurred, voicing similar sentiments.

"Sorry, fellers. I occasionally get lost in flights of fancy."

He took the opportunity of the interruption to hotten up his coffee. He settled in once again and asked, "Now, where was I? Oh, right, here's what happened.

"See, right in the middle of that dark storm, I had this brainstorm that fully illuminated our situation and cast light on the way out. So, when lightning next flashed, I spied the nearest man on horseback and set coordinates to reach him.

"As it happened, it was a cowboy name of Bobby Lee Beauregard, a freed slave from the Deep South somewhere who made his way to the Lone Star State and took up cowboying. And I'm here to tell you, no finer cowboy ever plugged his feet into a pair of stirrups."

"Get on with it!" came the urgent request from the audience there assembled.

"Take it easy, boys. We'll get there. Anyway, I rode up right close to Bobby Lee and had to darn near stick my nose in his ear to be heard, so loud was the racket of that storm. But Bobby Lee finally figured out what I was after and nodded in agreement.

"We unleashed our lariats from our saddles and each shook out a loop. When next a lightning bolt bounced out of the sky to the ground, I managed to get my rope around it and take my dallies—this being an occasion, you understand, when dally roping seemed to me the wiser course as compared with tying off hard and fast.

"That lightning bolt was more than I could hold, so thank goodness Bobby Lee was quick with his rope, and accurate as well. He cast as pretty a loop as you please and jerked his slack and dallied so fast his hand was but a blur. And, keep in mind boys, it was easy to observe his lass-rope skills as that lightning bolt we'd dallied onto brightened things up like noontime for at least a half-mile in every direction.

"Now, that lightning bolt was sizzling and popping and pumping out heat like a bonfire, but we figured if we didn't get too close—which no one was of a mind to, mind you—it wouldn't do us any harm. Our horses never did get used to the idea of roping lightning, but with a firm hand on the bits they bent to our will, as good cow ponies will.

"Bobby Lee and me stumbled around for a while figuring out how to control that lightning bolt and soon enough sorted out the fact that if we stayed on opposite sides and kept our ropes taut and worked in unison like a well-broke team of horses hitched to a wagon we could drag that thing about anywhere we wanted to.

"And so we did. We spent the rest of that night towing that lightning bolt around while the other hands on the crew used its light to gather the herd.

"Of course it helped that the cattle was so confused by the whole situation that they were more likely to stare slack-jawed at that lightning bolt than hightail it and run."

With that, Rawhide Robinson leaned back against his saddle and took a long sip of coffee.

"Well?" Zeb Howard asked.

"And then?" Tony Morales said.

"Then what?" Arlo Axelrod wondered.

"That's it boys. We gathered the herd and from that night on the drive proceeded as planned."

"But what about that bolt of lightning? Did it just fizzle out, or what?" Sop 'n Taters said.

"Oh, no," Rawhide Robinson said. "It was burning bright as ever. When we was done, me and Bobby Lee unwound our dallies and pitched the tail ends of our twines loose, and that lightning bolt zipped back up into the sky in the blink of an eye, dragging two perfectly good ropes along with it.

"The trail boss agreed it was a small price to pay, and stood us both to the cost of a new rope."

And, with that, Rawhide Robinson stretched out until fully prone, plopped his thirteen-gallon hat over his eyes, and drifted off to dreamland with a smile on his face.

Johnny Londo voiced an opinion shared by the rest of the crew when he said, ". . . !"

CHAPTER TWENTY-NINE

It took some looking, but Buckskin Zimmer found the Comanche camp he sought. After the usual hobnobbing with the band's leader and socializing and smoking with the men, the Indians' suspicions waned and the old trapper was given access to the healer whose expertise had brought him to the camp.

Through a lengthy exchange of signs, halting English, limited Comanche, and stumbling Spanish the pair finally arrived at the particular medicinal herb Buckskin was looking for. The old woman bored the old man with detailed instructions for preparing and brewing the plant, and schooled him in its many beneficial uses, from reducing fever by causing sweats to aiding relaxation and sleep to improving digestion to repelling flies and mosquitos.

None of which was of interest to Buckskin Zimmer.

His interest in the herb was spurred by memories of its use by Celestials—Chinese immigrants—who had come to America by the boatload to work the goldfields and build the railroads. While hanging about their camps years ago, he had watched pet cats, of which the Orientals were fond, come running at the slightest whiff of the herb. And he had watched felines hop, skip, and jump, run and roll, writhe and wriggle, twist and turn, frisk and squirm, even go catatonic after ingesting the magic plant known as catnip.

So the scheming mountain man bargained and bartered for a supply of sufficient size, he hoped, to lure gangs of cats away from Rawhide Robinson's herd. While rustling mousers was not an occupation he had heretofore considered, Buckskin was an opportunistic sort and convinced himself that feline fleeces must have market value somewhere. And he fully intended to test the market.

Stuffing his bundle of catnip into a parflêche on his packhorse, Buckskin Zimmer rode west in the general direction of the Santa Fe Trail at the Rock Crossing of the Canadian River, where he planned to launch his evil scheme.

Unsure as yet exactly how he would go about the nefarious deed, he had no doubt the wherewithal would come to him at the appropriate time, as it had on so many occasions over the years. He seemed always to find a way to fill his gullet with an extra helping of food from some other hungry person's plate and varnish his tonsils with trade whiskey that, somehow, magically appeared in his tin cup. He somehow managed, on a frequent basis, to charge his firearms with purloined powder, lead lifted from someone else's supply, and caps pinched from any unguarded tin he encountered. And, if one looked carefully among his possibles, it is altogether likely one would find any number of items carved or etched or otherwise marked with names and initials not his own.

But, being such a lovable old cuss, Buckskin Zimmer was seldom, if ever, caught or even accused of helping himself to the belongings of others. Still, the suspicion was there, and a talent for tongue wagging would only make him welcome for so long before being invited to boil his coffee on another fire somewhere far away.

And so it should come as no surprise that his packhorse, in addition to the catnip to which he was entitled, also carried away from the Comanche camp a battered but serviceable coffeepot to replace his with the split seam, and a sizable sack of jerked venison. While not among his most lucrative takes, the future prospect of the cat hides to come put a smile on the old man's grizzled face as he ambled across the plain.

CHAPTER THIRTY

Benedict Bickerstaff rode into camp early one morning, jingling in the horses for the day's work. He slid off Brownie, the wagon horse he always rode, hitched up his britches, and did not stop stomping until he stood but six inches away from Rawhide Robinson. The trail boss kinked his neck to look into the fiery eyes of the boy, whose neck was craned upward at a painful-looking angle.

"I need a horse of me own!" Bicky said, with more vehemence than was his custom when addressing the boss.

"Oh, you do, do you?"

"I do, and I want it now."

Rawhide Robinson took a step back to ease the slant in his upper spine. "What brought this on all of a sudden?"

Bicky took two steps forward to reclaim the uncomfortable—and, he hoped, intimidating—distance. "It ain't all of a sudden. I've needed me a horse for a long time, ain't I. A long time!"

"But you ain't said anything."

"Of course I haven't said anything, have I. I been keepin' myself to myself, ain't I. 'Seen but not heard,' like whelps of my station are supposed to be. But you're the boss of this outfit and you should notice who ain't well-mounted, shouldn't you."

Then, if such a thing were possible, Bicky's face turned an even darker, deeper shade of scarlet.

And he continued. "That harness horse ain't fit for ridin'. Why, he's so broad in the beam my knees won't bend and my

141

toes point straight up at the sky! I been watchin' you lot ride, and I know what I been doin' ain't no way to do it. Why, even that there old mule Mr. Hawken put me on to go huntin' antelope was better'n that wagon horse."

The trail boss lifted his lid and raked his fingers through his hair.

He kneaded his bristly chin with a thumb and forefinger.

He hitched both thumbs into the armholes of his vest.

He stuffed his hands into his pants pockets.

He removed his thirteen-gallon hat and scratched his head.

He checked the knot on his wild rag as if it was, all of a sudden, tight enough to restrict breathing.

Then he dropped his hands uselessly to his sides and studied the toes of his boots.

"Well . . ." he finally said.

Bicky waited for the boss to go on. He didn't.

"Well, what!?" the boy said.

Rawhide Robinson lifted his lid, then screwed it down tight as if he expected a sudden wind to come up, or a raunchy bronc to come unglued underneath him.

"We'll talk about it tonight," he said, then turned on his heel and marched away, leaving Bicky standing there as if nailed to the ground. Some who witnessed the event swore you could see wisps of smoke wafting out from under the kid's hat brim.

After a while, Sop 'n Taters rousted the boy and reminded him of his camp duties. The kid went through the cleaning up, packing up, and loading up with his jaws locked so tight the cocinero feared his teeth might shatter. And little changed throughout the day. When holding the lines, Bicky seemed to slap the backsides of the draft horses with them a little harder and a little more often than absolutely necessary—evidence, the old cook thought, that the boy was not himself.

Still, the cook allowed the boy to stew, figuring he would

either boil over or simmer down, eventually.

Without a word, Bicky helped make camp that afternoon, doing his part with the unloading and unpacking, fetching water from the nearby creek, scrounging the watercourse for firewood, laying the cook fire and the campfire, and seeing the remuda settled into suitable graze.

Before making his way back to camp, he gave the horses the once-over, eyeballing each at length and choosing, in his mind, which one should—could—would—be assigned as his mount.

If only.

Once supper had settled, the drovers took up relaxed positions around the campfire, settled onto their bedrolls, tin cups of coffee in hand, to ruminate on the day's events and swap story and song.

Across the campsite, next to the chuckwagon, Bicky, elbow deep in the wreck pan scrubbing supper dishes, stared at Rawhide Robinson with heat so intense that it liked to have raised blisters on the back of his neck. The trail boss, immersed in small talk, paid the boy no attention.

He did, however, wriggle and wiggle his neck from time to time, occasionally reaching back to give it a rub, wondering all the while why it felt like a hot iron fresh from the branding fire hovered just shy of the bare skin between his shaggy hairline and ragged collar.

Finally, the discomfort drove him to turn around and seek out the source of the spectral sparks discomfiting his nape.

Bicky's eyes glowed with the penetrating yellow fire of an alley cat's optics.

"Boy, you 'bout done with them dishes?"

Bicky only nodded in reply.

"Well, then, dry your fingers and rattle your hocks on over here."

And so he did.

"Now, why is it you think you need a saddle mount?"

"That wagon horse just plods along. Can't heel him out of a walk no way, can I. Me feet don't even reach deep enough to kick him, anyway. If ever I needed to hurry, say to head a horse trying to quit the bunch, I'd be in a right pickle, wouldn't I."

"Think you're up to handling a livelier mount?"

"Why not?"

"Well, you know, a cow pony can get a mite feisty from time to time. You don't always know what it's going to do, let alone when or where. And you ain't exactly got a lot of experience a-horseback. You might just end up in a heap on the ground."

"That's all right. You lot have all been bucked off and lived through it if them stories you tell is true, so I guess I can, too."

Rawhide Robinson nodded. "I reckon. And bein' young and all, you'll heal. But horses pitchin' a fit ain't the half of it. There's runaways. 'Fast' ain't all it's cracked up to be. Oh, I'll admit, breezin' across the plains with the wind whipping your wild rag and your hat stretchin' its stampede strings and bugs splattin' against your smiling teeth has its charms. Speed surely can be exhilarating. But there is danger involved when the horse takes on a notion of his own. Ain't that right, boys?"

"Oh, you bet," said Arlo Axelrod.

"Hay que tener cuidado," said Tony Morales.

"A man could get hung up and drug," said Zeb Howard.

"There's prairie dog holes to trip you up," Johnny Londo offered in a rare display of elocution.

"One time I was swept off by a low-hangin' limb," said Longshot Hawken.

"As a boy one time, a runaway horse did not stop with me until I took a spill into Bayou Teche!" said Frenchy Leroux.

"Oh that's nothin'," said Sop 'n Taters. "I once got piled when a pony on the go refused to jump a sodbuster's little ol' irrigation ditch and stopped up short!"

The stories morphed into tales of other wrecks, horse races, and feats of remarkable equine speed.

"The fastest horse I ever rode," Rawhide Robinson said, "was this red roan cribber that was in my string one time."

"Cribber?" Bicky said. "What's a cribber?"

"Cribbing is a habit some horses take up sometimes. Don't know why—it's a mystery to me, as I cannot see any advantage in the practice. Be that as it may, some horses are cribbers. Which means they grab ahold of a mouthful of fence rail or somesuch and suck air. They bow their neck and huff in wind and it fills their lungs and guts and, I suspect, every empty space inside the animal. Them horses is called cribbers. It's a nasty habit, but there you go."

"So?" Bicky said. "What's that got to do with fast horses?"

"Yeah, Rawhide," Zeb said, "what's the connection?"

Other cowboys chimed in with, "What's the big deal?" and similar sentiments.

"Here's the thing," Rawhide Robinson said. "I'd catch that cribbing horse out of the saddle string from time to time and use him for a day of riding circle, or maybe to move cattle onto fresh grass. He was a passable pony, but sometimes a mite sluggish, with a hump in his back as if he had a bellyache—which didn't surprise me, given all the air he sucked up and swallowed with his cribbing."

The raconteur rested, as if collecting his thoughts.

"Come on, Rawhide!" Frenchy Leroux finally said to break the silence. *"C'est quoi l'histoire?"*

"Tell it!" Longshot Hawken said.

"Now, boys, keep your shirts on. 'How poor are they that have not patience,' the great Bard of Avon had that feller Iago say one time. I think he was talking about you-all," the cowboy said as he ambled over to the coffeepot for a refill.

Settled again on his bedroll, with his saddle as a backrest,

Rawhide Robinson tipped his thirteen-gallon hat back on his head, took an experimental sip of coffee, and carried on.

"I was ridin' that horse on a gather one day—a day much like any other," he said, easing back into the story. "Until, that is, a yearling steer decided he didn't want to be gathered and turned tail and ran. I wheeled that horse around and put the spurs to him. That's when it happened."

Again, he paused. And, again, his impatient audience urged him on, this time in no uncertain terms.

"Get on with it, &$%@*!" Arlo Axelrod said.

Rawhide Robinson smiled.

"What happened was," he said after a lengthy sip and slurp from his coffee cup, "was that that horse took off like one of them Chinese rockets. See, all that air that went in through the front end came out the back end in a long blast. Shot that horse—and me, being in the saddle pulling leather and pinching that apple for all I was worth to keep from blowing out the back door—across that ground at speeds that plumb curled my eyelids. Why, his feet weren't even touching the ground but maybe once every half mile or so."

"Nonsense!" someone said.

". . . !" said another—in this case, the effusive Johnny Londo.

"It's true, boys! I swear to it. And I'm here to tell you, I'm glad that saddle of mine is equipped with a breast collar. See, as that air rocketed out of that horse, his belly shrunk up and my cinches went slack and that saddle—and me that was in it—was riding on nothin' but faith, balance, and a breast collar."

The cowboy crew pondered on that for a time, the result of which contemplation was a question: "So what happened?"

"Oh, nothing much. That horse eventually expelled all that pent-up air and came to a halt. Took me two-and-a-half days to get back to the gather, but I got the cattle rounded up. Including, I might add, that bunch-quitting steer that eventuated the

146

whole affair."

He sipped some more coffee and squirmed into a more comfortable position.

"I did, however, take that horse all around that country for a while fixing up match races and made me a pretty packet of money. I never did get beat, so long as I could run on a straight course—I never did figure out how to turn that horse when he was on the fly."

Again, a pause.

And, again, "So what happened?"

"Oh, I was racing him against this pinto pony out in the Indian Territory one day. My horse got up a head of steam and we were leaving that paint behind when a buckle on my breast collar failed. Well, that horse kept going, but me and my saddle didn't. He shot right through the cinches and left us plowing a real pretty furrow through the grass. Thing was, without the extra weight of me and the saddle, that horse lifted off the ground and just kept on rising. Shot off into the sky until he weren't nothing but a speck, then disappeared altogether."

The raconteur paused for a taste of coffee, then concluded his tale. "Like I said, cribbing is a nasty habit in a horse."

No one said anything for a while, all lost in their own thoughts.

Bicky broke the silence.

"Sir?" he said.

"What is it, son?" Rawhide Robinson said.

"Don't mean to be disrespectful, sir. But what's all that twaddle got to do with me gettin' a horse of me own?"

"Just a cautionary tale, lad. Just so's you know that speed in a horse ain't all it's cracked up to be."

"But I ain't wantin' no rocket-powered race horse, am I. I just want me a pony who ain't ten yards wide and what can move beyond a plod."

Rawhide Robinson kneaded his chin for a moment. "I reckon you're entitled to one. Come morning, when you bring in the horses, have Arlo rope out that little ewe-necked dun. Then— after your chores are done and we've got the cats on the trail— one of the boys will help you get a kack on him and take the buck out of him. You ride him alongside the chuckwagon all day for a day or two and get his saddle blanket good and damp and you'll get used to the feel of each other. Just don't get in a hurry."

"No, sir. I won't, sir. Thank you, sir."

And, as the cowboys snuggled into their sougans and snored themselves off to dreamland, Benedict Bickerstaff stole away from camp, raced out to where the remuda grazed, and squatted in the grass studying a certain scrawny dun horse.

Tomorrow, he thought.

Tomorrow.

CHAPTER THIRTY-ONE

The herd reached the Rock Crossing of the Canadian River without incident. But the stream, although not formidable as crossings go, again intimidated the cats. There being no alternative ford—sandy, boggy bottoms upstream, deep canyons and a gorge downstream—Rawhide Robinson knew they must find a way.

He and Longshot Hawken scouted around for a deadfall tree to use as a ferry as they had on the Arkansas, but no suitable candidate had succumbed nearby. But, there was plenty of driftwood and remains of wrecked wagons in the neighborhood, so they opted to build a raft the horseback cowboys could tow. It would be slower, requiring multiple trips to ferry all the cats, and would likely prove chaotic—but, it would work.

And so they set to and, in the true Cowboy Way, did the job that needed doing.

As they pulled away from the river and started the herd along the trail toward Wagon Mound, Bicky said to Sop 'n Taters, "What's that out there?"

In the distance, the Sangre de Christo Mountains lifted off the horizon.

"Why, that looks like mountains, boy. You ain't never seen a mountain?"

" 'Course not. Not like them. I'm from England, ain't I. Didn't see anything like that between here and Chicago, neither."

Rod Miller

"Well, son, truth be told I ain't seen no mountains like those, either. Not in all my born days. Accordin' to ol' Longshot, them's part of the Rocky Mountains and we'll be going right through them. But it'll be a good long while before we get that far."

The trail boss signaled a stop not far beyond the river to rest the cats and cowboys from the crossing. As they made camp, Sop 'n Taters did a quick inventory and came up short a half sack of beans. After a session of "%&#@?" and a bout of "@!*$+" he sat down on the wagon tongue to contemplate the quandary.

"Here's what must have happened," he said. "When we unpacked the wagon to get to the toolbox to bang that raft together, I must have missed that sack. I ain't never done such a thing before, but there ain't no other explanation."

Rawhide Robinson scratched his beard as he considered the situation and the remedy. "Bicky," he said after a time. "How you gettin' along with that cow pony I mounted you on?"

"Fine as frog hair," the boy said. "Ain't been on him since two days past, but he's a right fine horse, ain't he."

"Reckon you could ride back down to the river, cross over to the other side, and hunt up that bag of beans?"

Bicky stretched himself up to his full height, then strained out a half-inch more. "Why, sure I can. I can ride, can't I? And the trail won't be nothin' to follow. And I can get across that water without even gettin' me feet wet. And if there's any beans there, I'll find 'em, won't I. Yes, sir, Mr. Robinson, sir, I'm your man."

The boss sent Johnny Londo to fetch the dun pony from the remuda and cinch up the saddle the boy had been riding. While that happened, Sop 'n Taters gave the boy his best guess as to where the beans might be, figuring the bag must be hiding behind a boulder there where they had unloaded the wagon,

150

and had somehow escaped detection during repacking. The red-faced old man encouraged the boy to be careful and, while he didn't say it with words, all present could tell he was grateful for the boy's willingness to correct his error.

"Just heft them frijoles on behind your saddle and lash 'em down," Rawhide Robinson offered by way of last-minute instruction. "Don't push your pony too hard, but keep up a good pace so's to get back here before dark."

With that, Benedict Bickerstaff reined his horse around and heeled him into a trot, back held straight and head high, as if he were Lancelot sent off to slay the dragon and save the fair Guinevere.

All went as planned. At first.

Bicky rummaged around the staging area for the crossing and did, indeed, find the half-bag of beans slouched behind a big rock. It looked to him like it had slithered off the top of the rock in all the excitement and thus remained concealed in the shadows. He parked his pony near the boulder, hefted the bag onto the big rock, then climbed up with it and lifted it higher onto the horse's back. As he lashed the saddle strings to secure it, he imagined hearing meowing cats in the distance.

He stopped. He listened. He held cupped hands behind each ear and turned slowly from side to side. And he heard it again.

Sensing something wrong—for cats had no business being there and could only be escapees from the herd—he leapt into the saddle (easily done, as he was standing on the rock, but satisfying to his heroic sensibilities nonetheless) and rode off in the direction he sensed the sound of meowing was coming from.

The direction was downstream, where the river soon cut into a gorge. He rounded a narrow tongue of land on the riverbank and found himself at the mouth of a narrow box canyon. The cat racket came from within.

Suspecting no danger, he rode boldly into the ravine, all the while imagining the heroic reception he would receive back at camp when he arrived, not only to return the missing beans but retrieving felines no one even knew were missing. He swelled with expected pride just as he negotiated a bend in the low gorge and came upon a campsite.

Someone had taken a good deal of trouble in the setup. A picket corral made from riverside willows held what he guessed to be about a hundred cats (although he did not follow the prescribed procedure of counting ears and dividing by two). Two horses were picketed nearby, and a cone-shaped canvas tent sat near the cat pen, with tendrils of smoke snaking out the top.

Bicky sat in shocked silence, trying to understand what he was seeing. One of the picketed horses whinnied and his pony replied.

The tent flap exploded outward and a bear of a man all dressed in leather burst through. "Hey!" he shouted, "what are you after?"

Bicky could say nothing. He sat in the saddle and stammered as if he had swallowed his own tongue.

Buckskin Zimmer recognized the boy from his surveillance at Round Mound. "Say," he said. "Yer that flunky from Rawhide Robinson's outfit, ain't you?"

"Y-y-yes-s-sir."

"What are you doin' here?"

Bicky had no answer, but the man's abrupt manner triggered something in him.

"What are you doing with these cats? Them ain't your cats, are they. Them's Mr. Robinson's cats! You swiped them—you're a thief!"

"Just never you mind, kid. You best ride on in here and get off that horse. I never planned on company but it looks like I'm stuck with you fer a spell. Come on."

"No. I'm goin' back to Mr. Robinson. And I'll be tellin' him what I found."

"Oh no, you won't. Yer stayin' right here with me."

"Ha!" the boy said. "Just see if I am!"

And with that, he spun the pony around and slapped it across the hip with the tail end of his reins as he pounded its flanks with his heels. The horse responded by leaping into a high lope, eating up the ground with long strides. He kept up the pace back to Rock Crossing and barely broke stride as he splashed across the Canadian River.

Just as Bicky reached the verge of the river channel and sky-lined on the crest he heard a zip and whistle past his ear, fol-lowed by the sound of a gunshot somewhere behind. He turned in the saddle to see Buckskin Zimmer on the opposite bank standing in a drift of powder smoke. The old mountain man swung aboard his bareback horse, rifle in hand, and splashed into the river.

Bicky ducked low in the saddle and urged the dun pony along. He told himself he was glad he was not aboard the old wagon horse for he knew he was in a race for his life.

CHAPTER THIRTY-TWO

Sop 'n Taters stirred the pot of boiling beans, then ambled over to the drop-table at the back of the chuckwagon to slice bacon for the evening meal. Surprised in mid-slice, he stabbed the butcher knife blade into the tabletop.

"Rawhide! Somethin's wrong! Lookee there," he hollered, pointing down the back trail.

A cloud of dust followed a running horse in the far distance. The trail boss's sharp eyes recognized Bicky's dun horse and could see the boy was flogging him for all he was worth.

"Mount up, boys! Looks like we got trouble." It was evident by then that Benedict Bickerstaff wasn't alone—another horse was in the race, and gaining.

"Arlo, you and Zeb and Tony beat it out there and put a stop to whatever it is that's about to happen," Rawhide Robinson said. "Frenchy, Johnny, you two get mounted and keep an eye on the cats. Longshot, cap that long-distance rifle of yours and be ready to shoot should the need arise."

The cowboys were mounted and on the run in no time, and as they left Longshot Hawken said, "Thunderation! I'll be jiggered if that ain't Buckskin Zimmer!"

"Why do you suppose he's after our Bicky?" Rawhide Robinson said.

"Couldn't say. But you can bet your boots he ain't droppin' by for a cup of coffee."

Bicky's pony managed to stay ahead of his pursuer until help arrived. When he saw the cowboys coming, Buckskin Zimmer wheeled his horse around and headed for the river. But his horse was winded and the cowboys' mounts were fresh and they soon pulled even.

Tony Morales, whose favorite tool for most any occasion was a sixty-foot reata, punched a hole in his rope and cast as pretty a houlihan loop as ever you did see, settling it around the neck of Buckskin's horse as nice as the necktie on a Sunday-go-to-meeting suit. The vaquero reined up his horse, turning and slowing the mountain man's mount and discouraging further attempts at escape.

Meanwhile, Bicky reached camp and slid off his jaded pony, breathless. Sop 'n Taters could see conversation was out of the question and waved Rawhide Robinson away. He held the boy up and all but dragged him to the chuckwagon, then lowered the boy to the ground, propped him against a wheel to keep him upright, and hurried to the water barrel and filled a dipper for the fatigued flunky.

Knowing he was caught, and trusting his ability to talk his way out of any situation, Buckskin Zimmer handed his Henry rifle to Arlo Axelrod. Zeb Howard pulled a hogging rope from his saddlebags and jerked the loop—none too gently—over one of the old man's wrists.

"Reckon I ought to tie his hands behind?" Zeb asked Arlo.

"Nah. He ain't goin' nowhere. And him bein' bareback, he might fall off that horse. Come to think of it, that horse is plumb tuckered out. Don't seem right, him havin' to pack this sack of buffalo chips back to camp."

And so Zeb bound Buckskin Zimmer's wrists together, then, with a mighty shove, sent him tipping off the horse to land like a bag of beans falling off a rock. The captive struggled to his feet and snarled at the laughing cowboy—the only sound he'd uttered throughout the affair.

It was an unusual parade that made its way toward the chuck-wagon. Buckskin Zimmer led the way, sullen and stumbling along. Zeb rode behind, riding up beside him now and then to urge the old man ahead with the toe of his boot. Arlo followed with the mountain man's rifle across his saddle, then came Tony, followed by Buckskin's horse, towed along by Tony's rope. The procession reached the camp and Zeb hazed the captive over to where Rawhide Robinson and Longshot Hawken waited.

For a time, no words were spoken. The two men from the cat camp just stared at the old trapper they had exchanged an entire night's worth of words with atop Round Mound not so long ago. Buckskin Zimmer returned a glare of his own.

Finally, with the tension so thick you couldn't cut it with a Green River knife, Rawhide Robinson said, "What're you doing trying to run down my boy?"

Zimmer said nothing.

"C'mon, Buckskin, spill it," Longshot said.

Zimmer said nothing.

"What's the matter, cat got your tongue?" the cowboy said.

Zimmer said nothing.

Rawhide Robinson waited a moment, then said, "Well, I reckon he'll talk sooner or later. Zeb, keep his hands tied and truss up his feet so he don't get any ideas about walking out of here. He's likely thirsty after all that hard riding, but I don't believe we've got any water to spare just now."

Zimmer said nothing. Instead he snarled like a treed catamount.

Zeb poked a leg behind the man's feet and gave him a none-too-gentle shove. Buckskin Zimmer's backside hit the ground with a satisfying whump. He shot a wicked scowl at Zeb and snarled again as the drover took several wraps around the trapper's buckskin-covered ankles and finished off with a nice, tight knot that would make any sailor proud.

By now, Bicky's breathing had returned to normal, or nearly so. Rawhide Robinson took the dipper from the boy and refilled it, then squatted before him, handed him the water, and said, "You in any shape to tell me what happened, son?"

The boy thrust his chin in the direction of his horse, standing nearby in the fading light with head hung low. Through the entire affair, the half-sack of beans had stayed tied behind the cantle of the saddle. "I found them beans, didn't I," he said.

Rawhide Robinson laughed. "I guess you did. But I got me this feeling that tracking down missing Mexican strawberries ain't all you been up to."

In the best Rawhide Robinson tradition, Benedict Bickerstaff delayed the story by taking a leisurely sip from the dipper.

"Here's what happened," he said. "I got across the river without no trouble and found the beans right about where Mr. Sop 'n Taters said they might be. Whilst tying them on me horse I thought I heard cats. Real quiet-like, see. I wasn't even sure I heard it, was I.

"But then I heard it again and climbed back on the horse and rode to where I thought that mewling was comin' from. Downstream a ways there was this little alley-like thing goin' back between these steep hills. Back in there a bit, I sees this little pen made out of sticks and it's all full of cats, ain't it."

By now, Bicky was feeling better and once again he imagined himself a heroic figure of Sir Lancelot proportions.

"I started over there for a closer look when that there rotter over there started emptyin' his lungs at me. He told me to stay put, but I could see he wasn't wanting to feed me tea and biscuits so I lit out of there. 'Bout the time I was crossin' back over the river, that yob took a shot at me. Missed, though, didn't he.

"Anyways, I kept on keepin' on, not wantin' to test his shooting abilities no more. 'Fore I knew it, he was after me horseback. Couldn't catch me though, could he—not with me on that dun horse of mine."

Rawhide Robinson laughed again. "You say he's got some of our cats corralled back there?"

Bicky nodded.

"They look like they was faring all right?"

Bicky nodded.

"Did you see any water there?"

"Well, there was this little ditch thing running down through there. Mostly mud, wasn't it, but maybe some water."

Rawhide Robinson tipped his hat back and kneaded his forehead. He stood up and addressed the members of his trail-driving crew, all of whom had circled up nearby to hear the boy's tale of woe. "Fellers, it looks like that ingrate old trapper over there rustled some of our herd. Don't know how he did it, but he must've lured them away somehow during the chaos and confusion of the crossing. By tomorrow, the old reprobate might be thirsty enough to trade his story for a taste of water."

All assembled heard Buckshot Zimmer snarl.

"Anyway," Rawhide Robinson said, "I reckon them cats will be all right right where they are until morning. But most of you'll be goin' back for 'em at first light."

CHAPTER THIRTY-THREE

By the time the ribbon of dawn started its climb up the eastern sky, Buckskin Zimmer was spitting dust. When Sop 'n Taters cast him a nasty glance while filling the coffeepot with water—taking care to splash and slosh plenty of liquid onto the dusty ground—the antique trapper couldn't muster the saliva to snarl.

Bicky stoked the cook fire, taking the opportunity to toss a fragment of petrified buffalo dung toward his erstwhile pursuer before riding out to round up the day's saddle mounts. (He pocketed a purloined palmful of precious sugar to pamper his dun pony.)

The cowboys went about their business as usual upon rising, stretching and twisting out the kinks of a night spent on hard ground. They snorted and spat, huffed and hacked, and paid no more attention to the bound outlaw than they would to a pile of horse apples.

On the other hand, Rawhide Robinson and Longshot Hawken took a special interest in the tied-up and thirsty thief. They walked to the edge of camp to map out their approach to interrogating the old man and to decide a course of action.

The trail boss assembled the crew and lined out the day's tasks, assigning Frenchy Leroux to keep track of the cats at camp, while Arlo, Zeb, Johnny, and Tony would ride back to the Canadian crossing, pack up Buckshot's camp, and bring the stolen cats back to the herd. Benedict Bickerstaff's chest swelled and his gait took on a higher step when Rawhide Robinson told him to saddle up and show the crew the way—not that they needed the help.

Longshot Hawken carried a dipper full of water from the barrel to where Buckskin Zimmer sat, letting some of the tempting liquid slosh out onto the ground as he came. "You want this, you old ingrate?" he said.

Buckskin Zimmer nodded and reached out with bound hands.

"Not so fast. I'll give you a taste if you give me your word—not that it's worth a wormy hide—that you'll tell us what you're gettin' up to stealin' our cats."

The old trapper nodded again and extended his reach. Longshot let him grasp the bowl of the dipper and watched as the captive poured the water down his throat in one long gulp. He coughed. "More," he said.

Rawhide Robinson joined the pair as Zimmer downed his second serving of sweet water, then said, "I don't suppose a man could get a bite to eat."

"Nope," the trail boss said. "I got other plans for your mouth right now. Talk."

"Suppose I do? Then what?"

Longshot Hawken said, "Just never you mind. We'd be within our rights to hang you right now. And we might, if we take such a notion."

"Thing is," Rawhide said, "it don't make no never mind whether you talk or not. Don't make much difference why you did what you did—you're guilty as sin, no matter. I just want to satisfy my curiosity as to why—and how."

"Then you'll string me up, I suppose."

"Maybe so, maybe no."

The old trapper squirmed and stretched his limbs as much as the constraints allowed. "I don't suppose you'd loosen these fetters—I'm a mite stiff and sore."

"Quit bellyachin'," Longshot said. "Start talkin' or you'll find yerself discomforted by a rope of another kind."

Buckskin took a deep breath and let it out in a long sigh. "Couldn't see as I had any choice," he said. "Beaver's been trapped out fer years. Buffalo's all killed off. Wolves is unreliable. And there ain't even hardly no bears no more. Too bad nobody wants the skins off sodbusters. That's about the only thing there's a whole lot of in the West these days."

"What're you carryin' on about?" Rawhide Robinson said. "What's that got to do with my cats?"

"I'm a hide and fur man! Have been for more years than you been drawin' breath, I reckon. Skinnin' critters has made me an honest living all these years—"

Longshot Hawken laughed.

"—and the truth is, I don't know nothin' else."

"What's that got to do with my cats?"

"They got fur don't they? Ought to be able to sell their hides somewheres."

Rawhide Robinson laughed.

Longshot Hawken laughed.

Even Sop 'n Taters, listening in from his place at the chuckwagon work table, laughed.

"Who'd buy cat hides?" Longshot asked. "I ain't never heard tell such nonsense!"

Buckshot snarled. "I don't know! But you can see how desperate I am. And you gotta admit them cats come in pretty colors, and their hair is nice and soft. I figured maybe some Indians somewhere would take an interest in them. Or maybe someone down south of the border in Old Mexico. Maybe some seamstress for bangles on ball gowns. I don't know—but a man's got to do somethin' to earn a honest dollar."

When the laughter subsided, Rawhide said, "Enough of that drivel. Tell me how you did it."

Buckskin told about how he had seen Chinese miners and

railroad workers in the Sierra feed their felines catnip years ago, and how the cats craved it. He told how he obtained a bundle of the plant from the Comanche medicine woman. He told how he wrapped a handful of the herb in a scrap of cloth tied to a length of twine.

And how he crushed the leaves in the bag to release their potent smell, and how he tossed the bag out toward the clowder of cats amidst the chaos and confusion of the crossing, luring small bunches away and leading them into his makeshift pen hidden away among the river gorges.

"Why, you're a regular Pied Piper of pussies, ain't you," Rawhide Robinson said with a laugh.

Buckshot's visage went blank at the suggestion.

"Just an old story. Don't make no never mind. Now that my cats is out of danger—assuming the boys get them back here safe—I confess the whole situation seems somewhat comical."

"So what you gonna do with me?" Buckskin said.

"Don't rightly know," Rawhide said. "Hanging is the usual remedy in situations such as this when it's cattle or horses that's been rustled. When it comes to cats, there ain't no conventions I'm aware of."

He took a moment to scratch his head and whiskers, face twisted in thought as he squatted before the bound-up Buckskin Zimmer.

Finally, "Longshot, didn't you tell me there's a town here-abouts?"

"Few days farther on," the scout said, "where the Santa Fe mountain route and this one here join up. La Junta, they used to call it."

"Any law there?"

"Don't rightly know. Ain't been there in years. Might be a whole city, for all I know. Might be nothin' but memories."

Rawhide Robinson thought some more, then said, "I don't

suppose it'll hurt anything to keep this scapegrace till we get to that town. We can always hang him later."

Buckskin Zimmer snorted. "You'd hang me for a bunch of lousy cats?"

"We'll see."

"You at least gonna untie me?"

"When we're ready to hit the trail, we'll turn loose your feet so's you can stroll along. I'll be darned if I'll waste horsepower hauling you in the wagon. But your hands will stay tied. Not only that, you'll be tethered to the chuckwagon."

"You're makin' me walk?"

Longshot said, "Hush up, Buckskin. You're lucky to be alive and able to walk, to my way of thinkin'."

Rawhide said, "And there ain't no sense scheming on some way to escape. That boy you shot at and Sop 'n Taters will be keeping an eye on you. And when they ain't looking, ol' fat cat Percy will be watching you from his perch. I don't suppose he's any happier than I am that you made off with them cats."

Buckskin Zimmer snarled.

From atop a keg lashed to the side of the chuckwagon, Percival Plantagenet snarled right back at him.

CHAPTER THIRTY-FOUR

Benedict Bickerstaff carried the Henry rifle confiscated from Buckskin Zimmer like a badge of honor. He caressed its wood and brass and steel as it sat across his lap on the ride back to the river. Rawhide Robinson had instructed him in its use, which was much simpler than Longshot Hawken's Hawken. Rather than a single shot muzzle loader, the Henry was a lever-action repeating rifle that fired brass cartridges—and fired them as fast as the shooter could jack the lever.

While not in the same league as the Hawken when it came to power and distance, the trail boss figured it a better weapon for the job he'd assigned Bicky. The cats, Rawhide figured, would be hungry after their confinement in Buckshot Zimmer's corral. Bicky's job, along with acting as "guide" for the cowboys, was to bag as many comestibles for the cats as he could along the way.

Unfamiliar with the gun's idiosyncrasies, the boy missed his first shot at a prairie chicken.

"Well, kid, I guess them cats'll stay hungry," Zeb Howard said.

Bicky laughed. "Poppycock. This ain't Longshot's gun. I got me more than one bullet."

And he put the bullets remaining in the magazine to good use. By the time they reached the river the fledgling sharpshooter had bagged four prairie chickens, ten prairie dogs, and a Gila monster. He liked the Henry, he decided. It might not work for

164

long-range shots at antelope but when it came to hunting feline fodder it more than served the purpose. Besides, it didn't strain his muscles to lift and steady, or hurt his shoulder with its recoil.

The crew reined up at the crossing.

"You boys get your ropes around that raft we built and tow it back across. It ought to be good for another trip or two, but give it a look-see and make sure it ain't gonna fall apart on us," Arlo Axelrod said. "Then follow our trail. Me and the kid will go feed them cats."

Rawhide Robinson had correctly surmised the pent-up appetites of the cats. The fur and feathers flew (and a lesser amount of reptile hide) as Arlo and Bicky hurled the fare into the feline enclosure. By the time the rest of the crew arrived, the pussies were preening their paws in reposed bloated bliss and purring up a storm.

Bicky helped Arlo arrange the camp goods into bundles for loading onto the packhorse while Zeb and Johnny emptied and struck the tent and Tony cinched on the packsaddle.

"I don't know why we're goin' to all this trouble," Zeb said. "We oughta just burn the whole lot of it."

"Rawhide said so, that's why," Arlo said. "Besides, there might be something here we can use if we end up hanging that lowlife rustler."

"I got dibs on the gun," Bicky said.

"Why you?" Zeb said.

"I'm the one that got shot at with it, ain't I."

Arlo found a scabbard for the Henry in the pile, fished it out, and strapped it to Bicky's saddle. "There you go, kid. Now you don't have to carry it all the time."

The segundo also located a box of 44-caliber rimfire cartridges and the boy fed the magazine full and stowed the rifle. The young flunky admired the look of the sheathed rifle hanging on the dun horse. But, inside, he wasn't sure he was ready to forgo the feel of the Henry rifle in his hands.

Buckskin Zimmer's possibles piled high on the packhorse, with his worn McClellan saddle perched on top. Tony Morales, as always a top hand with rope, threw a perfect diamond hitch over the load, then handed the horse's lead rope to Bicky.

"Here you go, *muchacho*," he said. "We'll be busy towing the ferry and herding cats, so you get the honor."

Bicky climbed aboard his pony and double half-hitched the lead rope to his saddle horn. He felt the satisfying bulge of the holstered Henry beneath his right leg as he watched the cowboys start the herd toward the crossing.

Ferrying the cats across the Canadian went off without a hitch (except the half-hitches the cowboys took around their saddle horns so they could tow the raft with their reatas). And the journey back to camp proved uneventful.

At first.

By now, the cats, accustomed to the ways of the trail, plodded along passively in a loose bunch. The cowboys, as a result, rode along without paying much attention, lost in thought and daydreaming and nodding off and otherwise engaged in inattentive activities.

And so it was that no one noticed, at first, the antics of the cats when first they occurred.

Nor, when they did notice, could they imagine how and why it happened.

Maybe the relatively small size of the band—100 cats, as opposed to the usual 1,000—allowed an enhanced level of camaraderie and cooperation.

Perhaps the relaxed pace of the passage back to the main herd provided the inspiration.

Possibly it was to relieve boredom.

Or it could have been the lingering effects of the alluring catnip.

Whatever the reason, at some point the pusses proceeded to march as an organized unit. It started with a simple assembly into columns of four, then moving in and out of ranks in both loose and close-order drill. It evolved from simple motion "to the front" to inclines and turns both right and left, then an about-face or two.

Tony Morales, lazing along at drag, first noticed the activity when his horse snorted and shied when an "about-face" on the part of the cats put his horse and the herd on an uncomfortably close collision course. He whoaed up as he woke up, shaking away the cobwebs and trying to convince himself he was seeing what he was seeing.

"Arlo!" he hollered.

Arlo Axelrod turned in the saddle from his position riding point. Tony was pointing frantically at the cats, but the action was in vain as the segundo was already agape at the parading pussies. The other cowboys, too, alerted by Tony's shout, were likewise enthralled.

"*Híjole!*" Tony said.

"Well I'll be," Arlo said.

"*@#(%!" Zeb said.

"Blimey!" Bicky said.

". . . !" was all Johnny Londo could muster.

After sitting dumbfounded for a few minutes watching the cats at their maneuvers, Arlo realized the herd was getting ahead of them and spurred the drovers into action. And so they trotted along for a few miles as the herd—which seemed too imprecise a term for the cats in the current circumstance—executed increasingly complex drills.

They high-stepped. They glided. They pranced. They marked time. They quick-timed and double-timed. They floated and rotated. They marched with eyes left, and eyes right. They zigged and they zagged. They formed ever-shifting geometric patterns.

They displayed synchronous tail positions, both static and dynamic.

And then, for no apparent reason, they fell out of ranks and back into the chaotic placement and irregular pace of an ordinary trail herd, with no apparent order or organization.

It was as if it never happened.

And the cowboys could not believe it had happened.

Arlo collected his thoughts for a few minutes, then commanded, "Head 'em, boys."

The awestruck hands complied, turning the herd into a slow mill. Once the cats stopped and plopped down to lick their paws or maybe enjoy a catnap, the segundo signaled the crew to assemble.

"I don't know what that was, boys," he said. "But I suggest we keep it to ourselves. We say anything about this to Rawhide—or anybody, as far as that goes—they'll think we're plumb loco."

They talked about it, hashed it out, chewed it over, bandied it about, wrestled with and broached the subject. They agonized, argued, bickered, cogitated, contemplated, considered, debated, disputed, deliberated, negotiated, reflected, ruminated, and wore the issue at hand to a fine frazzle.

In the end, they all agreed Arlo was right. This episode, this occurrence, this incident, this improbable eventuality was best left to itself.

No one would ever speak of it again.

And so as they arrived back at camp and pushed the previously pilfered pussies into the main herd, unsaddled their horses, grabbed much-needed cups of coffee, and squatted near the fire. Their responses to Rawhide Robinson's request for a report on how things went were uniformly reserved.

"Fine," Arlo said.

"No problems," Zeb said.

"Peachy keen," Bicky said.

"Magnífico," Tony said.

". . ." Johnny said.

Despite it all, owing to the stunned expressions on the cowboys' faces, Rawhide Robinson had a sneaking suspicion there was something they weren't telling him.

And they never would.

CHAPTER THIRTY-FIVE

Sop 'n Taters wheeled the wagon into La Junta and parked in an alley beside a likely looking mercantile establishment. The small town, where the Santa Fe Trail's mountain and Cimarron routes rejoined, offered traders and travelers supplies of all sorts, and the cocinero hoped to obtain fresh fruits and vegetables along with fresh meat, and to replenish his supply of staples.

The cat herd was sequestered well out of town in an out-of-the-way area. Rawhide Robinson thought it best to maintain a low profile and avoid curiosity seekers. His concern extended to the cats—being city dwellers by nature, they might be attracted to the streets and alleys and houses and buildings, and getting them back on the trail might prove problematic. So only Sop 'n Taters, accompanied by young Bicky, made the trip to town.

The cowboys would get their shot at the town later, but their destination would likely be the local saloon, seeing as it had been many a week since any libation beyond creek water and coffee had moistened their mouths, wet their whistles, and sloshed in their stomachs.

And Longshot Hawken and Rawhide Robinson would escort the rascally rapscallion Buckskin Zimmer to the offices of whatever law resided in La Junta and explore the possibilities of punishment for the cat kidnapper.

All that would come later.

But for now, Sop 'n Taters filled his list with all anticipated supplies at the store. Throughout the visit, the overwhelming presence of chili peppers—in bins and barrels, boxes and bags, crates and cases, pokes and pouches, racks and ristras—aroused his curiosity. He soon learned that asking about chili peppers in New Mexico Territory is a mistake, as it is certain to prompt a protracted explanation of the fruit in its many varieties, its unlimited uses in the cooking pot in all its fresh, roasted, and dried incarnations, and, mostly, a lengthy discourse on the superiority of the red chili over the green chili—or vice versa, depending on the predilections, partialities, and preferences of the present pontificator.

In an effort to escape, he laid in a store of chili peppers fresh and dried, and even purchased a pot of a ready-made stew brewed from the stuff, having wasted so much time listening to the dissertation on chili pepper products that he would have insufficient time to organize a proper meal for the crew. The storekeeper threw in a stack of tortillas to save the kitchen mechanic the trouble of whipping up a batch of biscuits.

And so it was a relief to the ravenous cowboys when the late-arriving cooking crew rolled into camp with the announcement that supper was served.

Hailing primarily from Texas, the cowboy crew—and, for that matter, the cook—were not totally unfamiliar with Mexican cooking and the presence of the chili pepper therein. But, the fact is, chili peppers in New Mexico and chili peppers in all the rest of the world are an altogether different animal—or fruit, if one wants to be picky.

And so it was that as the steaming chili stew hit the lips, tongues, and throats of the hungry hands, it was immediately followed by hoots, howls, and hollers. Some exhaled smoke. Others spit flames. Sparks danced across Frenchy Leroux's tongue, despite its familiarity with spicy Cajun cuisine. Even Tony Morales, raised on the results of fiery Tex-Mex recipes, withered at the inferno that was his throat.

The crew emptied the water barrel in a matter of seconds. The contents of the coffeepot, despite being boiling hot, seemed cool in comparison to the chili and was soon drained in an effort to quench the fire. Then it was headfirst into the creek, soon reduced to a trickle as the cowboy crew swallowed water as fast as they could while the remnant rose as steam.

When finally the flames blazed out and they could breathe again, the cowboys gathered around the fire, the heat of which they barely felt. And, of course, the conversation started.

"Man, that stuff is hot!" Longshot said.

"Burned all the hair off my tongue!" Zeb said.

"*Très chaud!*" Frenchy said.

"Blazes!" Bicky said.

". . . !" Johnny Londo said.

"*Muy caliente!*" Tony said.

"So hot it sunburned my eyeballs!" Arlo Axelrod said.

" 'Twere a mite spicy," Sop 'n Taters said.

Even the captive Buckskin Zimmer pitched in: "Hotter'n a buffalo hunter's gun barrel!"

"Oh, that stuff weren't all that hot," Rawhide Robinson said. "Why, boys, did I ever tell you about the time—"

"Hold it right there, Rawhide!" someone said. "You don't mean to tell us some tale about eatin' somethin' hotter than that chili, do you?"

"Sorry, boys, but it's true," the trail boss said, launching a raucous chorus of disbelief.

"Here's what happened. Late one fall I was working a roundup out on the Llano Estacado somewhere. You boys know how that country is—you never can tell exactly where you are. Me and a cowboy name of Curly Carlyle had thrown together a good size bunch of bovines when a blue norther blew in one afternoon and darn near made an end of us.

"When that wind started whistling the temperature must have dropped a hundred and fifteen degrees. Now, I'll admit that might sound like an exaggeration, but had you been there at the time you wouldn't think so. That's sure enough what it felt like.

"Then it started spitting ice at us, and that stuff would stick to you like the diamonds on a rattlesnake's back. It started plugging up the nose holes on the cattle—the horses we was riding too—so there weren't nothing we could do but turn tail to the wind and let the cattle drift through the night, which we did. Had we not, we'd have frozen plumb solid and turned into ice statues out on that plain.

"The ice storm finally blew on past us and, as it will in a blue norther, it turned clear and cold—as if it wasn't cold enough already. The sun came up that morning, but for some reason it wasn't working properly. Oh, it was bright enough, but there wasn't a degree of heat in it. Me and Curly didn't know where we was or where we ought to be going, so we just kind of kept on drifting.

"Then, lo and behold, we came across something right curious."

With that, Rawhide Robinson rose and moseyed over to the coffeepot, which was, by then, bubbling away with a fresh batch of bean juice. He offered a cup to anyone who called for it but all declined, opting to let the skin lining their mouths recover before exposing it to anything warmer than chilled milk. (Which, as it happened, to the delight of all, was among the fresh goods Sop 'n Taters hauled back from town.)

"It started out as a smudge on the horizon that as we got closer resolved itself into three big old freight wagons, just a-sittin' out there all by themselves. No trace of oxen. No sign of bullwhackers. No wagon master. No nothing but those three big old wagons. The only thing we could figure was that they had all abandoned the wagons so as to save themselves and their animals from the storm.

"After rummaging around in the jockey box on one of those wagons, we found some paperwork and saw that they were hauling various and sundry goods from Santa Fe down to San Antonio, but that's neither here nor there so far as this story goes.

"Anyhow, them wagons was, like everything else, coated with a thick layer of ice, especially on the windward side. That's probably the only thing that kept us from setting a match to them in an effort to thaw ourselves out and maybe warm up them cattle a little.

"Then I noticed something even stranger," Rawhide the raconteur said.

And, with that, he yet again halted the telling to top off his coffee cup—a job at which he took his own sweet time.

"C'mon, Rawhide. Leave off with the coffee and get on with the story," Zeb said, a sentiment with which all assembled voiced agreement.

Rawhide Robinson said, "All right, all right—as Homer wrote in the *Iliad*, 'hold your horses.' Now, where was I? Oh, yes—I noticed the side of one of them wagons was bare right down to the boards. Not a sliver of ice on it at all. I stepped over and put my hand on it and I'll be darned if it wasn't hot to the touch. Then I got to looking around, and saw that the grass underneath that wagon was bare, and even the canvas on top was clear.

"So, of course, being inclined to curiosity—I ain't never held to that old saying that curiosity killed the cat, or I'd be dead nine times over—I climbed atop that wagon and peeled back the cover. There amongst the other goods was stacks of crates with *'Pimientos de Santa Fe'* and *'Cuidado! Caliente!'* writ on them.

"I'll tell you boys, and don't you doubt it, it was so hot in that wagon I started in to sweating like a Missouri mule. I tore into one of them crates and started tossing these big old dried red pepper pods out to them cattle. They nosed them around a bit, and gave them a lick or two, then started wolfing them down like a buzzard on a bloated buck deer. The ice started falling off their hides in chunks and slabs, steam started rising off their backs, and smoke billowed out their nostrils like from the stacks on a locomotive.

"We et some ourselves. Can't say we enjoyed it right off, as they singed our insides all the way down. But it sure beat freezing to death, and being warmed up from the inside out was a lot more efficient than a-huddling next to a fire.

"Speaking of fires, old Curly gathered up a handful of them peppers—he was wearing gloves, of course—and laid them out like kindling wood. And darned if they didn't burst into flame when he fanned them with his hat.

"After that, it was high living for a while. We offloaded a case of canned oyster stew, heated it up, and savored every bite of every bit of it. Another thing we learned—you didn't even have to heat it on the fire. You could just peel the lid off the can, stick one of them pepper pods in and stir it around some, and it'd warm right up.

"We stirred up some fat and flour and baking powder from the stores in those wagons and made us some biscuit dough, which we then wrapped around pepper pods to bake. Breadstuff was passable, but the peppers inside was a challenge to chew, hot like they was. But we got used to it. Even got to where we liked it.

"Anyhow, after a day or two the wind let up and the sun remembered what it was supposed to do and things warmed right up. Ain't much more to tell, except me and ol' Curly Carlyle finally managed to get them cattle back to the ranch. They was the only ones in that whole country to survive that storm, by the way, and we owe it all to chili peppers."

The cowboys took turns expressing disbelief and doubt, suspicions and skepticism, reservations and uncertainty.

"Think what you will, boys. But you all ought to know better, having yourselves had a taste of a somewhat milder version of chili peppers. Speaking of which, I believe I'll just have me another helping of that stew made from them chilis before I turn in."

And so he did.

CHAPTER THIRTY-SIX

The effects of chili peppers, while intense, are fleeting. And so it was that Rawhide Robinson's cowboy crew recovered after a restful night's sleep, then quaffed coffee, bacon, beans, and biscuits (all passed on the offer of a helping of the chili stew for breakfast), then saddled up in the early morning light and rode out to sample the amusements of La Junta. The town was no Dodge City, but it had been a good long time since the men had seen a town of any kind so the burg would serve.

Rawhide Robinson and Longshot Hawken left young Benedict Bickerstaff and ol' Sop 'n Taters to tend the camp and the herd dogs to tend the cats while they contemplated the fate of Buckskin Zimmer.

The cowboy squatted near the campfire. "What do you reckon we ought to do with him?"

Longshot lowered his wiry frame to sit cross-legged on his bedroll (his significant height meant a measurable length of time passed before all of him reached the ground and got settled) and sipped his coffee. "Don't rightly know, Rawhide. I've thought on it considerable and it is a quandary."

"I ain't sure turning him over to the law is the thing to do."

"You're thinkin' we hang him, then?"

Rawhide Robinson scraped up a handful of pebbles from the dirt between his toes and pitched them away one at a time. "No. Even though we caught him red-handed, I can't see it. On the one hand, rustling is rustling. On the other hand, cats ain't cows nor horses. Even a hundred of the little critters don't seem a fair trade for a man's life."

"The law, then?"

"Like I said, I can't quite get my mind around that, either. What's your thinking on the subject?"

"Just this: I reckon lockin' the old man up would be akin to stringin' him up. He's a mountain man and free trapper, Rawhide, and bein' confined ain't somethin' he could tolerate."

The trail boss pitched a few more pebbles. "Then again, I can't see just turning him loose."

"Me neither."

More pebbles skittered across the ground. "What would the law do if they didn't lock him up?"

"Don't ask me. What I know about the law could be writ upon a kernel of rice."

"Well, I've seen the law at work in some of them trail towns. Sometimes for minor infractions—stuff not worth a jail sentence—a judge might levy a fine."

"How much?"

"Depends on the seriousness of the crime, I reckon. Might be set by statute. Could be based on what side of the bed the judge got out of that morning, far as I know." Rawhide Robinson tossed the last of his pebbles and dusted off the palms of his hands. "Let's go talk to the old geezer."

Buckskin Zimmer sat tied to the front wheel of the chuckwagon. Through slitted eyes, he watched the trail boss and scout approach. Longshot Hawken landed a swift kick on the sole of the mountain man's foot. "Wake up, you ornery old reprobate!"

"I ain't asleep," he snarled. "Every time I nod off, that cat up there on that keg reaches down and smacks me upside the head. Been that way all night."

Rawhide Robinson laughed. "Sounds like ol' Percy ain't too pleased with you."

"Hmmph. Cat's got paws nearly the size of a grizzly bear's. Swats near 'bout as hard, too."

The two men squatted before their captive, with Rawhide Robinson settling in long before his gangly companion, owing to Longshot's length.

"What're you intendin' to do with me?"

"As it happens," Rawhide Robinson said, "we are contemplating that very thing."

"I can see why it ain't easy."

"Why's that?"

"Any man dumb enough to herd cats can't have too much in the way of brains."

Quick as a cat, Longshot Hawken lashed out and boxed Buckskin Zimmer's ear. Almost simultaneously, Percival Plantagenet's outsized mitt landed a swift blow on the other ear.

"Mind your manners," Longshot said, waggling a finger in Buckskin's face. "You ain't in no position here to be actin' rude."

Buckskin Zimmer snarled.

Percy pounded him again.

"Here's the thing," Rawhide Robinson said after an uncomfortable span of silence. "You've done us wrong. You stole from us, shot at us, swore at us, and otherwise sullied the social niceties. Not to mention violating any number of the tenets of the law, both codified and common. We ain't inclined to just let you skate."

"So what're you gonna do to me?"

"Rather than turning you over to the law and the courts, I reckon we'll try you right here."

"Sure you will. You'll pronounce me guilty and swing me from one of them cottonwood trees yonder. Ain't nothin' but mob justice."

Rawhide Robinson shook his head. "If we was of a mind to hang you we'd have done so long before now. What I aim to do is levy a hefty fine to see you pay for your crime, fix it so you can't do us any more damage, and send you on your way."

A "hmmph" from Buckskin resulted in another swift swat from Percy.

Rawhide Robinson rose from his squat. "Bicky," he called. "C'mon over here."

Sop 'n Taters followed on his heels.

"Son, how's that Henry rifle of ol' Buckskin's shoot?"

"Right fine, sir."

"You hit anything with it?"

"I hit whatever I aim to shoot, don't I."

"Here's the deal, Buckskin. That rifle now belongs to young Bickerstaff here, along with all the cartridges you've got for it."

Buckskin snarled.

Percy the cat clouted him.

"And I want that catnip. Whatever's left of it."

Buckskin snarled.

Percy pummeled him.

"Then you'll pack up your stuff and hit the trail. We'll be heading south. You'll go north. And just to make sure you don't start taking potshots at us, we'll confiscate all the powder and caps and cartridges and other ammunition you've got."

Buckskin snarled.

Percy pasted him one.

"You can't leave a man alone out here without no protection! Them guns of mine won't be no more use than a willow switch if'n I can't shoot 'em!" Buckskin said, punctuating his protest with a snarl.

Which, of course, resulted in another pussy-paw pasting from Percy.

Rawhide Robinson said, "Longshot tells me Fort Union ain't

but a few miles up the trail. You can resupply there. And make sure you pay for what you get—don't let them sticky fingers of yours be doing anything but counting out money."

Buckskin snarled.

Percy whopped him with a fat paw.

"That's about it, I guess. Except for this: If ever I see you again anywhere within a mile of this herd, I'll shoot you down and feed you to the cats."

Again, Buckskin snarled.

And again, Percy cuffed him on the *cabeza*.

"One more thing," Sop 'n Taters said, to the surprise of all. "I can't let you leave here hungry—"

"Now wait just a minute!" Longshot said in protest. "He don't—"

The cocinero would not be interrupted. "Before you go, you'll polish off that pot of chili."

"What?! I'd as soon you hang me!"

Rawhide Robinson laughed.

Longshot laughed.

Bicky laughed.

Percy purred.

A satisfied smile spread across Sop 'n Taters's face.

The old trapper tromped around the camp in a huff, heaping stuff in a pile on the packhorse and tying things to the rings on his scruffy McClellan saddle. Despite being unbound for the first time in a long time, and out of reach of Percy's punishing paws, his attitude remained raunchy.

The trail boss, the scout, the cook, and the flunky watched the show, standing next to the stack of powder and cartridges and caps it would take for Buckskin to put his arsenal to use. Under Rawhide Robinson's arm was a bundle of catnip wrapped in buckskin. Bicky proudly held the Henry rifle, now his by right, propped on his hip in case the mountain man's anger got the better of him and he attempted an attack.

Finally, they all heaved a big sigh of relief as they watched the backside of Buckskin Zimmer ride off up the mountain route of the Santa Fe Trail, trailing smoke and steam that streamed from his mouth and his nose—and, as those assembled would swear ever after—his ears.

Longshot said, "I'm glad to be rid of him."

Sop 'n Taters said, "I'm glad to be rid of that chili."

CHAPTER THIRTY-SEVEN

Not long after leaving La Junta and skirting Las Vegas, mesas and mountains swallowed the trail drive. The Sangre de Christo Mountains that started as a blue smudge on the horizon days ago at the crossing of the Canadian River lifted from the earth in folds and wrinkles and creases and crinkles that unnerved the flatlanders herding the cats. Only Longshot Hawken and the well-traveled Rawhide Robinson had seen the like, and their experiences taught them that these mountains, while formidable, were small potatoes compared to other ranges that framed the Mountain West.

Still, no one would argue with the awe-inspiring sheer granite wall of Hermit Peak, or the impressive rise of Starvation Peak. As the mountains rose off to the right, Glorieta Mesa loomed to the left and the prairie dwellers felt hemmed in by the cliffs and crags and crevices that surrounded them. Only the cats seemed unimpressed and unworried as their paws continued their relentless plodding, day after day, along the last leg of the trail to Santa Fe.

One night they camped near the Pecos Pueblo, whose crumbling stone walls glowed eerily in the warm light of the campfire as the crew sat clutching their coffee cups.

"What's that noise?" Sop 'n Taters said, jumping up and looking around for some sign of threat.

"It's my knees a-knockin', ain't it," Bicky said.

"This place is a mite spooky," Arlo Axelrod said.

"Makes the hair on the back of my neck stand up," Frenchy Leroux said.

"It is a bit unnerving," Longshot Hawken said.

"&*@#$ scary is what it is," Zeb Howard said.

"Plumb petrifying," Tony Morales said.

". . ." Johnny Londo said, too terrified to talk.

"Ah, boys, this ain't nothing," Rawhide Robinson said.

Sop 'n Taters snorted. "I suppose you're gonna tell us about someplace you been that's more frightening than this."

"Why, yes, as a matter of fact. I one time encountered the devil himself. And if that ain't about as fearsome as it gets, then I don't know what is."

With that, the trail boss ambled to the coffeepot as he was inclined to do in such situations and topped off his tin cup. He walked to the edge of the firelight to stretch his legs and stood studying the starry sky.

"Well?" he heard, and turned back to the fire.

"Well, what?"

"What about you meetin' up with ol' Lucifer?" Sop 'n Taters said.

"What about it?"

"What happened?" someone said.

"And when?" another asked.

"And where?" someone else said.

Rawhide Robinson strolled leisurely back to his bedroll by the fire and took his own sweet time settling in. With each passing moment, the impatience of the crew grew. But, with impeccable timing, the storyteller launched his tale mere moments before the mutiny.

"Me and this cowboy name of Gail Gardner was working a cow camp up in the Sierra Prieta Mountains—Sierry Petes, they call them—out there west of here in the Arizona Territory. Well, one day Gail decided he'd seen enough of the backsides of cows for a while and talked me into taking a trip to town. Which we did. Had us a right fine time, too, as far as I can remember.

"Anyhow, after we'd paid a visit to every whiskey mill in that town we set off for home in the wee hours of the morning. It was a moonless night, so it was dark as the inside of a black cow on that trail up through them mountains. We was just riding along trying to keep our eyelids from slamming shut when things started going wrong."

Rawhide Robinson shuddered. He sipped his coffee and allowed himself a moment to gather his thoughts. His audience protested.

"Well, what went wrong?" Arlo said, a sentiment expressed by the others in turn.

"Gail, he whoaed up his horse and said, 'Can you smell that?' So I takes a big sniff and says, 'Yes, I reckon I do. Smells like someone struck a whole passel of Lucifer matches,' and he said, 'That's what I thought.'

"We rode on along a ways and Gail stopped again and said, 'You feel that?' and I said, 'I don't know what you mean,' and he said, 'That heat—can't you feel that heat? Why, it feels like we're a-sittin' next to a stoked-up cookstove' and I gave the notion due consideration and said, 'By golly, Gail, I believe you are right. It does seem uncomfortably warm' and he said, 'What do you suppose it is?' and I said, 'Well, Gail, I don't rightly know.'

"And so, lacking any reasonable alternative we rode on— which wasn't easy, because by then our horses were getting spooked and wanted to go anywhere but up that trail. Along about that time we heard this otherworldly scream—not a scream really. More like a screech, maybe. Or a shriek. Well, words can't describe it, I guess. It didn't sound like anything I ever heard before. Or anything I ever want to hear again."

Again Rawhide Robinson paused. The cowboys took the opportunity to build up the fire, and all seemed to edge a bit closer to its light and away from the darkness. When all were comfortable—in a manner of speaking—the cowboy continued.

"About the time that infernal noise went echoing away through the mountains, this apparition appeared."

"Appa what?" someone said.

"Apparition," Rawhide replied. "A specter, you know. A phantom. Anyway, whatever you call it, it started to take form right there on the trail in front of us. Boys, you can't imagine how scared we was when we seen what it was."

Another pause.

"Well? What was it?" came the question.

The answer came from Rawhide Robinson: "Oh, it goes by lots of names," he said. "The Devil. Lucifer. Satan. The Prince of Darkness. The Serpent. The Beast. Beelzebub—I could go on, but you get the picture.

"He looked about like you'd expect. Red as a ripe tomato. Hoofs and horns, long tail with something like a spearhead on the end, big wicked eyes—fiery yellow, they was—and a pointy mustache and chin whiskers that looked like they was fashioned from sliced steel."

Rawhide Robinson paused again, but this time the cowboy crew sat in stunned silence. The shock and awe wore off eventually, to be replaced by the customary impatience.

"Really?"

"You saw him?"

"What happened?"

"What did you do?"

"Gail, now he was a reata man like Tony here. A fine and fearless roper, he was. He'd put a loop on any critter anytime, anywhere, under any conditions and hope for the best. Which is what he did that night on that trail up there in the Sierry Petes.

"And once Gail had him headed, I didn't figure there was anything for me to do but put a heel loop on that evil imp. Which is what I did."

Another pause. Another encouragement, in no uncertain terms, to continue.

"Boys, I'll let Gail finish the story. He wrote it down something like this:

> 'Oh, we stretched him out and we tailed him down,
> While the irons was a-gettin' hot,
> We cropped and swallow-forked his ears,
> Then we branded him up a lot.
>
> We pruned him up with a de-horning saw,
> And we knotted his tail for a joke,
> We then rode off and left him there,
> Necked to a blackjack oak.' "

The cowboys unleashed a cacophonous chorus of incredulity.
"You expect us to believe you left the devil tied to a tree?"
"No way did you dehorn the devil!"
"You didn't really whittle on his ears, did you?"
"A knot in his tail? Not a chance!"

Rawhide Robinson smiled. "It's the honest truth, boys. Every word of it. If you don't believe it—which I cannot imagine— well, ol' Gail Gardner wrote:

> 'If you're ever up high in the Sierry Petes,
> And you hear one Hell of a wail,
> You'll know it's that Devil a-bellerin' around,
> About them knots in his tail.' "

And, with that last piece of advice, Rawhide Robinson snuggled into his sougans and started snoring the night away.

Rod Miller

For their part, the cowboys huddled ever still closer to the campfire, casting, from time to time, apprehensive glances into the darkness and hoping against hope the sun would waste no time in rising.

CHAPTER THIRTY-EIGHT

The drovers were pleased to leave the eerie ruins of the Pecos Pueblo and get the cats back on the trail. All hurried through breakfast and did not even linger over coffee. Every sound incited anxious glances, with the cowboys, the scout, and the kitchen staff expecting, fearing, what they might see.

If the cats noticed anything untoward in the vicinity it was not evident.

The crew, however, remained edgy and the plunge into the defile of Apache Canyon did nothing to relieve the anxiety. Bicky, horseback on this day to bring up the rear of the parade and ensure no cats escaped or were left behind, whooped and hollered as cowboys often do to encourage the herd to keep moving.

Then, the echo of his voice bounced off the canyon walls. He reined up his horse in fear.

The boy perused the promontories in every direction but saw no one. He rode on. When another yell to discourage a bunch-quitting cat answered itself, fear got the better of him. He pulled the Henry rifle and piled off the horse, dropped to one knee, and scanned the cliffs and crags and crevices. He chambered a round on the rifle and in response heard the jacking of a lever off to the left. Another cocking rifle to the right, farther away.

Try as he might, Bicky could not find a target. He did see the trail boss down the canyon. "Mr. Robinson!" he yelled. He heard someone else call. And another.

Seeing the lad dismounted with gun in hand, Rawhide Robinson spurred his mount into a high lope and swung out of the saddle as the horse came to a sliding stop inches from Bicky.

"What is it, son?"

"There's somebody out there!"

"Who? Where?"

"I don't know, sir! I can't see them, can I."

"How do you know they're out there? What happened?"

Bicky thought for a moment, wondering how to explain the situation. "Well, sir, I could hear them. When I shouted at the cats, someone up there did too. Over there, and over there," he said, pointing with the barrel of the rifle.

Rawhide Robinson ruminated on the situation as he studied the surrounding cliffs. When he hollered "Hey!" at the top of his lungs, Bicky just about jumped out of his boots—and it's likely he would have had not all the blood in his body pooled in his feet and held him down. When the answers to the man's shout came echoing back the ghostly white boy said, "See! You hear that?"

The trail boss laughed. According to the flush climbing back up the boy's neck and face, he failed to see the humor in the situation.

"What's that all about?" he said.

"Bicky, there ain't nobody out there."

"But you heard them, didn't you, same as me!"

Rawhide Robinson laughed again. "It's an echo, boy."

"A what?"

"Echo. It's when sounds bounce off cliffs like these and come back to you. So, when you let out a beller, it hits those walls and rebounds, and that's what you hear—your own voice coming back to you."

"Yeah, right. You're pullin' me leg."

"No, it's the truth," he said. Then, "Hello!"

". . . Hello . . . hello . . ."

"See, Bicky—it was just me. Every voice you heard was mine."

Bicky echoed Johnny Londo when ". . ." was all he could say.

"Ain't you ever heard an echo before, boy?"

Bicky dropped his chin until all Rawhide Robinson could see was his hat brim as he shook his head in the negative.

"Not even when you was in among all those tall buildings in Chicago?"

Again, Bicky shook his head.

Rawhide Robinson mulled that over for a few moments.

"That is a curiosity," he said. "I reckon it's because it's always so noisy in the city that echoes just get lost in all the clamor. Can't think of any other explanation. Anyhow, not to worry, son. Echoes can't hurt you—although I can see how they could be a mite unnerving.

"Let's get these cats out of this canyon and bedded down. After supper, remind me to tell you about this ranch I worked on one time where echoes were a part of everyday life."

And that's just what Bicky did. With supper out of the way and cleanup complete, while still wiping dripping dishwater from his elbows, he walked over to the campfire and reminded Rawhide Robinson of his promise.

Not being the sort to pass up an opportunity to enjoin an audience with an anecdote, Rawhide Robinson launched his tale—following brief introductory remarks concerning the afternoon's incident in Apache Canyon to set the scene, which caused Bicky's face to turn an embarrassed shade of crimson.

"Anyhow, here's the deal. I was working on this ranch up in the Sawtooth Mountains of Idaho. It sat in a place called Echo Valley and was called, oddly enough, the Echo Ranch. Now that valley was unlike any valley I—or you—have ever seen. All around was these big, tall vertical cliffs that hemmed in that valley like the rim on a skillet, with ranch headquarters sitting smack-dab in the middle like a leftover bean. There wasn't but one way in or out—just a narrow gap in the cliff wall.

"Cowboying there wasn't like anyplace else I have ever worked. There was thousands of cattle spread out across that spread, but since they couldn't wander it didn't take but a few cowboys to ride herd on them. Come morning on the days I was on duty, I'd saddle up and see where the herd was—they'd be right close by every day—and ride in the opposite direction of what grass I wanted them to graze that day. Then I'd just let out a long holler like you was calling hogs or something, and that would chouse them cattle away from me and toward where I wanted them to go. And boys, that was it for the day. That's all I ever had to do."

Arlo Axelrod asked, "But you said them cattle would be bunched up near the bunkhouse every morning. Did somebody else ride out and drive 'em back?"

"Oh, no! That was the beauty of the place, see. Remember, it was called Echo Valley. The place was so big it would take most all day for my holler to get across the valley. Then it would hit that there wall and bounce right back. So, along about late afternoon, the echo would arrive and drive them cows right back toward headquarters."

"Ah, Rawhide! I ain't never heard such nonsense!"

"Well, Tony, had you been in Echo Valley you would have heard it—twice. And that ain't the only way them echoes came in handy. About the time we'd finish up with breakfast, the kitchen mechanic there would step out onto the porch and clang away on the dinner bell. Just like clockwork, the echo would come back in the early evening and call us to supper. Worked like a charm, it did."

"Sounds handy," Sop 'n Taters said, "if it didn't sound so crazy."

"I'll admit it was a crazy place. But even that ain't the craziest thing that happened." Rawhide Robinson rose from his bedroll and stretched to his full height, massaging the small of his back with both hands. He fetched his coffee cup and refilled it at the pot and, with no sense of urgency, wandered back to his bedroll to sit again.

"Et alors?" Frenchy said.

"C'mon, Rawhide! Tell it," Longshot said.

"I'm waitin', ain't I!" Bick said.

". . . !" Johnny Londo added, impatient despite his usual reserve.

"One time the owner of the Echo Ranch got wind that a band of rustlers had their eyes on his herd. Guess they figured them cows was sitting ducks in that big valley, especially with such a small crew on hand on account of—well, I already told you why there was a small cowboy crew. So, anyway, with some sleuthing—meaning I hung around the saloon in the nearest town and overheard them outlaws making plans—we knew when they planned the raid, which was at sunrise the next morning.

"So I beat it back to the ranch and got there in the middle of the night. I rousted everybody out of their bunks and we stepped outside packing every shooting iron we owned and started into shooting up the night like nobody's business. We put so much lead in the sky it fell like rain all the rest of the night—but that's neither here nor there.

"When the sun peeked over the cliff wall, that band of rustlers came storming out of the gap and into the valley in full force. Then, like clockwork, the echoes from all that gunfire came roaring back and them outlaws thought they were under attack by an entire army!

"Well, boys, they wheeled their mounts around and beat it back out of that valley like the Philistines leaving the Valley of Elah. We saved the herd without firing a shot—well, not without firing a shot, but by firing shots at nobody—oh, you all get the point."

The reactions bounced around the campfire like so many echoes:

"Pshaw!"

"Absurdo!"

"Poppycock!"

"Ridiculous!"

"Preposterous!"

"Sorry boys, but it's the truth," Rawhide Robinson said. Then, with a foolish grin, "You want to hear it again?"

CHAPTER THIRTY-NINE

The cowboy crew wandered the Santa Fe Plaza, overwhelmed by the onslaught on their senses. People of all kinds came and went, from the posh and perfumed and prosperous to the poor and impoverished peons. There were laborers and tradesmen, bullwhackers and muleskinners, caballeros and cowboys, farmers and merchants, and all other manner of humanity.

Longshot Hawken's big sombrero fit right in—but so did the cowboy hats that crowned the heads of the others. For that matter, headwear of any variety would blend into the mix, and, in fact, did. There were tattered forage caps and kepis from the late rebellion in both faded blue and gray, stovepipes and skimmers, bowlers and John Bulls, Panama planters and cloth caps. and more. Topping off the ladies were colorful scarfs and mantillas, bonnets and caps and boaters and fancy-brimmed hats festooned with feathers and fur and ribbons and bows.

Then there were the smells—food, both plain and exotic (with chili peppers in every stage of preparation predominant), humans and animals and their waste, hides and leather, dust and mud.

The sounds of trace chains and wagon wheels, hoofbeats and footsteps. And talk—every dialect and accent imaginable of English, Castilian and Mexican Spanish, German and Dutch, Jicarilla and Mescalero, Swedish and Sicilian, Navajo and Tano, and a polyglot of all combinations thereof and then some.

The plaza was the terminus of the Santa Fe Trail, but only a way station for Rawhide Robinson's trail drive. The herd would never set foot on the plaza, nor would the trail boss. For while the cowboys sated themselves in the city, he sat at a candlelit table at a hacienda outside town feasting on the beauty of his hostess, Magdalena Maria Martinez y Montez de Monterrey.

The name, too much of a mouthful for the cowboy, was immediately truncated in his mind and mouth to Maggie—short, he would say, for Magdalena—and magnificent. Rawhide Robinson was smitten, and had been from the instant he met the woman when he rode onto her ranch seeking a bed ground for the herd during their sojourn in Santa Fe.

"My apologies, señor," Magdalena said, "but we have not had rain for some time. Although our cattle are few, we have no grass to spare."

"Well, señora—"

"Señorita," she interrupted, bringing a smile to Rawhide Robinson's face.

"—that's just fine, as we won't be needing any grass."

That simple statement, of course, led to a lengthy explanation that had Magdalena, in turn, skeptical, incredulous, thinking this man crazy, understanding, and, finally, laughing.

"You are welcome to your rest your gatos on my rancho, señor—on one condition."

"And what might that be?"

"You must consent to dine with me. It will be a humble repast, but I cannot pass up an opportunity to visit with a man who would undertake such a preposterous operation."

Rawhide Robinson removed his hat. "Why, Miss, it would tickle me plumb pink to partake of comestibles with you."

Magdalena suggested a suitable location to pasture the pussies. The trail boss returned to the herd and he and the cowboys got the cats on the ground. The boys left for Santa Fe, leaving Arlo Axelrod and Sop 'n Taters and an assortment of herd dogs to hold down the fort. Rawhide Robinson dusted himself off and went to supper.

The meal was anything but humble. Rawhide Robinson had hardly ever seen so many eating utensils surrounding so many plates of assorted sizes and had no clue how to proceed. And so he set a pace that kept him consistently twelve-and-a-half seconds behind his hostess as he mimicked her every move as to what to eat when, and with what.

But when it came to conversation, the congenial cowboy more than held his own. He regaled Magdalena with amusing anecdotes and entertaining tales but, more than that, he imperceptibly extracted her own life story, subtly drawing out revealing details and closely held secrets. He learned the forebears on both the Martinez and Montez branches of her family tree had deep roots in New Mexico, having resided there since it was part of Old Mexico and even New Spain, with land grants from the King of Spain going back nearly two hundred years. The combined families had controlled vast swaths of land—or had done so before the Americans took over.

Now, conniving speculators were challenging land titles and demands from the tax man had depleted the family treasury. Magdalena, the last of her line since the death of her father and older brother at the hands of avaricious opportunists, was, in fact, hanging on by the skin of her pearly white teeth.

"Is there no help for the situation?" Rawhide Robinson asked with genuine concern.

Magdalena heaved a sigh.

"Perhaps," she said after an interval. "But I fear the cure would be worse than the disease. Don Carlos Valencia—from a family nearly as established here as ours—is a turncoat and among the worst of the capitalist pigs. He has offered to let me stay on the land with one small stipulation—that I do so as his wife."

Voicing the words stirred Magdalena deeply and, in a most unladylike gesture, she expectorated fiercely onto the floor.

"I would rather die," she said as her anger turned suddenly to tears.

Rawhide Robinson knew not what to do. As capable as the cowboy was in most any situation, he found himself at a loss. He walked to her side, placed a hand on her shoulder, removed it, returned it, removed it, and finally let it settle there.

"Don't cry, Maggie. It can't be that bad."

As if on cue, violent knocking on the door announced that it was, indeed, that bad.

The cowboy trailed Magdalena to the entryway and watched as she swung the heavy door open. There stood the man he would soon learn was the wicked Don Carlos Valencia himself. Behind him, two haughty bodyguards sat horseback, one holding the reins of the Don's high-strung stallion.

"Magdalena!" Valencia said. "I see you have guests—I hope I am not intruding."

"Your presence would be an intrusion if I were alone."

The Don smiled. "As fiery as ever, I see. Bueno. I like a hot-blooded woman."

Magdalena lashed out to slap Valencia's handsome face, but he caught her wrist before the blow landed.

Rawhide Robinson stepped forward. "I believe you had best unhand the lady."

"And who might you be? And why do you presume to instruct me? You appear nothing more than a common saddle tramp."

"Never you mind who I am. But if you don't let go of the lady's hand pronto, you'll find out more about me than you want to know."

With a villainous laugh the Don dropped Magdalena's hand and reached inside his fancy jacket to retrieve a document.

"Do you know what this is, Magdalena? It is the title to your land. All of it. I could wait no longer for your cooperation so I made the necessary arrangements to obtain the deeds."

"Arrangements? Surely you mean bribes," she said.

Again the vile laugh. "Not to worry about the details, my lovely. As you know, I am a generous man, and my offer still stands. Become my wife and this hacienda will still be yours—and more, so much more."

Now it was Magdalena's turn to laugh. "You have my answer. I have given it to you more times than I can remember."

Valencia slapped the paper against his thigh, wheeled on his heel, and with surprising grace swung into the saddle.

"And so, señorita, again we part. This time, forever. You have until week's end to remove yourself from my rancho."

Magdalena stood stunned in the open doorway as the three men rode away. Rawhide Robinson stood beside her.

And they were still standing there some minutes later when his segundo, Arlo Axelrod, rode up.

"Rawhide, we got a problem."

"Oh? What's that?"

"All them cats—well, some of them cats—is having kittens."

CHAPTER FORTY

Awash in the golden light of a new day, Rawhide Robinson and his crew walked among the cats. There were kittens everywhere. It seemed that half the cats were curled around tiny furballs. Some had two or three. Most had four or five. Some had six or seven.

"Cattle ranching would surely be a more lucrative pursuit if cows birthed that many babies," Rawhide Robinson observed.

The stunned crew agreed, with a series of silent nods and vocalized affirmations. Then the questions and comments concerning the current circumstance commenced.

"X#$%&@!" Zeb Howard said. "What on earth are we gonna do?"

"Good question," Tony Morales said.

"I am wondering the same thing myself," Frenchy Leroux said.

"Land sakes!" Sop 'n Taters said. "Their eyes ain't even open!"

"They sure can't walk on them stubby little legs," Longshot Hawken said.

". . . !?" Johnny Londo would have said if he could have found the words.

"There's sure a lot of them," Benedict Bickerstaff said.

"Well," Arlo Axelrod said in summary, "we've got to think of something."

Ever the optimist, Rawhide Robinson said, "What I'm think-

ing is how much more money we'll make from all these extra
cats when we get to Tombstone."

The cowboys concurred, but the question remained: "How
are we going to get them there?"

Rawhide Robinson removed his hat and scratched his head.
He stood for a moment, the brim of his thirteen-gallon hat in
hand, aimlessly rotating it around and around and around, his
brow furrowed and lips pursed.

He smiled. He plopped the hat on his head and pulled it
down tight. He said, "Boys, I've got it. We'll get us a calf wagon,
just like on spring roundup! And I think I know just where to
get one. Zeb and Bicky, you two come with me. Rest of you
keep an eye on these mama cats. They're likely to be a mite
nervous or cantankerous or something, so don't press 'em any.
But keep a close eye out for varmints and raptors that might
mistake those little kitties for a meal."

Soon, the trio rode into the yard at Magdalena's hacienda.
They had barely alit when Magdalena Maria Martinez y Montez de Monterrey came out of the house, wrapped in a rebozo.
To Rawhide Robinson, it looked like she had not slept. But,
even through red-rimmed eyes and a paled complexion, her
remarkable beauty gleamed, glowed, and glistened.

Zeb Howard swallowed hard at the sight of her and instinc-
tively removed his hat.

Even at his tender age, Benedict Bickerstaff was stunned, his
visage taking on a blood-bay blush, his tongue tighter than a
toenail in a too-small boot. Zeb whacked the infatuated boy on
the chest with his hat, and signaled Bicky to remove his own
head cover.

"Señor Robinson," Magdalena said. "I did not expect to see
you so soon. It is a distinct pleasure to welcome you and your
cowboys."

She smiled, and any rigidity remaining in Bicky's (and, we

suspect, Zeb's) bones melted away, rendering him a sagging, lovesick husk.

The trail boss, likewise smitten, but more functional owing to earlier experience and exposure to her mind-boggling beauty, spoke. "Maggie," he said, removing his hat and holding it over his heart, "I have come to talk business."

Dismounted and seated on the veranda, Rawhide Robinson explained the situation and asked Magdalena about the availability of wagons and, perhaps, mules to draw them.

"Sí, señor. In our wagon yard are conveyances of many kinds. And, of course, we have mules with much experience on what you call the Santa Fe Trail, as well as El Camino Real de Tierra Adentro to the City of Mexico."

Magdalena looked troubled. "But Señor Robinson—you are aware that the evil Don Carlos Valencia now lays claim to my rancho."

"I know it, Maggie. But as I recollect, he said he would take possession at the end of the week. Until then, I expect it's still yours. And if you choose to sell me some wagons and mules, well, that's your choice, to my way of thinking. Should the Don object, I reckon me and my boys can deal with him."

"Then consider it done."

"Oughtn't we discuss terms and such?"

"No, Señor Robinson—"

"—Call me Rawhide."

"No, Señor Rawhide, we can discuss that later. I am confident we can arrive at a disposition that will be to our mutual benefit. For now, let us select the appropriate *medios de transporte*."

From among the many possibilities, Rawhide Robinson selected a high-sided freight wagon of massive proportions. With the canvas cover deployed, it would stand nearly fourteen feet high, nearly as tall as it was long. The rear wheels themselves would overtop a tall man. He chose a smaller freight wagon to hitch behind as a trailer.

"We'll pull some of the boards off the sides to let air in and keep things cooler. Them kittens weigh next to nothing, so I expect three spans of mules can pull the train all day without breaking a sweat. With spares, let's say ten mules to throw in with our remuda, Maggie."

"Sí, Rawhide. The mules will do the job. They are strong and reliable. My father's teamsters trained them well."

"Bicky, you recall them shelves I hammered together in that railroad car?"

The boy nodded in the affirmative.

"We'll have to build something similar in these wagons."

Bicky nodded, thought, then said, "But these kitties can't hold on like big cats, sir. And they ain't got no balance. They'll be fallin' off the shelves and doin' themselves a-damage, won't they."

Rawhide Robinson scrunched up his face into a thoughtful posture and considered the boy's comment. "I suspect you're right, son. We'll have to devise some way to keep them from bouncing around and slipping and sliding and skidding and falling. Little rows of boxes, or some such."

"I have the thing, Señor Rawhide," Magdalena said.

"And what might that be, Maggie?"

"You see over there," she said, pointing with her chin. "The long building beyond the *caballeriza*—the horse barn? That is the hen house, mostly empty now. Our family once supplied many *huevos* to the people of Santa Fe. Inside are just such boxes as you describe. Rows and rows of them. More than enough for your *gatitos*."

"Sounds perfect to me. Zeb, you take young Bicky here and get these wagons outfitted. Think you two can handle it?"

"Darn tootin'."

"Maggie, can I leave it to you to cut us out ten head of your best mules?"

"Sí. And you?"

"Me, I got an errand of a different kind. Can you point me to a healer hereabouts? One who uses plants and such?"

"Oh, Rawhide! You are ill?"

"No, I'm fine, Maggie. But I think I had best lay in a supply of catnip. Unless I miss my guess it'll help keep the mama cats happy whilst being away from their babies most of the day. We got a bit of it, but it won't be enough."

Magdalena directed him to a *curandera* who resided on the outskirts of Santa Fe. He rode away to the sound of hammers and pry bars as the refitting of the wagons got underway. He returned, hours later, to find the work nearly finished. In his absence, Magdalena had supervised several modifications to the original plan, including the addition of a spring seat to the big wagon, with a walled-off area beneath and behind the seat.

He looked the situation over and said, "What's all this, then?"

Zeb merely looked sheepish.

Bicky said, "It was her idea, wasn't it!"

Rawhide Robinson didn't even dismount, instead reining his horse around and riding off toward the house.

Magdalena's startled heart pounded at the loud knock on the door. She feared the evil Don Carlos Valencia was back to beg her hand in marriage yet again, and offer insults and threats when she refused. But when she opened the door, there stood Rawhide Robinson.

"Señor Rawhide!?"

"Maggie, I think I know what you got in mind, but maybe you had best tell me yourself."

"It is simple. My price for the wagons and the mules is that I go along on this fool's errand of yours."

"But, Maggie, that just can't be."

"Oh? And why not?"

"We'll be weeks on the trail, yet. Eating dirt all day and picking it out of our beans and bacon and biscuits at every meal and sleeping on it at night. You'd be in the company of uncouth men—good-hearted, and harmless, but they are cowboys, and, on the trail, well, men will be men. Which ain't so far distant from hogs. Why, a fragile rose like yourself would wilt in such harsh and unwholesome conditions."

"You think me a delicate flower. But like all plants that survive in this high desert, I am strong and resilient, I assure you. And like the rose, I, too, have my thorns."

"Judging from the seat you had the boys put on that wagon, I take it you intend to drive."

"Sí."

"Can you handle a team?"

"Sí."

"Six up?"

"Sí."

"You've done it before?"

"Sí. Well, no. But I have driven a pair, both mules and horses, many times. How much more difficult can it be?"

"Well, if it happens you get into a jackpot somewhere on the trail, I can tell you it ain't three times harder . . ."

"Aha! See!"

"More like six or eight times the challenge. That many animals is mighty powerful and can be a handful for a strong man to control, even if he's an experienced muleskinner."

"I can do it, Señor Rawhide."

"I can't allow it, Maggie."

"You are determined?"

"I fear so."

"Fine. Then the deal is off. You are free to look elsewhere for wagons and the animals to pull them. And, I might add, nests for your gatitos."

"Aw, Maggie, you don't mean that," Rawhide Robinson said, even as the firm set of Magdalena's jaw and the steel in her gaze told him otherwise.

He took off his thirteen-gallon hat.

He scratched his head.

He studied the toes of his boots.

He rubbed his whiskers.

He said, "You are determined?"

She nodded.

He nodded.

"We'll be going back to the herd now to sort things out there. I'll be back at first light to hitch up the wagons and help you pack up and load whatever you intend to take along."

She nodded and closed the door.

CHAPTER FORTY-ONE

The latigo on Rawhide Robinson's saddle was drawing up snug when he heard the rattle of trace chains. With dawn just encroaching on the morning sky, he had intended to get to Magdalena's ranch plenty early.

But now, with the coffee still hot in his stomach, he dropped the latigo strap (and his jaw) as she drove into camp perched on the spring seat on the tall wagon with six prancing mules well in hand. The smaller wagon rattled along behind, trailed by four mules tied head to tail, the leader tethered to the endgate. She turned the train in a tight circle (likely to demonstrate her mastery of the hitch) and whoaed up inches from Rawhide Robinson's mount.

"Sakes alive, Maggie! What in blazes are you doing here this time of day? I meant to ride over and lend you a hand."

"I have two hands of my own, Señor Rawhide. I find that sufficient for most tasks."

"I didn't mean to imply you weren't handy. But you had quite a task at hand, and, well, as that old English writer John Heywood said, 'many hands make light work.' "

"That is wisdom. But I was unable to sleep so thought to make use of the night. Now, I would like nothing more than to get down from here and enjoy a cup of coffee. Give me your hand."

Rawhide Robinson helped Magdalena off the wagon. In the growing light, he admired her flat-crowned, flat-brim hat, riding breeches tucked into knee-high boots, and a high-waisted jacket decorated with floral stitching and silver conchos.

"Coffee's already hot, and I suspect the biscuits are just about ripe. Let me introduce you to our cocinero, Sop 'n Taters, and the rest of the hands."

If there was any sleep left in the eyes of the crew it was not evident. All stood wide-eyed in the presence of such beauty. You would have thought Johnny Londo's reticence was catching, as their response upon being introduced to Magdalena was identical:

". . ." from Sop 'n Taters.

". . ." from Frenchy Leroux.

". . ." from Tony Morales.

". . ." from Longshot Hawken.

And, of course, ". . ." from Johnny Londo.

Rawhide Robinson said, "You've already met Arlo Axelrod there, and Zeb Howard and young Bicky."

"Surely 'Bicky' is short for something young man," Magdalena said. "What is your proper name?"

"B-B-B-B-B-B-B—" he said, stuck in a most unfortunate embarrassment and unable to extricate himself.

Magdalena smiled. Bicky's face flushed a deeper shade of scarlet, whether from humiliation or the rosy glow of the morning sky no one could say. But the kindness in her eyes urged him on, and he finally managed to say his name.

"B-B-Benedict Bickerstaff!" he said, then nearly collapsed from the effort.

She placed a hand on his shoulder and said, "I can tell we shall be great friends, Señor Bickerstaff. Now, did someone say something about biscuits?"

While the crew filled their plates—with Magdalena served first, of course—and emptied them—with less clamor and more care and a more calculated attempt at manners than usual—

Rawhide Robinson looked over the calf wagon. Magdalena had stuffed the nest boxes—every one of them—with bedding straw and covered the floor of the wagons with enough of the stuff to allow regular replenishment. The walled-off area at the front of the tall wagon held her clothing and heirlooms and keepsakes from the hacienda. She had filled the rear of the small wagon with foodstuffs, apparently emptying the pantry of everything edible. The chuckwagon would be better provisioned—and overflowing—once the goods were transferred.

"Maggie, you've done more than your share in filling these wagons—way more than I have any right to expect. *Muchas gracias.*"

"De nada. It is nothing, Señor Rawhide. The gatitos must be comfortable. As for the rest—better to share with the fine cowboys on this absurd expedition of yours than leave it for the evil Don Carlos Valencia."

"Thanks just the same. Boys," he said, "here's the plan. Over there at the cook fire, Sop 'n Taters has a big kettle of catnip tea brewing. What I figure is this: we each of us fill a cup and take a spoon. We'll work through the herd, feeding each mama cat a dose of the drink. That ought to calm them down enough so's they'll let us gather up their litters and stow them in those nests in the calf wagons."

"*Uno momento, por favor,*" Magdalena said. "These gatitos, these kittens, seem to be a surprise. Did you not expect this to happen?"

Rawhide Robinson studied the toes of his boots. Finally, "Well, miss, it just never occurred to me . . ." He looked to the crew. "None of the boys mentioned it, either," he said, prompting a sheepish interest among all of them in the toes of their boots.

Magdalena laughed.

"What's so funny, Maggie?"

"You worried about my presence as an unchaperoned woman among these men, Señor Rawhide. Surely it is of no concern, as you plainly see."

"What do you mean?"

Maggie laughed again. "It is obvious. Even the blind can see that you men are unfamiliar with the interactions of males and females and the consequences. I believe I shall be perfectly safe among you innocents!"

The interest of the men in the toes of their boots intensified, whether that interest was real or feigned to conceal their florid physiognomies.

After a moment, Rawhide Robinson came to his senses and said, "C'mon, boys. We got work to do." Not a one of them raised his eyes until well clear of the amused gaze of the lovely Magdalena.

But soon, kittens by the handfuls were ensconced in the nest boxes in the calf wagon. The blissful mother cats seemed content, with not a one raising a fuss. The chuckwagon and calf wagon pulled out, tongues pointed southwest toward the Rio Grande. The remuda followed along, and the mounted cowboys and herd dogs got the cats on the trail.

Nested next to radiant Magdalena rode a purring Percival Plantagenet, the polyamorous puss and proud papa of many of the offspring riding behind.

Some who saw him there swore he wore a smile.

CHAPTER FORTY-TWO

The herd plodded along the high ground above the Rio Grande. Off to the west, five low and blackened hills lined up as if for inspection, and the crew did give the curiosity due attention, wondering at the origin of the dark cones. Not far ahead lay Albuquerque, but Rawhide Robinson asked Longshot to avoid the city, so the guide angled the drive eastward toward the base of the looming Sandia Mountains.

Bicky handled the lines on the chuckwagon as it led the parade while Sop 'n Taters snoozed as much as he could on the jerky, jarring, bumpy, bouncy, rough, and rugged ride. Next in line, Magdalena drove the calf wagon, with the remuda moseying along beside and the cats behind, with the drovers trudging along horseback.

The three horsemen startled Bicky as they thundered out from behind a low ridge, leaving their dust to cloud his vision as they raced past the chuckwagon to slide to a stop in front of the calf wagon. Magdalena had no choice but to check her teams, her surprise turning to shock, then rage as she identified the evil Don Carlos Valencia and his brace of bodyguards.

Bicky circled the chuckwagon and stopped, facing the standoff as the Don and Magdalena barked insults back and forth. He elbowed the cook—although the old man was well awake—and reached under the seat for his Henry rifle.

With each insult, the Don rode closer to Magdalena, threatening with every breath to remove her bodily from the wagon and

211

carry her bound and gagged back to Santa Fe and his marriage bed.

As the inflamed Magdalena hissed and spat at his entreaties, he rode ever closer until his face was so near she could smell the onions and garlic—mixed with the rank and rancid odor of *aguardiente*—on his breath.

His henchmen sat their horses, hands on the grips of the pistols in their sashes, and laughed. But their humor was cut short when Percival Plantagenet, without warning, lunged from his perch upon the seat next to Magdalena with fur flared and claws bared and lit in the middle of Don Carlos Valencia's face with a howl and a yowl that caused the evil interloper to roll backward off his horse and hit the ground on the flat of his back, stirring up a choking and blinding cloud of dust and causing a tremor felt far and wide.

Once he deemed his mistress safe, Percy bounded back to the wagon seat and took over the hissing and spitting duties. Magdalena gladly relinquished the chore.

By the time Don Carlos regained his breath and gained his feet, Bicky stood nearby, rifle at his shoulder and aimed at the middle of the raging ranchero.

Don Carlos laughed. "Get out of the way, muchacho, before I crush you like *la cucaracha*."

Bicky jacked the lever and filled the chamber of the rifle in response.

Don Carlos laughed. "You must be loco," he said. "Surely you see you cannot shoot us all. My men will kill you."

"I don't have to shoot all of you, do I. I only have to shoot you."

The smile left the evil Don's face.

His two plug-uglies bit off their wicked grins when, from behind, they heard the ratcheting of the hammers on Sop 'n Taters's double-barreled shotgun.

It seemed to Bicky hours later—although it was a matter of moments—when Rawhide Robinson rode in at a gallop, with the rest of the cowboy crew, from Arlo to Zeb, hot on his horse's heels.

He laughed, but there was no humor in it.

"Looks like you're in a bind, Carlos," he said.

The infuriated Don did not reply.

Rawhide Robinson dismounted. "Johnny, disarm those two," he said. "And while you're at it, dismount them."

As Johnny went about his business with his usual reticence, the trail boss, with his accustomed loquaciousness, removed a pair of silver-plated, pearl-handled Colt 45 Peacemaker revolvers from Don Carlos's gunbelt, a similarly fancy Webley Bulldog pocket pistol from a shoulder holster, a nasty-looking knife from a belt scabbard, and another from concealment in the throat of his boot.

"Quite an arsenal you got there, Carlos."

"More than enough to kill you."

Rawhide Robinson laughed. "Not this time. In fact, I suspect it would take a lot more than this collection of weaponry in your nefarious mitts to do away with me—or to convince the lovely Miss Maggie to do your bidding. So, I'm a mite suspicious that you might have even more armaments hidden away somewhere on your person," he said.

"Boys, do you think we ought to risk it?"

"Non!" Frenchy said.

"Not a chance," Arlo said.

"I'd check him thoroughly," Zeb said.

"Right down to his miserable skin," Tony Morales said.

". . . !" Johnny Londo said.

Rawhide Robinson smiled. "All right, you cantankerous curs, peel off them duds."

All three men protested, of course, but the pampered patrician pouted most vociferously.

"Quit your bellyaching and shed your apparel. Otherwise, I'll sic Percy on you. Worse still, I'll let Maggie have at you."

Don Carlos snarled, but undressed. Soon, the three evildoers were attired in nothing but boots and underwear, the pain of embarrassment plain on their faces while ire enflamed their eyes.

"Say, coosie, anything left of that roll of twine you had in the wagon?"

"Sure thing," Sop 'n Taters said. He produced the spool.

"Mount up, you sorry scalawag," Rawhide Robinson said as he used Valencia's knife to slice off short lengths of the lightweight rope while Don Carlos complied with the order.

"Now, turn around backwards," he said.

Valencia started to protest, but the prick of the knife on his barely covered backside cut off the complaint. With the Don facing rearward in his fancy hand-tooled saddle, the trail boss tied his wrists together and bound his ankles to the stirrup leathers. He unslung the fancy canteen with its tooled leather cover from the saddle horn and hung it around the Don's neck.

"Being a kind-hearted soul, I wouldn't want your throat to parch on the ride home," he said. "Boys, truss them other two up likewise, and shoo their horses off towards Santa Fe."

As the ne'er-do-wells rode off to the north, Longshot Hawken rode in from the south. He studied the situation, but did not comment. Instead, he hoisted his thumb over his shoulder and said, "There's water about a mile yonder way."

Rawhide Robinson said, "All right, boys, let's push the herd that way and call it a day. We'll water the cats, then let the mamas into the wagons to mother up and get these little kitties fed."

"Wait!" Magdalena said as she scrambled down from her high seat on the calf wagon. With a few quick and purposeful strides she reached Benedict Bickerstaff and enfolded the boy in her arms.

"You are *muy valiente*, Bicky!" she said. "If not for you, even now I would be in the clutches of the evil Don Carlos. Forever I am in your debt."

With that, she planted a kiss on the young boy's cheek, whose "smack" resounded in the still air and seemed to hang there like the haze of dust.

The cowboys fidgeted in their saddles.

The horses pawed the earth and rattled their bits as they shook their heads.

Magdalena climbed back onto her wagon.

Young Benedict Bickerstaff's face glowed as rosy red as the beautiful Magdalena's lips, the tender feel of which was now seared forever into his soul.

And, from his perch on the wagon seat, Percy appeared miffed that he was not the object of Magdalena's attention and affection.

CHAPTER FORTY-THREE

One day along the trail down the Rio Grande, Rawhide Robinson decided the cats—young and old alike—could use a day of rest and recreation.

Most of the cowboys appreciated a day of forced idleness around the campfire and spent their time swapping stories and songs and deceits and ditties while repairing tack.

Bicky cleaned and oiled his beloved Henry rifle, while Magdalena laundered clothing—an activity the cowboys could not understand, as she changed apparel so regularly her duds had no opportunity to become severely soiled.

Rawhide Robinson and Longshot Hawken drew maps in the dust and discussed the route from here on to Tombstone—the distance now growing short—and contemplated the crossing of the Continental Divide that would be required. Then, they took some time to examine the crowns of their hats for holes in the sunlight by assuming a reclined position and placing the headgear over their faces.

Sop 'n Taters spent the afternoon sitting on the riverbank threading bits of bacon fat on a fishhook and dangling it in the stream. A nice mess of crappie and bluegill resulted, and he used the catch to whip up a dinner of fried fish for all assembled.

"Très bon!" said Frenchy Leroux. "Haven't had any fish since I left the bayou. Takes me right back home, it does."

"I ain't so sure about this," Zeb Howard said. "Closest I ever come to eatin' fish was on a drive one time when we butchered a steer that drowned in the Red River."

"Wish we had some chips," Bicky said as he licked grease off his fingers and mopped it off his chin.

"*Muy bueno,*" said Magdalena.

"Sí," agreed Tony Morales.

Longshot belched, but did not excuse himself as he considered it high praise.

". . . !" said Johnny Londo.

Rawhide Robinson said, "Say, did I ever tell you boys about the time I caught me a fish?"

All agreed he had not, and so he did.

"At least I think it was a fish," he said. "For all I know, it might have been the riverine equivalent of a sea monster, or one of them submarines like that Hunley machine they had back in the war. Never did see what I snagged, whatever it was. Since it was in a river, I naturally figured it was a fish.

"Anyway, here's what happened. I was working on this ranch up on the Montana plains one time. Place was owned by this Englishman who wasn't never there in all the time I was. He had this fishing rig just laying around catching nothing but dust so I thought I would give it a go. There was this big bamboo pole with a fancy reel and all kinds of hooks and such. There was even this pair of India rubber britches with boots on the bottom, but I couldn't see wearing anything like that.

"I dug me up a worm and stabbed a hook through it and after a couple of tries managed to get it tossed far enough out into the Yellowstone River to where I figured there might be a fish. Nothing happened for quite a spell so I was just sitting there by the river and sort of dozing off. At the time, I was thinking this fishing was a fine enough pastime.

"Then, all of a sudden, the twine on that reel started unwinding at a furious rate. I jumped up and grabbed that pole but didn't know what to do—couldn't find anything to dally to so as to stop that line from feeding out so fast. But, finally, I managed to get a grip on the little spinning handle and slow it down some. I dug in my heels like you would when you're afoot with a recalcitrant horse or cantankerous cow critter on your reata, and darned if that fish didn't start dragging me along the edge of that river.

"Well, not wanting to lose that fishing rig I got me a death grip on the handle and vowed as how I wouldn't turn loose no matter what."

Rawhide Robinson paused in his tale to top off his coffee cup. As was his wont, he took his own sweet time doing so, stirring the impatience of his audience until it started rising like sourdough.

"Well, what happened?" someone said, prompting others to voice similar queries.

"Be patient, boys. Fishing is a patient man's sport, and so is talking about it. Just bide your time and I'll get to it," he said, sipping the hot off his coffee. "Now, where was I? Right. There I was, getting dragged along that riverbank, grinding the heels of my boots off in an attempt to rein in whatever species of Pisces I had on the line."

"What?"

"Huh?"

"Que?"

"Pisces. Ain't you ever read them old Greek stories? Like that one about Aphrodite and Eros? Or looked up at the stars?"

"What?"

"Huh?"

"Que?"

"Oh, never mind. I figured it was a fish, but didn't know what kind, and naturally figured it was some mythical variety given the current state of affairs. Which was, as you recall, me being dragged along the bank of the Yellowstone River on my boot heels. Sad to say, boys, that situation was short-lived, as soon enough that sea monster headed for deep water and towed me right out onto the river."

The storyteller paused again and the cowboys chewed on his choice of words.

"*Onto* the river?" Arlo said. "Now, I ain't no linguist, but I believe you mean *into* the river."

Others there assembled bore witness to the veracity of the observation.

"Not at all, boys, although I see your point. Thing is, that water trotter was moving so fast I couldn't have sunk *into* the river had I wanted to. Instead, I just skimmed along the surface, and not an inch of me got wet save the soles of my boots."

"Never!" Bicky said.

"No way!" Longshot said.

"Not a chance!" Tony Morales said.

"Fat chance!" Zeb said.

"*Ni loco!*" Magdalena said.

"Non!" Frenchy said.

Johnny Londo said ". . . !" and Sop 'n Taters stirred the beans.

"It's all true, boys, and I'll swear to it to my dying breath. Which, by the way, I expected to draw that very day as I slid down that river. Along about Miles City, some cowboy saw the fix I was in and shook out a loop to try to rope and rescue me. But, I was moving a lot faster than his horse could run and was farther out in the stream than the length of his rope. But, his intentions was good and if ever I see that cowboy again, I will surely thank him for his effort.

"But, on we went. And I must admit, it was an interesting way to see the country. I saw soldiers drilling off in the distance at Fort Buford about the time the Yellowstone joined up with the Missouri. Before you know it, there was Fort Abraham Lincoln and them Mandan dirt houses on the bluffs above the shore. I flew—leastways it seemed I was flying—past miles and miles of grass and a ranch now and then. One place I saw looked familiar, like an outfit I once worked cattle for, but I only got a glimpse of it so I wouldn't guarantee it. There was all manner of creatures, deer and elk and water birds and such along the way. And I'll tell you boys, they stood stock still and wide-eyed when I went by, as they had never encountered anything like me, and I came and went faster than they even had time to spook.

"Things got more settled-like when we got down around Nebraska and Iowa, then Missouri—farms and towns and all that. Things was right busy down around Independence, both ashore and in the water. There was times I was right scared we'd crash into one of them riverboats or barges or keelboats, but by that time I was right handy at maneuvering around on the water.

"We made it through that maze and headed east across the state of Missouri at a frightening speed. By now, I confess I was getting a mite worried. I was fatigued and dozing off from time to time and worried what might happen if I we ended up in the Mississippi. If I was to fall down in that big river—or even in the Missouri, for all that—I did not imagine I would have the strength or energy to swim to shore.

"As I contemplated my fate, I must have fallen asleep on my feet, if only for an instant. When I woke up, I lifted my eyelids and there was a big ol' steamboat staring right at me. That finned critter that was towing me must have dived deep, for my line went underwater straight ahead of that paddle wheeler and there was no time for me to slide to either side. Wasn't anything I could do but brace myself for the crash and smash that was sure to come."

Rawhide Robinson rose from his bedroll roost, tossed the dregs of his brew into the campfire, and refilled his tin cup with fresh coffee from the steaming pot. He hitched up his britches, stomped his feet to restore circulation, adjusted the wild rag around his neck, reset the slant of his thirteen-gallon hat, and took an experimental sip of his java.

As he intended, anticipation flogged his audience into a frenzy.

"C'mon!" one said.

"Get on with it," said another.

"*Raconter!*" was heard.

"Talk on," someone said.

Rawhide Robinson took another sip of coffee. "Keep your pants on," he said. "Ain't nobody going anywhere and we got all the time there is."

It took another round of encouragement to spur him to action, but, finally, the fabulist forged ahead.

"Well, just as I figured it was time to cash in my chips, the line went slack. In thinking about it afterward, I came to the conclusion that it got severed by the paddle wheel on that riverboat. But whatever it was that caused it, I quit being towed and starting coasting. The closer I got to the boat the slower I'd go. So, when we met, it was just a matter of stepping off the water and on to the deck.

"Of course my mode of locomotion and my means of arrival on board caused an outbreak of excitement among the passengers and crew. Even the captain climbed down from the pilot house to shake my hand and slap me on the shoulder. I was a sure-enough celebrity and even something of an object of worship aboard that boat, no question about it."

Another pause.

And more impatience.

Finally, "So what did you do?"

"Just went back to work as if nothing had happened."

"Nonsense! You was durn near halfway across the country!"

"Oh, I didn't get back right away. As it happens, that steamboat was bound up the Missouri and Yellowstone for Billings, Montana, so I went along for the ride. When we passed the ranch the captain put me ashore—with that bamboo pole still in hand, I might add. I gathered up the rest of that Englishman's fishing gear and put it all away and went back to punching cows, as I had determined in the interim that I was better suited to that line than a fishing line.

"And, I ain't sorry to say, I haven't wet a line since."

Rawhide Robinson swallowed the rest of his coffee and stretched out on his bedroll. He rested his head on the seat of his saddle, tipped his thirteen-gallon hat over his eyes, and said, "You boys had best get some sleep. We'll be back on the trail come morning."

Of a sudden, he lifted his lid, looked around the sky, and pointed at a cluster of stars. "By the way, boys—that string of stars there, that's the constellation Pisces. Means fish."

As the cowboy crew studied and discussed the arrangement of heavenly bodies, Rawhide Robinson settled back down and slept the night away with a smile on his face.

CHAPTER FORTY-FOUR

As is often the case on a trail drive, things became routine.

The tedious and tiresome sameness, the dull and humdrum monotony had the cowboys falling asleep in the saddle.

The herd plodded toward and along the Rio Grande day after day, their little cat feet barely raising dust or even precipitating a perceptible sound.

The remuda dragged along, grabbing mouthfuls of grass as they went, so entrenched in the routine that straying went unconsidered.

The chuckwagon wheels rotated and rolled in their endless rounds as if Sop 'n Taters and Bicky, although on board, had no role in their motion or direction.

And the calf wagon train trundled along, seemingly independent of Magdalena and Percy rocking in rhythm atop the high seat.

Then one day, as had happened countless times on countless other days, the passing parade jumped a jackrabbit. Stirred from his siesta in the scraggly sward, the leggy hare hopped away. Whether hunger or the need of the mother cats for enhanced sustenance to aid nursing or mere boredom triggered the attack cannot be known, but the fact is one of the cats—a tortoiseshell tom, as it happens—launched a pursuit of the retreating rabbit.

Now, by any measure, the feline was on a fool's errand. With a top speed—and that for a pitifully short distance—of thirty miles an hour, an alley cat—even one trail-hardened—is no match for a well-rested jackrabbit, whose pegs can propel him to speeds approaching forty miles per hour. Besides, agile though the feline species may be, the zigging and zagging, ducking and diving, twisting and turning of the hare can knot up a cat's legs and send him rolling, embarrassed, across the unforgiving ground.

But, for reasons known only to themselves, the cats collectively concurred that this particular rabbit was destined to be lunch for a few or a snack for many, and simply would not be permitted to escape. As one cat flagged, another angled into the attack to take over the pursuit. Others headed off the hustling hare, forcing unexpected changes of direction, upsetting momentum, and keeping the coney in proximity to the herd and the attendant reinforcements. Eventually, in a remarkable display of cooperation and teamwork, the cats outlasted their prey and the bushed bunny succumbed.

The cowboys were amazed—awestruck, actually—at the event, and it engendered comment for days to come. Even the herd dogs were enthralled, and did not stir as their charges, in singles, pairs, and small groups, quit the herd to participate in the coordinated quest to best the bunny. (Whether or not the horses noticed is unknown; if they did, their reaction or regard is unrecorded.)

From that day forward, the feeding habits of the cat herd changed. Now appreciative of the profitability of hunting as a pack, the pusses pursued bigger game on a regular basis. Oh, they would continue to roust rodents and badger birds and harry reptiles individually when feeling peckish, but their newfound power and prowess as a pack improved productivity as well as pleasuring their palates through variety in viands.

The days and weeks to come would see the pussies pull down rabbits regularly and coyotes occasionally. They dined on diminutive deer, even a beleaguered bear. And, in one noteworthy encounter, took a buffalo. (Now, granted, it was an aged bull and in no condition to deflect a determined attack by dogged cats. But, still, the gang of alley cats brought the bison to bay, and, with the able assistance of Longshot's Hawken and well-honed skinning knife, and a butcher knife wielded by ol' Sop 'n Taters, they dined on bits of buffalo cut into cat-sized chunks for several days. And while the cowboy crew might have enjoyed a repast of fresh buffalo flesh at the time, no one considered the notion of cooking so much as a cutlet, as all agreed the cats were entitled to their take in toto.)

And there, on the southernmost reaches of the trail to Tombstone, the hunters also found success stalking javelina and feral hogs, hunting the rare ringtail and coati, even feeding on ferrets and foxes.

In years to come, the cowboys—Rawhide Robinson foremost among them, being of a reflective nature and a noted anecdotist—would contemplate the cunning of the cats and spin many a campfire tale and bunkhouse legend about pack-hunting pusses, most of which stories engendered disbelief among the hearers.

Still, the drovers had seen, and the drovers believed. And, on many a future occasion, usually after seemingly endless episodes of staring at the backsides of bovines, would yearn for those long-lost days on the adventurous tabby trail.

CHAPTER FORTY-FIVE

The drive left the Rio Grande at the fertile berg of Hatch—but not before replenishing the supply of chili peppers, for which the area was famous. The spicy pods had become a regular ingredient in Sop 'n Taters's recipes, encouraged by Magdalena's gentle advice and assistance. The hide on the drovers' tongues had toughened up in the interim and they appreciated—no, were addicted to and demanded—the fiery flavor the flaming fruit lent their food.

Ahead lay wild and arid country seldom traveled by man or beast. Longshot Hawken had once, long ago, followed a trail blazed by the Army with a battalion of Mormon recruits looking for California way back during the Mexican War, and that was the route the herd pursued.

Long, dusty days would fill the remaining time on the trail. At Cow Springs—Ojo de Vaca—the crew filled water barrels before lumbering over a broad plain to cross the Hatchet Mountains, then trudge across the playa of an ancient lake. Climbing out of the valley to the summit of the Animas Mountains, the drive crossed the Continental Divide. Longshot Hawken and Rawhide Robinson sat horseback in the swale of the summit, and signaled the drovers and wagons to stop there and let the dogs prod the pusses over the top of the continent.

"Boys—and Miss Maggie—" Rawhide Robinson said, removing his hat as he addressed the lady, "Longshot tells me, and I concur, that this here place marks the Continental Divide in this part of the country."

"What's that mean?" Arlo Axelrod asked.

"So what?" Zeb Howard said.

And so on through the crew, until Johnny Londo finished up the series of queries with ". . . ?"

"Well," the trail boss said, "it means if you was to spit behind you, that moisture would eventually find its way to the Gulf of Mexico. But spit in front of yourself—taking care not to do so into the wind—that liquid would ultimately end up in the Pacific Ocean."

The cowboys looked around, studying the terrain, which appeared little different from any number of other places they had passed over.

Zeb Howard said, "Can't see that it matters. There ain't no water nowhere around here to run anywhere."

That astute observation prompted agreement throughout the crowd.

Rawhide Robinson removed his thirteen-gallon hat and scratched his head, replaced the lid, and snugged it tight. "I reckon you're right. But you-all are looking with limited vision. If you look at the big picture, you can see why it matters. The Continental Divide once saved a lot of lives—I know, for I was there at the time and lent a hand."

"Do tell," Frenchy Leroux said.

"Remind me after supper," Rawhide Robinson said as he heeled his horse into action to catch up with the herd.

And he did tell.

With the mother cats and kittens curled in their nests and the rest of the felines grooming and purring on that night's bed ground, the cowboys downed a meal of bacon, beans (liberally seasoned with chili peppers), and biscuits, with spicy rice and tortillas to fill the gaps and sweet empanadas stuffed with preserved fruit for dessert. Hot coffee, of course, accompanied and followed the meal, with all clutching a steaming cup.

"Zeb!" Tony Morales said. "What on earth are you up to?"

"You got a pair of eyeholes bored into the front of your head. Surely them orbs in there can see what I'm doin'."

"Sure I can. But the question is, why are you doing it?"

What he was doing was stirring his coffee with a long slice of peeled chili pepper.

"Obvious, ain't it? Keeps my coffee hot."

The cowboy crew contemplated that for a time as they settled in for yet another in a long, long line of evening assemblies around the campfire.

"Rawhide," Frenchy said. "You promised to tell us about this here Continental Divide."

"That I did. And so I will." He sipped his coffee to lubricate his talking tools and launched the tale.

"Years ago, it was, whilst I was on one of my many sojourns in the north country. Up near the Canadian border, I was, working on a Montana ranch. It had been a horrid winter, with snow piled up on the plains deeper than I ever seen. Why, I was line riding one time and spied this fine-looking Stetson hat lying on the snow out there in the middle of nowhere.

"I climbed off my pony and picked it up and lo and behold there was a head under it. I scraped the ice and snow away from the feller's face, fearing the worst, but darned if he didn't start sputtering and swearing up a storm.

"I asked him, 'Are you all right?' and he said, 'I reckon so. But I'm worried about this horse I'm ridin'.'"

A wave of guffaws and cussing, disbelief and hilarity made its way around the campfire.

Rawhide Robinson talked on.

"But, that's neither here nor there. The thing is, that snow on the plains wasn't nothing compared to the mountains of it in the mountains. And it was that way all the way south through

228

Colorado and even down here into New Mexico—not quite this far south, I'll grant you, but there was more snow everywhere than was customary.

"Well, when all that snow started melting, the rivers were soon out of their banks. The Missouri, the Yellowstone, the Platte, the Arkansas, the Canadian, the Red, the Brazos, the Rio Grande—they was all filled to overflowing and flooding the country for miles and miles. Them that joined the Mississippi had that big river spread out across the country, making the whole of the Midwest a big ol' lake. Towns and cities underwater, farms flooded, folks losing everything. And then it started raining.

"Came a telegram one day from Washington, D.C. It was the federal government requesting my assistance," Rawhide Robinson said.

And then he stopped to swallow off the rest of his coffee, amble to the pot for a refill, rummage through the remains of supper searching for an overlooked empanada, and otherwise aggravating his waiting audience.

"Well?" someone finally asked.

"And?" asked another.

"Then?" someone said.

"What did they want?" one asked.

"Oh, nothing in particular," Rawhide Robinson said as he nestled his way into comfort on his bedroll seat. "They just asked if I had any ideas—them knowing I was an imaginative sort—and if there was anything I could do—them knowing I was a resourceful sort.

"I put on my thinking cap—speaking figuratively, of course, as I never wear any headgear save this beloved thirteen-gallon hat you see on my head—and cogitated on it for a time. The solution came to me in a flash, and I went to work on it right away, time being of the essence."

Rawhide Robinson waited.

But he did not wait long, for the urgent question, "What did you do!?" soon rang out from a choir of curious cowboys.

"Now, I'm the first to admit that working behind a harness is not to my liking, whether walking or riding. But there was work to do, so I got to it. I acquired a stout team of draft horses and hitched up a Fresno scraper and went to digging."

He told how he filled up mountain passes and buried canyons, remodeling the Rocky Mountains practically from border to border, creating the very Continental Divide so recently crossed. Waters that once babbled happily downslope to the various rivers flowing to the Gulf were cut off, forcing the relentless liquid to find another way. And the way Rawhide Robinson arranged it, at least according to his account (which, we should add, is difficult to verify in the annals of history), was down the western slopes of the Rockies and the various sub-ranges that form that impressive crest.

"What happened was," he said, "was a whole new crop of rivers got made—the Columbia, the Snake, the Green, the Colorado, the Gila, and a whole passel of other streams that feed them major rivers. All that water now found its way to the Pacific Ocean, relieving the streams flowing east to the Mississippi and south to the Gulf of Mexico. It was just enough diversion that the floods east of the Divide receded and saved all that country and all those folks from permanent ruin."

The spellbound cowboys were as speechless as Johnny Londo, with ". . . !" being the only comment. Only Bicky was skeptical.

"That's a lot of codswallop, ain't it."

"Why would you say so, Bicky?" Rawhide Robinson asked.

"If you had done such a thing, why, you'd be celebrated, wouldn't you. You'd be rich and famous and livin' in the lap of luxury. Instead, here you are herdin' cats."

"You've hit the nail on the head, young'un. The reason I ain't enjoying the fruits of my labors is that I made a mistake that is just too big to ignore," the tale-teller said softly, a measure of melancholy in his voice.

"What was that?" said the cowboys, stirred from their reverie by this turn of events engendered by Bicky's skepticism.

"The Great Basin," Rawhide Robinson said, and once again paused—supposedly to refill his coffee cup; more likely to collect his thoughts.

"What about it?" came the question.

Came the answer: "The Great Basin, you see, is a huge chunk of country that encompasses most all the state of Nevada, a broad slice of Utah, a good-sized swath of Oregon, and even bits of Idaho and Wyoming."

"So?" came the question.

Came the answer: "It's called the Great Basin 'cause it's like a big bowl—you know, a basin. Water gets in and can't get out, on account of there ain't no outlet to the sea. What happened was, after all my landscaping all the water out that way ran off the Wasatch Mountains and other ranges in the area and rushed westward, only to run smack into the Sierra Nevada Mountains. It couldn't get past them, so it just bottomed out in all the low spots to evaporate and seep away into nowhere. Most of it ends up in the Great Salt Lake, some in other sinks.

"Anyhow, the powers that be decided that that geophysical accident—the unforeseen formation of the Great Basin—was a major flaw in my Continental Divide plan and could not be overlooked. So they gave me a handshake and helped me out the door. And they informed me they would look elsewhere in the future for hydrological engineering and advice.

"A major failure on my part, boys. One I am not proud of, and one I cannot forget. A persistent smudge on my otherwise spotless record of public service."

Some who were there that evening were so touched by

Rawhide Robinson's tale of woe that tears fell. And, falling west of the Continental Divide, those tears would, someday, find themselves afloat in the vastness of the Pacific Ocean.

Chapter Forty-Six

Like water bound for the Pacific Ocean, the drive made its way down the Animas Mountains to the Animas Valley. But down was only a temporary condition, as it was soon uphill again to cross the Guadalupe Range.

While the cats and horses pawed and hoofed it along as usual, these mountains proved a challenge to the wheeled vehicles. The downslope was treacherous in places as they dodged dangerous defiles and scary escarpments. Rough-locked wheels and braking assistance from reatas dallied around saddle horns were sometimes required to negotiate grades where the possibility of an upset proved extreme.

But these obstacles, like all encountered to date, were overcome with bravery and aplomb and the herd proceeded apace. Although there were no signs or other markings to make the point, the faint trail now left the bootheel of New Mexico and entered the long-sought Arizona Territory, wandering across the border into Old Mexico and back on the way to the San Pedro River.

The stream created a most welcome verdant ribbon through the otherwise dun-colored countryside and the drive soon bedded down to take advantage. Lolling in the shade, bathing, and laundering (an activity engaged in only by Magdalena, save the odd sock or two rinsed by the cowboys) proved a welcome break for the two-legged members of the company. The four-legged critters, cats and *caballos* alike, likewise seemed to enjoy the respite.

Around the campfire that night, Longshot Hawken related a tale as unlikely as any offered by Rawhide Robinson, but the well-traveled trapper swore to its veracity and challenged doubters to "look it up," as the event was well documented.

"That battalion of Mormon soldiers who blazed the trail we've been followin' camped somewheres along the San Pedro—can't say exactly where, but it couldn't have been far from here," Longshot said. "And there they fought the only battle and shed the only blood spilled during their long march back in the Mexican War.

"Seems they was minding their own business when a big herd of wild cattle showed up and objected to their being there. Them boys' efforts to shoo the cattle out of the way only made the critters mad, and before you know it they was stampedin' and stompin' and hookin' Mormons right and left. Wrecked some wagons, they did, killed a few mules, and gored two or three men bad enough to bust bones and draw blood.

"So the soldiers started shootin' 'stead of shooin'. Killed a bunch of them cattle before the beasts quit the field and beat a hasty retreat. 'Battle of the Bulls' is what they called it."

The story prompted the usual round of unconvinced commentary from the cowboys, although their personal experiences chousing mostly wild and often ornery cattle out of mesquite thickets in Texas tempered their skepticism, and lingering thoughts of Longshot's tale accompanied the crew along the trail to dreamland. More than one slept with one eye open, just in case a wild cow or irate bull should pay a visit.

As usual, the night seemed short.

Some roused from slumber at the sound of Sop 'n Taters starting breakfast. Others awakened when Bicky jingled in the remuda. A few slept until the cocinero took to pounding the lid of a Dutch oven with a heavy spoon, announcing the availability of the accustomed hot and stimulating beverage and the imminent arrival of the morning meal of bacon, biscuits, and beans (with the added improvements—owing to the influence of the lovely Magdalena and her gustatory gifts—of *tortillas, chorizo,* and *queso*).

After breakfast, Rawhide Robinson lined out the crew for the day.

"Tombstone ain't that far away, boys. The end is nigh."

The announcement engendered a round of hearty cheers and hoorahs.

"From here we head north and follow the river downstream to where there's a mill town where they crush ore from the Tombstone mines. I make it about twenty, twenty-five miles as the crow flies; maybe two days as the cat walks. You boys move the herd thataway and I'll meet up with you there."

"Where you a-goin' Rawhide?" came the question from more than one mouth.

"I'll be riding on ahead into Tombstone to see to the disposal of the herd. Should make it easy before nightfall, if my calculations are correct. Anyhow, find a likely spot to bed down the cats and kitties and wait for me there by the mills. I don't know what kind of town there might be there, but you boys behave yourselves. There'll be plenty of time to celebrate after we deliver the herd to Tombstone." Finally, "Bicky, you come with me."

"Have you gone barmy, sir?" Bicky asked.

"Not at all, son. You want to come along, or don't you?"

"Sure I do! It'll be the bee's knees, won't it! But why?"

Rawhide Robinson tipped back his thirteen-gallon hat and smiled. "The way you skinned me back in Chicago—and, I suspect, fleeced all them street urchins I recruited to collect cats—tells me you know how to drive a hard bargain. Your negotiating skills might come in handy in Tombstone."

Benedict Bickerstaff wasted not a second saddling his pony and stowing his beloved Henry rifle in the boot and he and Rawhide Robinson headed north.

They made the mill site that straddled the river by afternoon. Charleston sat on the left bank where a few hundred folks lived and Milltown lay opposite, where they crushed ore. The travelers stopped only briefly; long enough to be directed to a well-traveled wagon road angling northeast toward Goose Flats.

There, a dozen miles up the hill, they would find Tombstone.

CHAPTER FORTY-SEVEN

Man and boy sat horseback, silent and open-mouthed at the end of Allen Street. The cacophony of the city overwhelmed them. It appeared that all of Tombstone's thousands and thousands of residents were on the street. Commercial establishments of every variety lined the thoroughfare—hardware and dry goods and drug and cigar and clothing and grocery stores, eating houses, hotels, barber shops, butchers, banks, theaters, saloons—lots of saloons.

The attack of agog abated and Rawhide Robinson and his young companion rode down the street, dodging carts and buggies and wagons, other horsemen, and pedestrians crossing the street in both directions at every angle. Finding someone not in a rush took some time, but, finally, they spotted a man on a bench in front of cigar store enjoying at leisure an odiferous example of the tobacco merchant's wares.

Rawhide Robinson reined up at the edge of the sidewalk. "Pardon me, Mister," he said. "Can you tell me who's in charge around here?"

The man pursed his lips and puffed out a perfect ring and watched it float away, then exhaled a long stream of malodorous smoke. "That would be Mr. John P. Clum. He's the mayor."

"You wouldn't happen to know where I might find him, would you?"

The smoker repeated his prowess producing smoky circles. "Most likely at the newspaper office. *Tombstone Epitaph*. He runs that, too. Just follow Allen Street here down to Fifth Street," he said, pointing the way with the smoldering cigar. "Turn left and you'll find it in the middle of the block on your right. Can't miss it."

Rawhide Robinson tipped his hat in appreciation.

The man replied with another smoke ring.

"You gentlemen hungry?" Clum asked when located in the newspaper office and told a proposition was in the offing.

He led them to Nellie Cashman's Rush House restaurant. "Nothing fancy," he said as they sat, "but the grub can't be beat."

They ordered dinner, and Rawhide Robinson threw out the first conversational ball as Bicky looked on, silent and wide-eyed.

"Epitaph. Kind of a dismal name for a newspaper, don't you think? How'd you come by it?"

Clum's response was automatic, as if he had offered the same explanation on many an occasion. "When I was leaving Tucson to come here, this town didn't amount to much. Folks figured the silver would play out and Tombstone along with it. Some business acquaintances in Tucson allowed as how I would not be writing a newspaper here in Tombstone, I'd be writing an epitaph. Thought I'd use it for a name, and rub their faces in it when this town, and my newspaper, left their city in the dust."

"Town seems a prosperous enough place," the cowboy said. "I heard the rats are doing well, too."

Clum's face turned rosy from embarrassment or anger or both. "It's true. The town is overrun with the vile vermin. Don't be surprised if you spy one of the beady-eyed little buggers before we're served dessert. Despite our best efforts at trapping and poisoning and shooting and paying bounteous bounties, we can't get ahead of the filthy pests."

"What about cats?"

"Cats are in short supply in Tombstone. Isolated as we are, it's a challenge. Businesses are already overburdened paying exorbitant freight rates for necessary goods. And cats are not exactly at the top of any miner's list when he's traveling to the latest boomtown to work or prospect. I editorialize on the aggravation of rats regularly, the town council discusses it *ad nauseam*—all to no avail. The problem seems insurmountable and the solution beyond reach."

"Well, Mr. Clum, this could be your lucky day."

Rawhide Robinson explained the nature of his visit, related tales of the trail, and finished off the story with the fact that the arrival of some fifteen-hundred cats of various ages and breeds, sizes and shapes, colors and conformation was in the offing.

John Clum rose to his feet, unable to contain his excitement. "Mr. Robinson," he said, "that news relieves me of such a burden that were I not wearing suspenders I would shoot right up into the sky!"

"Don't get too excited, Mr. Mayor. There's yet the matter of money to be discussed."

"Money! Money! Why, if there's one thing we've got more of in Tombstone than rats, it's money. Name your price."

Rawhide Robinson tipped back in his chair to contemplate that comment. He came expecting negotiation and bargaining, haggling and wrangling, give and take, wheeling and dealing to arrive at a price that would cover his costs and return a modest profit. Instead, the opportunity for abundant wealth lay before him. And Bicky's sharp trading skills weren't even required to achieve it.

Visions of luxury and ease filled his mind. He entertained thoughts of extravagance and indulgence. Ideas of castles for when he felt settled, and lavish travel when he felt footloose crossed his mind. He imagined himself swaddled in silks and decorated with expensive doodads.

Then he came to his senses.

Rawhide Robinson was, after all, an ordinary cowboy. None of that foofaraw appealed to him, really. He had been rich and he had been poor, and he liked being an ordinary cowboy better than either.

And so he lifted his thirteen-gallon hat and scratched his head. He stroked his chin. He interlaced his fingers and untangled them. He tapped his foot and drummed his fingertips on the tabletop. He thought. He studied. He contemplated. He considered. He calculated. He cogitated. He deliberated. He reflected. He ruminated.

Then he suggested a price per cat that would recover his original investment, cover expenses incurred to outfit the drive for the trail and replenish supplies along the way, pay generous cowboy wages, allow each crew member to pocket a hefty bonus, and pay himself a tidy—but reasonable—sum.

"You're altogether too modest, Mr. Robinson. I'll accept your price—plus a dollar a head."

Surprise opened Rawhide Robinson's eyes to the size of the dinner plates on the table. Bicky choked on a bite of pie.

"You drive a hard bargain, Mr. Clum," the cowboy said when once he caught his breath. "But you've got yourself a deal."

In the morning, following a restful night in Tombstone's finest hotel and a sumptuous breakfast in its Continental dining room—all at the city's expense—Rawhide Robinson and Bicky spent the rest of the morning hours following the energetic Mayor Clum from place to place as he made arrangements for the arrival of the cats.

Everywhere they went, everywhere they looked, bulletins all but wallpapered the town. Overnight, the mayor—in his role as publisher—had inked up type to produce the handbill on the *Tombstone Epitaph*'s press:

CATS! CATS! CATS!

Visionary Entrepreneur to Relieve Tombstone of Persistent Problem with Rats!

More Than 1,000 Cats Arriving Tomorrow P.M.! Available for Distribution to the Public the Following A.M., O.K. Corral, Allen Street Between 3rd and 4th Streets!

By Invitation of Mayor John P. Clum and the Tombstone Town Council, All are Encouraged to Assemble Midafternoon Along Allen Street to Welcome Our Feline Liberators in a Grand Parade!

"By tomorrow morning, I'll have an extra edition of the *Epitaph* on the street giving more details," Clum told the cowboy and his companion. "Mark my words, Rawhide Robinson, you will dominate the news in this town for weeks to come. Your money won't spend here, and neither will that of your brave cowboys!

"Newspapers throughout the Territory and from coast to coast will pick up this story, spreading your fame from border to border and shore to shore.

"At long last, the news out of Tombstone will be good news, and our city on the hill will shine as a beacon to the nations.

"And—you can mark my words concerning this detail—the name and fame of the O.K. Corral will live in history for the ages owing to its role in this momentous event."

Overwhelmed by the enthusiasm of Mayor Clum—and the entire town, for that matter—Rawhide Robinson and Benedict Bickerstaff snugged up the cinches on their saddles, screwed their hats down tight, and rode out for Charleston where they would meet the herd and, come the morning, see to its delivery to Tombstone.

CHAPTER FORTY-EIGHT

The cats were already bedded down when Rawhide Robinson and Bicky arrived at the camp on the San Pedro near Charleston. The cowboys—along with Longshot Hawken and Sop 'n Taters—were huddled around the fire wrapped in hen skins peeled from their bedrolls, cowboy hats being the only other article of attire to adorn their persons.

"What on earth is going on here?" the trail boss asked.

"Hmmph!" the cocinero said.

"Bah!" the trapper said.

"Ugh!" Arlo Axelrod offered.

And so on, all around the campfire until all had expressed displeasure in no uncertain terms without uttering an actual word.

Down on the riverbank, the lovely Magdalena had a fire going, ringed with steaming Dutch ovens and kettles from the chuckwagon, and suds peeked over the rim of Bicky's dishwashing tub. Draped over nearby bushes were the cowboy clothes that normally covered the crew from chin to ankles and from the hide out.

"Aah, I see," Rawhide Robinson said with a guffaw and a grin. "Maggie's sprucing you-all up some."

"Don't laugh," Zeb Howard said. "You're next."

Realization revealed itself on Rawhide Robinson's reddening face. But he saw no means of escape as Magdalena was already on the way, toweling her wet forearms.

243

"Get off that horse and out of those filthy rags you call clothes, Señor Rawhide. If we are to arrive in town tomorrow, it is only fitting that we be presentable." She eyeballed an embarrassed Bicky, attempting to hide under his hat brim. "You too, Bicky. Here," she said, tossing a cake of soap to the trail boss. "I will wash your clothing, but you two will wash yourselves."

"But I had a bath, only just the other day. Down where that battle of the bulls was."

"You went swimming in your clothes. That does not count."

"She made us all take a bath," Tony Morales said. "You ain't gettin' away with any less."

Rawhide Robinson cast a nasty glance that nearly knocked the drover over, then pleaded with the lovely Magdalena. "Aah, Maggie! C'mon!"

"Now!" she said with the stamp of a shapely foot.

Without another word, Rawhide Robinson dismounted. Bicky followed, still unwilling to look in any direction but down. Soon the dripping duo stepped out of the water at a concealed cove around a bend in the river, screwed their hats down tight over wet hair, wrapped themselves in blankets, and joined the others at the fire.

Once settled in and warmed up with hot coffee, the trail boss said, "I hope you boys are set for a celebration. Bicky, fetch that handbill from my saddlebags, why don't you."

The cowboys passed around the printed announcement.

"You weren't kidding back in Dodge City when you said they'd throw us a parade," Frenchy said.

"To tell you the truth, I said that out of sheer desperation. None of you appeared too willing to go to herding cats, so I was grasping at any straw I could come up with. Fact is, I'm as surprised as anybody at the enthusiasm these cats is causing up there in Tombstone."

He sipped some more stimulating brew. "I guess it ain't such a bad thing after all that Maggie's making us look halfway decent. We might as well take a few minutes in the morning to curry and brush our mounts to a right fine shine. They'll gather a little dust on the way, but they'll look better for the attention anyway."

Magdalena arrived about that time and started tossing long johns at the cowboys. "Tonight," she said, "you sleep in your undergarments. I will not have you soiling and wrinkling your clothing in those filthy blankets. In the morning, you may dress." She started back toward the San Pedro, stopped, and said, "And do not flatter yourselves that I will peek." Then, with a toss of her magnificent ebony mane, she walked away.

"Land sakes," Zeb said. "I could take a bath every week and not smell as sweet as that woman!"

Johnny Londo nodded with enthusiasm and added, ". . . !"

With that, the cowboys curled into their respective bedrolls to rest up for tomorrow's promised excitement. And it was not long in coming, as it seemed to some they had barely shut their eyes when Sop 'n Taters took to clanging on his pan lid to rouse them for breakfast. The meal disappeared in record time, owing to the cowboys' eagerness to hit the trail and hit the town.

As requested by Rawhide Robinson, they took a few extra minutes to groom their mounts. Frenchy Leroux braided his horse's tail. Tony Morales tied a curly red ribbon (where it came from no one knew, Tony did not say, and its origin remains a mystery to this day) to his horse's forelock. And Longshot Hawken brushed trusty mule Number Fourteen to a high gloss and dressed all four delicate hooves with bacon grease blackened with soot scraped from the bottom of pots and pans and ash from the fire.

Even the cats, sensing something special was up, tidied themselves and each other a little extra that morning, the mothers giving added attention to the grooming of their offspring.

The dogs, too, licked and pawed themselves to tonsorial perfection.

Thus it was a fine-looking procession that made its way up the hill to Goose Flats that morning. And if their anticipation and excitement were at a fever pitch, it was nothing compared to the enthusiasm that gripped Tombstone.

The herd was in sight of the city but still some distance away when they first heard the murmur of voices emanating from the town. The noise grew as they drew nearer, but then fell silent when they hit town.

As if by prearrangement, which it was not, the drive organized itself into an orderly parade. Sop 'n Taters led the way with the chuckwagon (Bicky opted to go mounted for the occasion), followed by the lovely Magdalena and her six-up prancing mules pulling the pair of calf—or kitten—wagons, the young pusses alert and attentive and eyeing the crowds with as much interest as the crowds showed them. Percival Plantagenet, the Polyamorous Puss, struck a regal pose on the seat next to Magdalena.

(A side note: all along the route that day, men could be seen fanning themselves with hats and were heard catching their breaths at the very sight of the magnificent Magdalena Maria Martinez y Montez de Monterrey, while their envious wives responded with whacks with parasols, smacks with reticules, the occasional sharp kick on the shin, and a plethora of slaps, cuffs, and clouts.)

Next in the "catalcade" came the cats themselves, followed by the priceless pack of cow dogs. The cowboy crew came next: Rawhide Robinson and Arlo Axelrod, Frenchy Leroux and Tony Morales, Zeb Howard and Johnny Londo, Longshot Hawken and young Benedict Bickerstaff. The remuda brought up the rear.

Then, as the parade turned off the Charleston Road onto Allen Street, something magical happened—the cats started performing feats few had ever seen.

Like that long-ago day on the way to rejoin the herd from the Rock Crossing on the Canadian River when the rescued cats took to marching, the herd assembled itself into rows and ranks. The crowds lining the streets (as did the cowboys riding behind) looked on slack-jawed and articulated "oohs" and "aahs" as the pusses marched in unison, paws pitty-pattering in perfect time.

Then the fancy maneuvers started, with columns of cats weaving in and out, executing precision turns, and otherwise amazing the thousands who watched and, later, the millions who would read and hear about an event in the history of the *felis catus* species that can only be described as miraculous.

And so the parade proceeded down Allen Street to Seventh Street, U-turned, and backtracked until, between Fourth and Third Streets, they all turned into the driveway that led to the soon-to-be-famous-for-their-presence O.K. Corral.

No one saw it happen, as all were entranced, mesmerized, by the cats and their keepers. But as the herd entered the alley, rats in mass quantities quit the town, escaping (if only temporarily) into the brush, under rocks, down mine shafts, and any other place their beady little eyes identified as a possible place of refuge.

Epilogue

Rats Eradicated!
Clowder of Cats Rescues City

TOMBSTONE, ARIZ. TY.—The plague of rats that has held our City hostage is on the run, thanks to the heroic efforts of one Rawhide Robinson, a cowboy.

Mr. Robinson, having read newspaper reports of the vermin overwhelming our fair City, purchased some 1,000 cats from the streets of Chicago and, over a period of months rife with danger and difficulty, herded the animals to Tombstone. Citizens of Tombstone turned out in numbers to greet the arrival of their four-legged saviors.

Attempts to locate Mr. Robinson for comment for this report proved unsuccessful as it appears the cowboy vacated Our Fair City soon after disposing of his cats. His absence is regrettable, as our citizens would rather have feted and honored him at length for his heroic effort.

John P. Clum, Mayor, negotiated a reasonable price for the cats and with the approval of municipal leaders purchased them with funds from city coffers for free distribution to citizens, deeming the expenditure to be in the public interest and the presence of the cats, even as private possessions of the public, a public service.

"This ordinary cowboy, this Rawhide Robinson, has performed an heroic feat for the people of Tombstone. His 'herd',

248

as he so cleverly termed it, relieved the City of a tremendous burden," the Mayor tells us. "Already, rats are a rare sight within the city limits. No doubt the comfort and health of our citizens will improve, businesses will benefit and the growth of our fair City will hasten forward in the wake of this important development."

Mayor Clum arranged with proprietors of the O.K. Corral, off Allen St. between 3rd and 4th Sts., to confine the cats on their premises until citizens availed themselves of the opportunity to acquire a cat to rid their properties, whether residential or commercial, of the aforementioned pestilence with which all are familiar.

"We are grateful to the proprietors of the O.K. Corral for their willing cooperation in this daring endeavor," Mayor Clum told the *Epitaph*. "No doubt that humble livery and wagon yard will be forever etched into the consciousness of our residents and recorded in the annals of history for its role in ridding the City of the late plague of vermin. Mark my words: when, in years to come, the history of Tombstone is discussed, as it no doubt will be, the name of the O.K. Corral will figure prominently in those discussions."

The *Epitaph* will continue to report on progress in the eradication of rats by our newfound feline wealth; a richness that will prove, beyond doubt, to be as important to the future of our fair City as the discovery of silver and other precious metals has been to our past.

POSTSCRIPT

As is usually the case at the end of the trail, the drovers spent some days in town devoted to celebration and profligate spending of their newfound wealth. (Although, in Tombstone, for this particular batch of cowboys, wasteful spending proved impossible as no one in town would accept their specie. The entire party was on the house—or, truth be told, several houses, as the cowboys made an earnest attempt to visit them all—still, they did their best to enjoy themselves despite the troublesome presence of the money burning holes in their pockets.)

Then, they mounted up and rode away to who-knows-where.

Sop 'n Taters opted to stay on in Tombstone and open a dining establishment where he could turn his newfound mastery of the chili pepper into recipes beyond bacon, biscuits, and beans—not that those staples of western cuisine would not be on the menu.

Magdalena and young Bicky had cooked up a scheme to settle in California, where she would see to his proper raising. The herd dogs, with Percy and a select few of the finer specimens of female felinehood withheld for the purpose from public distribution to the citizens of Tombstone, would accompany them. The animals would form the basis of a dog-and-cat breeding operation with the purpose of providing top quality dogs and cats to the growing population of the Golden State, both for performing useful work and the pure pleasure of pet possession. Longshot Hawken had consented to guide them to a suitably salubrious seaside site, with the possibility of joining the partnership should he find the labor—and leisure—agreeable.

And Rawhide Robinson?

As was his wont, he rode off into the sunset whistling a happy tune, continuing his quest for brave and daring adventures in the Wild West.

ABOUT THE AUTHOR

Multiple Spur Award–winning writer **Rod Miller** is author of the Five Star novel *Rawhide Robinson Rides the Range,* which won the Spur Award for Best Western Juvenile Fiction, as well as other novels, short stories, nonfiction, poetry, essays, and magazine articles. A former rodeo cowboy raised in a cowboy family, he grew up and lives in Utah. He is a member of Western Writers of America and can be found online at www .writerRodMiller.com.